Standing Alone

Other novels by Anne Melville
The Lorimer Line
The Lorimer Legacy
Lorimers at War
Lorimers in Love
The Last of the Lorimers
Lorimer Loyalties
The House of Hardie
Grace Hardie
The Hardie Inheritance
The Dangerfield Diaries
The Tantivy Trust
A Clean Break
The Russian Tiara

Short story collection
Snapshots

Standing Alone

Anne Melville

PIATKUS

First published in Great Britain in 1995 by
Judy Piatkus (Publishers) Ltd of
5 Windmill Street, London W1

**The moral right of the author
has been asserted**

*A catalogue record for this book is available
from the British Library*

ISBN 0-7499-0294-9

Set in 11/12pt Times by
Computerset, Harmondsworth
Printed and bound in Great Britain by
Bookcraft (Bath) Ltd

Chapter One

1

It is six o'clock in the evening of the third Monday in October. Candida Brown is feeding her baby. Only a few moments earlier Daniel's face was flushed dark red with hunger and indignation; but now, as he sucks contentedly, his cheek looks pale beside her smooth, brown breast. As she looks down at him, Candida is overcome by a love so fierce as to be painful, a longing to take him back inside her body again so that no one will ever be able to hurt him.

Did her own mother, she wonders, once feel like this as Candida herself sucked and gurgled, pressing a small fist against her skin? How does it happen that a loving girl can grow into a stern and unforgiving middle-aged woman? With a moment's uneasiness Candida wonders whether she herself will ever forget – as her mother must have forgotten – the joy of hearing that first cry, the protectiveness with which she and Tom, sitting close together, first embraced their newborn son, or the adoration which she feels each time she lifts him to her breast. No, she will never forget. She vows to love him for ever, however much in the future he may disappoint her.

It is disappointment, almost certainly, that has caused Mrs Brown to reject her daughter. 'After all I've sacrificed for you!' 'When I had such high hopes of you!' 'You could give it away instead of ruining your life.' Could she have given her own daughter away? Does she not remember how it feels to love?

The intensity of her feelings tightens Candida's arm and Daniel breaks off from his meal to protest, gulping in air and then regurgitating a little of the milk he has just swallowed. She dabs his mouth and chin dry and settles him comfortably back again. The whole of their home, she sometimes feels, smells of regurgitated milk; except

1

when she is with Tom, when it smells of love. There was another period, when they first started to experiment with Formula Four, when it tended to smell perpetually of something rather like spinach, but by now that has been banished to the barn.

Candida and Tom have made their temporary home in a building which fell into disuse ten years earlier, when four farms were amalgamated to create one huge orchard and all the storage was concentrated in one area. To call their home a conversion would be to conjure up a misleading impression of exposed beams, floor-to-ceiling windows and the other loving details with which architects transfer suburbia to the country. What they are living in is simply a stable, containing a tack room, a hayloft and six stalls which were once upon a time the homes of a farmer's plough horses and hunters.

Tom, although a brilliant scientist and skilful at fitting fiddly connections and valves on to tiny glass pipes, is surprisingly inept when it comes to DIY work. The task of homemaking has been left to Candida; but because they moved in on the day she left hospital, it has taken her a little while to recover her full strength – and because Daniel arrived early and was very small, he needed frequent feeds to start with, allowing her only short working sessions.

So they are still more or less camping out. But there is water and electricity, the roof is sound and the floor is solid and Candida, her mother's daughter, has made sure that the building is spotlessly clean. She has painted the walls of the stall which houses Daniel's cot pale blue and the woodwork dark blue, hung curtains over the open part of each side to reduce the draught and warmed the floor with carpet tiles; it is a perfectly adequate nursery for such a small person.

Their own living accommodation, hers and Tom's, is more primitive, since they had no money with which to set themselves up. Daniel's grandparents on both sides, achieving that status against their wills, have never been to visit and cannot be asked even for contributions of unwanted furniture. The grant with which Tom was expected to finance his work for a doctorate would not have kept even one person alive; and although by abandoning an academic career he has achieved the security of a salary, it is not a very generous one.

That, however, may be about to change – indeed, it may have changed already. Tom, swearing her to secrecy, has told her all about the negotiations which are due to come to a head today or tomorrow. The small business for which he works produces pure fruit juices from its own harvest and from fruit bought in from neighbouring orchards. It needs more modern machinery for bottling and labelling,

2

and to make the machines economic it would need to expand production. The business itself, which is personally owned by its executive chairman, has insufficient capital for the necessary investment, but an offer to take it over has recently been placed on the table by a large conglomerate. This – if the deal goes through – will hugely increase the scale of its operations and will open the doors of the giant supermarkets to its products.

An essential ingredient of any such deal must be an agreement for three of the key members of Purefrew's staff to remain in their posts. The men concerned will demand it, for the sake of their own futures, while the corporation will also require it as part of its policy of allowing successful small firms to expand under their existing management. So there is not likely to be any disagreement of principle, but only of terms. Tom has so recently taken up his employment that in ordinary circumstances he would not have been one of the élite who must guarantee to remain; but it is Tom who, if all goes well, will contribute Formula Four to the process of making everyone's fortune.

'We're going to be rich, Candy.' It was the last thing he said to her that morning. 'Not straight away, perhaps, but in time for Daniel to have a millionaire father one of these days. So think about it while I'm away. I can see that a gold-digger like you will never agree to marry a poor man. But once I'm rich, oh, then, Candy, marry me then!'

Candida didn't answer directly. 'Who is this stranger in a suit?' she said instead, laughing as happily as he and pressing her body hard against his as he kissed her goodbye. She remembers that kiss now as she finishes feeding Daniel, brings up his wind, cuddles him for a little and settles him back into the cot. Her love for her child merges into her love for Tom. It is all one. She feels as though she is hardly herself any longer, but only an amorphous emotion which stretches out to enfold these two people who are so dear to her.

It is then, as she stares down at Daniel, that she realises the time has come to change her mind. Her pregnancy was accidental and was a nasty shock when she first discovered it; but she was quick to come to two decisions. She wasn't going to have it terminated and wasn't going to use it as a lever to force Tom into marriage at an age when he was too young, too poor and too ambitious to be tied down.

These decisions didn't prevent her from feeling delighted when he insisted that they should set up home together. Had he told her in advance that he was going to abandon his doctorate and all thought of an academic career, she would have argued fiercely against it, feeling guilty that he should even contemplate taking such a step on her

3

behalf. But he found a job and a home – of sorts – without giving her any inkling of what he had in mind. By now she is no longer upset about his change of course and since the baby was born her gratitude has deepened into joy, as she sees how Tom adores him.

He has done his best to make an honest woman of her, pressing her both before and after the birth to marry him. Until now she has felt that only by continuing to say 'no' can she prove to herself that 'no' is what she always intended to say. Little by little, though, she has come to realise that this kind of strong-mindedness is selfish. Tom is an adult; he has the right to decide for himself how he wants to live – and he has made the decision. And Daniel – who is imperceptibly ceasing to be a baby and is becoming a person with a character of his own – deserves to have a secure family home, with parents who have committed their lives to each other and to him.

She has already made half of that commitment, when she chose to abandon her career ambitions rather than ask whether her pregnancy could be terminated. It is only fair that she should offer Tom the same sense of security. Perhaps it is because she is already feeling lonely at the prospect of a night without him that she at last makes up her mind. She has proved her point, such as it was, and now is simply being unreasonably stubborn. It is time to give in. The next time Tom proposes marriage, she will accept.

'That'll shake him!' she exclaims aloud, laughing so loudly and so merrily that little Daniel opens his eyes again for a few seconds and smiles. No doubt the smile signifies wind or a dirty nappy or merely the contentment of a full stomach, but Candida allows herself to interpret it as a sharing of her own happiness. She can hardly wait for Tom to get home.

2

At six o'clock in the evening of the third Monday in October Penny Martin cleans her paintbrushes and wipes her fingers down the side of her smock. The light has already, half an hour earlier, become too dim; but it doesn't matter, because what she is painting doesn't exist any more.

Her painting room – to call it a studio would be too pretentious – is at the top of the house: an attic which would have been inhabited by servants in the days, two hundred years earlier, when The Old Rectory was a new rectory. Penny particularly likes the attic because until she came to live in the house it was used just to store junk: it is the only room that holds no trace at all of Margaret, Clive's first wife.

4

It is also the only room high enough to allow a view over the stone wall into their neighbour's walled garden, and that is what she has spent almost the whole day painting – not as the jungle it is today, but as it must have looked at the turn of the century and as Clive, spending holidays in his grandparents' house fifty years later, might have seen it as a boy.

The Manor itself is out of sight, hidden by overgrown shrubberies and a high bank of rhododendrons as well as by some of the magnificent specimen trees – cedar and copper beech, chestnut and oak, grey poplar and sequoia – which were once upon a time carefully positioned in the park by a landscape gardener. Of its spacious grounds, all that Penny can see is the orchard, from which Clive has in his time scrumped apples, and the walled garden which immediately adjoins the tennis lawn of The Old Rectory.

The wall, which is almost two hundred years old and more than ten feet high, is made of very large pieces of stone which from a distance look simply grey. Close up, however, it is possible to distinguish traces of yellow and black, silver and green; even the greys are of four or five different shades.

Penny is fascinated by the subtle colours. Since coming to live in The Old Rectory she has spent hours sitting on the tennis lawn – no longer used for the playing of tennis since Clive joined a local club – and painting some minute section of stone, complete with its lichen, spiders and ladybirds. Clive, laughing affectionately, thinks she is mad when he sees her embarking on yet another study: what sort of a subject is that? He is right, of course. Watercolour is not a medium that Penny particularly enjoys using and these finished paintings are never likely to be of interest to anyone but herself. But the intense concentration of vision which is needed gives her pleasure in itself.

Today's work, however, has been different. The painting is intended as a Christmas present for Clive: that is why she is secretly pleased that the business negotiation in which he is involved today is complicated and important and likely to be protracted. Even if it doesn't in the end extend itself into a second day, it is expected to continue so late into the evening that the four men who are representing the company have decided in advance to stay overnight in London.

And so, with no danger that the painting's intended recipient will sneak silently upstairs to look over her shoulder, she has embarked on an imaginative reconstruction of the walled garden in its heyday. Although it has been neglected for years, the ground plan can still be identified; marked out by box hedges which would once have been neatly trimmed to a height of a few inches. In her painting she has

5

filled their triangles with leeks and lettuces, cabbages and carrots. The hoops which looped over one of the main cross paths are still furnished with roses which bloom, unpruned, each summer, and in the wide herbaceous border which originally provided flowers to be cut for the house, tall perennials still in their seasons force their way through a carpet of weeds.

There are further clues to help her. A rotten framework of wood which supports the last few panes of glass indicates the site of a greenhouse. Against the other three walls, many old fruit trees retain the shapes into which they have been trained, stretching their arms horizontally to touch their neighbours or lifting them towards the top of the wall in a fan. These also have continued to blossom and sometimes to bear fruit. The only occasion on which Penny has ever glimpsed the new owner of the estate, who recently inherited it from his grandmother, was when he appeared one day carrying a leaf-lined trug basket which he gently filled with peaches.

The garden is about to disappear. Not just the walled garden, but the whole of The Manor's extensive grounds will very soon now become a building site. The grandson, it appears, is an architect and intends to put his skills to use on his own land. A copy of the plans are in Clive's study at this moment, since as next-door neighbours the Martins have had the right to make comments on the application to develop the land and to ask for it to be rejected. They have not, in fact, put forward any objection, knowing that nothing they might say would make any difference. The land is zoned under the planning authority's local plan as being suitable for increased development and permission for the project has by now been granted.

And so before long The Manor itself will be divided into six luxury apartments for able-bodied and wealthy retired couples, and in its grounds will stand thirty-six units of sheltered housing – to which the retired couples may wish to retreat as time passes. On the acre of land now covered by the walled garden will rise a five-bedroomed detached house with double garage. It is all going to happen. The painting on which Penny has been working may prove to be the last record of a kind of modestly comfortable country life which is ceasing to exist.

Penny does not consider herself to be an artist, a word which she applies infrequently and with a sense of awe to those painters she particularly admires. Her training was in commercial art and design and during her eight years of employment in an advertising agency she almost always painted to order. It was someone else's responsibility to plan a campaign and produce the vague squiggles and incoherent descriptions which she would translate into eye-catching designs. Only infrequently, and almost in secret, did Penny herself conceive an idea for a poster or trademark and draft and finish the painting; and only very infrequently indeed did her idea progress even as far as the presentation to a client.

She enjoyed her years in the agency, though, and it is a matter of regret that Clive should so firmly have required her to stop working. In a sense, she realises, she has become a trophy wife. Not in the usual sense of being a beautiful blonde bimbo to be paraded by a sixty-year-old millionaire as a sign of his wealth and virility. She is blonde, certainly; but thirty-one years old and only five foot four tall. She dresses stylishly on social occasions, but no one will ever mistake her for one of the elegant clotheshorses who are photographed for magazines.

As for Clive, he is only forty-five. Because he inherited The Old Rectory from his grandparents he has not been crippled by years of mortgage payments but is not particularly highly paid – at least until today – and owns no great fortune. What he needs to prove to himself is that he can maintain the two sons of his first marriage and still be able to support a second wife as a lady of leisure.

Penny understands this need and has ceased to argue about it because, after almost three years of marriage, she is still head over heels in love with her husband. Whatever he wants he shall have, and she manages to convince herself that she wants it too. All the same, the sudden loss of an often frenetic working life and the distance which now separates her from all her London friends make the days seem very long. She has not really solved the problem of what to do with herself. As Mrs Clive Martin she is happy, deliriously happy, but she is not completely contented.

If any small cloud of discontent hovers over her now, she is quick to blow it away. She is missing Clive: there is no more to it than that. It hardly seems worth cooking an evening meal if Clive will not be there to share it, and there is no pleasure in the thought of going to bed when Clive will for once not be lying close against her back as she falls asleep. Oh, how much she loves him! But it is ridiculous to feel lonely when he is only spending a single night away from home. He will be back again tomorrow, and then they will continue to live happily ever after.

3

At six o'clock in the evening of the third Monday in October, an electric bell rings raucously in the indoor bowls hall to mark the end of a two-hour session. Madge Manderson shakes hands with the opposing skip and walks briskly down the rink to congratulate the rest of her team. They have won by four shots: enough to lift them to second place in the league.

Madge is a small, slight woman. Seen from the side she is – as Harry often affectionately remarks – as thin as a plank. At this moment she is wearing the neat but unexciting outfit prescribed for the bowling green: white blouse with set-in sleeves, grey skirt with two inverted pleats back and front and falling two inches below the knee, flat brown bowling shoes. Even in ordinary clothes her extreme thinness gives her the figure of a schoolgirl and the effect is accentuated by this uniform. But her schooldays are far behind her. Her hair, which rises in a thick wave above her forehead and is layered at the back into a short and almost boyish style, is grey. Neither the cut nor the colour has changed in almost twenty years. Madge has just passed her fiftieth birthday.

She is a skilled bowls player who would easily qualify for her county badge if she could spare the time to take part in matches. The two clubs to which she belongs – the outdoor village green in summer and this indoor hall from October to April – represent her private life. Harry never comes to watch her play. He is glad she has a hobby to amuse her, but would be surprised if anyone were to tell him that she is really rather good at it.

Madge is quite surprised herself. Before her marriage, she regarded bowls – if she thought about the game at all – as an undemanding pastime for pensioners. She took it up at the age of thirty-two only because the village of Lower Monckton proved to have little in the way of entertainment to offer a largely housebound mother. By now she is hooked on the subtle skills it demands and looks forward to her regular games.

For the past two hours she has been vigorous in giving her team instructions before delivering her own bowls either delicately or forcefully, as the position requires; but quitting the green she becomes once again the quiet woman whom Harry knows. In the locker room she exchanges friendly smiles with her fellow bowlers as she changes her shoes. The higher heels stretch her calf muscles and reveal that she has good ankles, but even these cannot take her over the five-foot mark.

'Ready, Madge?' asks her friend Gwen.

Without Gwen it would be impossible for Madge to play bowls in the winter. The outdoor green in the village is within walking distance of College Farm, but when the summer season ends the nearest indoor club is thirty minutes' drive away. Madge has no car and hasn't driven for years; and Gwen is the only member of the outdoor club who also wants to play indoors and is prepared to offer regular lifts. She often makes Madge anxious by her habit of arriving at the last possible moment to pick her up and of lingering to chat after the game is over, when Harry will be starting to worry about his supper. But for once Madge herself is in no hurry to get home.

'Fancy something to drink?' she asks.

'I wouldn't dare keep you from your kitchen stove.' Gwen is well aware of her friend's domestic arrangements. Harry Manderson is a Northerner, who regards six o'clock as the proper time to take what he still calls 'tea'. Since he doesn't arrive home from work until six twenty, he has long ago had to agree a compromise with his wife, who would prefer to serve dinner at eight. Seven o'clock prompt, though, is as far as he is prepared to go.

'No hurry today. Harry's staying overnight in London. A business meeting.' Gwen's generosity as a giver of lifts deserves to be recompensed for once. She asks only for a lime and lemonade, but Madge decides to be a dog and have a whisky Mac. Although Harry, a teetotaller, does not positively raise objections to her having a drink if she feels like one, she doesn't choose to attract his disapproval by asking – and in practice there is never anything in the house except a bottle of sherry to be offered to visitors. As the bell rings again to summon a new group of players for the beginning of the next bowling session, the two women, glasses in hand, join a group of their friends for a chat.

One of the group is the ladies' captain.

'We're losing our caterers at the end of the season,' she remarks. 'They've just given notice. If any of you know anybody who might take over, do please let us know.'

No one is surprised by this announcement. The task of providing low-priced hot meals twice a week, after matches against other clubs, is unattractive to professional caterers. Madge considers the appeal with particular interest. She once trained as a cook and, until her marriage, worked as a private caterer. That was in fact how she met Harry, when she was catering for his sister's wedding. He almost drove her mad with the way he fussed about details, checking on everything as though she had never undertaken such a job before. But

9

when it was all over, the sincerity of his thanks and apologies won her heart. Their courtship started there.

Marriage at the age of twenty-eight brought her brief career to an end. Harry, old-fashioned, made it clear that he could support a family and would prefer his wife not to work. Madge, who had every intention of continuing at least on a part-time basis, refused to be deterred; but, before she had time to establish herself in the new area where Harry already had a home and a job, she found herself pregnant, and the next seventeen years were devoted to keeping Julie alive. Three years have passed since she was last needed as a mother, but she has lost the confidence needed to run her own business again.

To provide hot meals for forty-eight people twice a week, in a familiar setting, would be well within her capabilities, though. She has often thought that she could do better than the present caterers. But almost as soon as the idea begins to seem attractive, she dismisses it as impractical. There is the transport problem and there is the Harry problem.

Well, they are really the same problem. If they were separate, the transport problem could be solved. The main reason why Madge doesn't drive these days is that they only have one car, which Harry takes to work; and even when they go out together he's not prepared for a moment to consider handing over the wheel. By now his nervousness is well justified: it is so long since she last drove that she would have no more confidence in her capabilities than he does. But it was not always like that. For eight years, after leaving college, she transported everything she needed for her catering engagements in her own van, weaving her way through the streets of London as expertly as any taxi driver. That, however, was a long time ago.

Madge is well aware that even her closest friends believe she has allowed herself to become the doormat kind of wife, and in one sense they are right. She is not a woman who enjoys quarrelling or even arguing, so it's true that she doesn't stand up for herself when she disagrees with her husband. But the reason is not as simple as they probably think. Harry is not a bully. He is overprotective, but that's a different matter altogether.

Madge's present lack of wheels is all her own fault. She continued to run the van after her marriage and the birth of her child. She was transporting Julie in an emergency dash to hospital when, with her attention distracted by the baby's struggle to breathe, she was involved in an accident. It was the smallest of accidents, and no one was hurt, but the van, already old, was written off by the insurance company.

That was when she discovered for the first time what a nervous man she had married. At work, as a factory manager, Harry is efficient and decisive; overmeticulous, perhaps, but for that reason making few mistakes. But as a man he seems to be frightened of life – and, in particular, terrified of being left alone. He needs his wife and has to look after her in case she is not careful enough about looking after herself. Madge suspects that the root of his fear lies in the death of his mother when he was only seven, but this essay in amateur psychology does nothing to change the situation and so over the years she has forced herself to accept it.

If she were to offer her services to the club as a caterer she would need some kind of vehicle, because the village shop would not be able to supply her in sufficient quantity or at an economical price; and also because she would be arriving earlier and leaving later than any of the playing members of the club and so could not expect to be given lifts. Her own savings are insufficient to cover the cost of a car, and she can't see Harry stumping up several thousand pounds for a venture of which he would certainly disapprove. Because the other thing is that twice a week she would be late home. He would have to take his own supper out of the oven and eat it on his own. And all the time he would be worrying about where she was. No, it would not be at all a good idea to volunteer.

There are times when Madge feels resentful at being treated almost like a child, but more often she recognises that this is her husband's way of showing that he cares for her and is anxious to protect her from the perils of dark streets and irresponsible drivers and her own possible carelessness. From time to time, when friends who have continued to live in London come to stay, chattering about their more exciting activities, she recognises silently that her marriage was a mistake. But she has a comfortable life and a kind husband. Although she had not expected him to become so protective, she knew before she married him that he was a fussy man; there are no reasonable grounds for complaint.

Because none of her fellow bowlers is aware that she was once a professional caterer, there are no meaningful glances in her direction as the club's problem is discussed. The subject changes to the prospects for the next round of the interclub Yetton trophy and Madge, since she will not be driving, has another whisky Mac.

Gwen notices this and laughs. 'Aha! I see the mouse is playing while the cat's away!'

Madge's smile is more restrained than usual. Gwen is too tactful ever to use her nickname openly, but is well aware that within her own family Madge is always known as Mouse. The name dates from babyhood, because she has always been both tiny and quiet. When

11

she first got to know Harry, he naturally called her Madge, the name on her business notepaper. It was when her hair turned grey within three months of discovering that her baby had been born, after an exceptionally long and painful labour, with cerebral palsy, that he picked up with affection the word which of course he had heard from her mother. 'Don't cry, my little grey mouse.'

It was a mark of love and comfort then, and she gratefully accepted it as such. But it is not an attractive nickname. She repeatedly asks Harry not to use it in public, but he rarely remembers the request. She cringes when she hears herself introduced to strangers, 'And this is Mouse.'

Gwen is ready to go. They drive back to Lower Monckton, chatting about the colours of leaves and the drawing-in of nights. Madge is dropped to walk up the track to College Farm.

The farmhouse, long ago separated from its land, is too large for two people; but from the first moment of seeing it Madge was delighted by the spacious and welcoming kitchen; and Julie, when she was old enough to sit in a wheelchair, could sleep in a downstairs room and be moved easily about the whole of the ground floor.

The hall, which has become shabby over the years, is cluttered with umbrellas and walking sticks and boots and pieces of old furniture which Harry has bought at country sales and restored. On top of a carved oak chest stands a photograph of Julie, placed there so that it will be the first thing Madge sees whenever she returns home. As always, she pauses for a moment to kiss the air towards it.

Taking off her coat, she stares at her reflection in the hall mirror. Is she really a mouse?

It's the greyness of her hair, she decides, that is to blame. When she was in her thirties that same grey hair looked striking because it framed young – well, fairly young – skin. But now it gives a certain drabness to her appearance, because so few fifty-year-olds these days allow themselves to go grey. Helen Cunningham, whom she knows for a fact to be ten years older than herself, looks far smarter – and it's all thanks to her hairdresser. Madge tells herself that she doesn't care. After all, she's happily married and has no wish to attract other men, so what's wrong with looking her age? Harry still comes home to her every night. Well, every night except this one.

All the same, the evening, with its break in routine, is proving an unsettling one. There is nothing to be cooked for Harry, and she can't be bothered to eat by herself. Although, as a skilled and imaginative cook, she enjoys the appreciation which Harry always shows when his meal is set before him, her own interest in food ends when it is served, and she rarely takes more than a mouthful or two of any dish.

12

So, instead of sitting down to supper, she pours herself a glass of sherry and switches on the television set. Harry is a man who looks through the coming week's programmes every Sunday. He marks whatever he decides they would be interested in watching, and is not easily persuaded that his wife might wish to make a choice of her own. Madge rarely expresses any preference, because she has little interest in television. She is a voracious reader, finding in books the only remaining link with the more sophisticated city life she once led. But tonight the unusual freedom to zap around in an undisciplined fashion persuades her to leave her book unopened. She is in the mood for simply being entertained and doesn't care what's on. She watches a game show, a police drama, the nine o'clock news. The bottle of sherry remains within reach.

4

At six o'clock in the evening of the third Monday in October, Helen Cunningham sits at her dressing table, wearing the lacy black underwear which she reserves for her little adventures. To the different scents of bath oil and talcum powder she adds generous touches of perfume, dabbing it on her wrists and behind her ears. She has read somewhere that it is a woman's natural smell that is most enticing to a man, but is not at all sure that such a generalisation still applies if the woman is sixty years old.

For a moment she stares critically into the looking glass. She has always taken care of herself and her life has gone smoothly, with no great tragedies or illnesses to etch lines of pain or misery into her face. Some women of her age become scrawny, but she has just enough flesh on her bones to keep her skin smooth. She is a tall woman who holds herself well; expensive clothes look good on her, and she has the money to buy them. Her hair would be grey by now if she allowed it to be, but she is sensible about disguising the fact. Resisting the temptation to become a blonde or redhead, she maintains the light brown with which she was born. As she skilfully applies her make-up– not too much but not too little – she doesn't look a day over fifty.

With her face and hair ready for the evening, she steps into a black dress. The dress has a sweetheart neckline, because her skin there can stand up to the exposure, but there are full chiffon sleeves to conceal the fact that her upper arms are not as seductive as once was the case. She clips on expensive jewellery: necklace, bracelet, brooch. Too much, probably, for a country restaurant, but the temptation to

13

make an impression cannot be resisted. She is giving a signal that she is available.

Derek Forsyth, who will be calling to pick her up at seven o'clock, is the secretary of her bridge club. He is a good-looking man of about her own age, with plentiful grey hair and a neat moustache. He has been divorced for at least twenty years and shows no wish ever to be tied down again. The members of the club whom he from time to time singles out for special attention are always married women who may be bored with their marriages but have more sense than to put them at risk by indiscreet behaviour. Helen knows that if this dinner date develops as she hopes, she will not be the first of his conquests, nor the last; but she can hardly complain about that since she has had previous affairs herself; and she can trust him not to make waves.

She intends to be equally discreet herself. Michael, her husband, is four years older than she is, but sixty-four is not really old. If he has ceased to come to her bedroom – and it must be almost six years since they last made love – it is presumably because he no longer finds her exciting. He doesn't explain it that way, but apologises instead for the fact that he can't manage it any more. She has assured him that she doesn't mind, and in one sense she doesn't. There is no reason to suspect that there is any other woman involved, and after thirty-five years of marriage she and Michael have an easy, friendly, social relationship. She doesn't even particularly miss the sex, as a physical experience. What she does need – and what she hopes this evening will offer – is the excitement of feeling herself desired. When she can no longer attract a man to her bed, then she will know herself to be old.

Soon – perhaps very soon – it will become more difficult to arrange these diversions. Michael is within a year of retiring age in any case, and if the takeover which he has been discussing today goes through he will almost certainly sell the whole of his interest in Purefrew, the business he founded and developed, in order that a new management setup can be put in place straight away. How will she cope with a husband who is at home all day?

Well, that's tomorrow's problem. For the moment she takes a last look at herself in the glass, smooths down her skirt and goes downstairs.

Derek arrives punctually at seven o'clock. Helen looks for the admiration in his eyes as he kisses her in greeting, and is not disappointed; he is playing his part as skilfully as she is playing hers. She invites him in for a drink. He has never been inside Monckton Hall before, and takes appreciative note of antique furniture and silver, expensive rugs, shelves of leather-bound books, cabinets of china.

There are collections on display. Michael is an obsessive buyer of miniatures and daguerreotypes, old truncheons and snuff boxes, button hooks and thimbles. A pretence of studying the miniatures allows Derek the opportunity to put a necessary question.

'Is your husband –?'

'Michael and some of his staff are spending the night in London. A big business deal. They need two days for it.'

'Ah, yes.'

There is no need to press the matter further. Helen hands Derek a gin and tonic and adds ice to her own Campari soda. Smiling, they lift their glasses to each other without bothering to put any toast into words.

5

At six o'clock in the evening of the third Monday in October the boardroom doors of Wright and King's City headquarters open. The meeting is over.

The Purefrew contingent is the first to emerge: Michael Cunningham, Harry Manderson, Clive Martin and Tom Harding. Negotiations which had been expected to continue over two days have been concluded in one long and arduous session. The afternoon's discussions have been prolonged and detailed and they all unconsciously show how much the tension has cramped them by stretching their arms, rotating their shoulders and breathing deeply. As one man they make for the directors' washroom and sigh with a physical as well as a mental relief.

Michael Cunningham is the first to speak, glancing round to see whether any of the other side's negotiators have followed them in.

'Well, I think that all went very well, don't you?'

Michael has reason to be pleased. Although they will all profit in the end, he is the only one who will become an immediate millionaire. He takes this as his due. Purefrew is his own private company. He inherited a large fruit farm while still a young man, but it was he who had the idea to start and expand the juice business which he is now passing into other hands. If his daughter had ever shown the slightest interest in taking it over, he might have hung on to it; but she has made her home in Washington and is unlikely to live in England again. He himself is practically at retiring age and quite ready to take life easily in prosperous circumstances. It has been clear to him from the start that Wright and King will want to buy him out.

The situation for the other three is different. They are employees and have not so far held any financial stake in the company. But their expertise is needed. The morning was devoted to accounts and projections and development plans for the business as a whole, but it is the discussion of terms and contracts which has taken much of the afternoon. The company taking them over needs to be sure that these three at least will stay and work hard and imaginatively; they for their part need assurances that their work will be valued.

The terms now agreed, although not yet written out and signed, are complicated but satisfactory. Harry and Clive and Tom are not, like Michael, being offered fortunes on the spot. But they will have security of employment at enhanced rates of pay and the prospect of generous incentive bonuses each year; and they have been offered share options in the parent company at an extremely favourable price.

Harry Manderson, a neatly-dressed man with a face so deeply lined that it could be described as wizened, looks tired and drained as he splashes his face with water in an attempt to refresh himself. He is fifty-five and more concerned with the terms of his future pension than with the glorious possibilities of ever-increasing bonuses. Although the Purefrew team were supposed to leave the negotiations as far as possible to Rufus Grant, their lawyer, Harry has been unable to refrain from continually interrupting to check that details are correct. He is not a good delegator, never quite trusting anyone to do a job as well as he could do it himself. Although Michael Cunningham owns the company and is theoretically in charge of it, Harry is the man who looks after its day-to-day running and he carries every detail in his mind.

Clive Martin has been watching Harry's defence of his pension with amusement. For his own part, he expects to do very well out of the new arrangements. Although to start with he will continue as marketing manager of the existing business, that business will now be part of a large empire and within it he may hope to expand his own domain. At forty-five, he is still young enough to look forward to a new career which will allow him to take advantage of the financial incentives. He smiles to himself as he rehearses the words with which he will break the good news to Penny. She wants to start a family, and now she can. Not tonight, since he will be spending the night in London with the others; but perhaps tomorrow.

For Tom Harding the lure of share options is not great. They are a gamble, and every gamble needs a stake. The options have to be bought and, although the purchase price is low, Tom has no savings at all except the pitifully small amount which must be kept and

16

increased if he is ever to put down the deposit on a house for Candida and Daniel.

He feels no bitterness about this restriction on his potential fortune. He has worked for Purefrew for less than a year and as a new boy would not normally have expected to be included in such a scheme at all. But he doesn't propose to belittle his own contribution. Although the takeover makes very good business sense simply on the figures which Purefrew has been able to produce from the past and their projections for the future, Tom is well aware that the joker in the pack is the new drink which is his particular baby: Formula Four.

Nobody has said in so many words that this may be a deciding factor. All over the country, no doubt, on hot summer afternoons, jugs of cool liquid made to some special family recipe are carried out into gardens. This one may be better than most; Tom certainly believes it to be. So do his Purefrew colleagues, who with unscientific enthusiasm assume that they are sitting on a gold mine.

The Wright and King negotiators are more realistic, resisting any suggestion that they should put large extra sums of money on the table in respect of something that may never reach a point of sale. They recognise that there must be a great deal of testing and analysis before Formula Four can take even the most tentative first step towards a commercial market. It may be necessary to add preservatives, and only time will tell how effective they are. There are health tests to be passed in a range of climatic conditions, and legal protection to be taken out all over the world – and all these hurdles must be successfully jumped before a single bottle can be produced for test marketing.

Research of this kind is not what the conglomerate is in business to do directly, although under the new arrangement its funds will become available to Purefrew. And so in the contracts which have been under discussion all day there has been no direct statement that Wright and King is buying Formula Four or that Purefrew is selling it.

Tom is right, nevertheless, to think that his contribution is an important one. There will be a schedule in the final contract which lists all Purefrew's present products and then adds a special clause on the subject of patent applications and future developments. A good deal of discussion has gone on about the precise wording of this clause.

In a confused sort of way Tom is aware that he would perhaps have been wise to have a lawyer of his own, if only to deal with the situation which might arise if Formula Four is not in the end successfully produced or adequately marketed. But he isn't a businessman. He would in no case want to set up a company of his own. As far as he is concerned, the new taste has got him a good job and an even brighter future. If the drink takes off, he will share, through bonuses, in the increased prosperity of the company. He is just as pleased as the others about the way the day has gone.

As they wash their hands, Clive comes to stand beside him.

'Well, young Tom, that was a very profitable game of tennis we played, wasn't it?'

Tom grins his agreement. He and Clive, as members of the same tennis club, have been friends and sporting opponents for several years. It was as they sprawled, panting, on the grass at the end of one particularly ferocious session on a hot and humid summer day that Tom produced a thermos flask and two glasses. 'Something you might find refreshing.'

The first sip was followed by a murmur of approbation. 'What's it made of?' But Tom wasn't saying.

He still hasn't said, and this may be why Michael Cunningham now takes him by the arm for a confidential word.

'This share-option business, Tom. If you haven't got any spare cash just at the moment, let me know. Out of all they're paying me for the business I could let you have an interest-free loan of a few thousand. You could pay me back when you take the shares up eventually.'

This offer is not quite as altruistic as it sounds. Michael is well aware that Tom, who has kept very quiet all day, could even at the last moment scupper the whole deal. He has kept the secret of Formula Four close to his chest, insisting that all the samples provided over the past few months must be drunk on the spot and not taken away for analysis. Michael believes it is not completely fanciful to envisage the drink as one day rivalling Coca-Cola, now that it is about to have the money and resources of an international company behind it. But . . .

The biggest 'but' is that the recipe does not yet belong to Purefrew, although Wright and King have been allowed to think that it does. Tom first poured the drink for Clive before he was employed by the business. In the interests of getting a good deal, he has agreed with Rufus Grant that he will lodge the recipe in a secure place approved by all parties before the documents are finally signed in four or five days' time and will relinquish any personal rights which he may have established; but nothing of this has been put in writing.

Michael doesn't doubt that the promise was sincerely made. It is probably because Tom is an academic scientist at heart, and not by nature an entrepreneur, that he is displaying such a marked lack of greed – apparently accepting the increased salary and security which the new arrangements offer him as being sufficient recompense for his contribution.

But he will go home tomorrow to his girlfriend and tell her what has been settled – and Michael has met Candida. She is a smart cookie. He wouldn't at all put it past her to explain to Tom that by allowing negotiations to progress so far he has in fact got his colleagues over a barrel. She could introduce the words 'royalty' or 'licence' into his mind, and the whole discussion would have to start again from scratch. Later in the evening Michael will suggest quietly to all the others that no word of the proposed arrangements should be passed to anyone at all until the papers are finally signed: not even in pillow talk. In the meantime, anything that Michael can do to keep Tom happy will be money well lent.

'Would you really? Well, thanks. That's very good of you.' Tom is naively enthusiastic. He is twenty-five years old, and in the laboratory, his forehead furrowed with concentration, is clever beyond his years. But in other respects he is still little more than a boy, rushing at life without too much regard for consequences.

Michael smiles in confirmation of his offer, hoping that he has bought the necessary three or four days. Candida may not have realised yet that she will have to provide the business head in her relationship with Tom, but that time can't be long in coming.

As they emerge into the open space which leads from the board-room, the four men are joined by their lawyer, who has lingered behind to agree the time of the next meeting.

Rufus Grant is an unlikely-looking lawyer. Take away the jacket and tie and unbutton the shirt collar and he would pass for a foot-baller. His hair, tousled now by much running-through of fingers, is on the red side of sandy and his face is freckled. Wide cheekbones and clear blue eyes give him an open-air look which has not been dimmed by many years of study and examinations. By the time he becomes an old man, his eyebrows will probably be described as beetling; but today he is in his early thirties and the strength of his features merely suggests that this is a man who can be trusted. As a rule Michael Cunningham turns to his senior partner when he needs legal advice, but in this specialised field of mergers and takeovers he has been advised that Rufus is the best man for the job.

'I'll spend a couple more hours here tomorrow,' Rufus tells Michael Cunningham now. 'Then it'll take a little time for the draft agreements and contracts to be prepared and for me to go through them. Once I've okayed them and the final version is ready, I'll give you a ring. I'll need you all to sign and then the whole thing will be buttoned up.'

By now the Wright and King contingent is emerging from the boardroom; their company secretary has a suggestion to make.

'Why don't we all go off for a drink and a meal? To celebrate. With a toast to our future partnership. It's a bit early, but I know somewhere that opens at six. Are you on?'

Yes, they are all on. Chatting together in small groups, they move towards the lifts. It has been a good day.

6

It is six o'clock in the evening of the third Monday in October. The soft murmuring of visitors' voices is interrupted by a rattling of trolleys and plates at the far end of the hospital ward, and the scents of the flowers which have arrived during the afternoon are overcome by the odours of fish and broccoli.

The trolleys will not pause beside the cubicle of Jarvis Elliott, for a placard hung above his head orders 'Nil by mouth'. But it is nevertheless, time for Pamela to go home. Gently he extricates his hand from her anxious grasp.

'Are you sure you've got everything you want?' she asks, not for the first time.

She is frightened. Well, naturally she is frightened. She has not yet recovered from the shock of the phone call which told her that her husband had been rushed to hospital after being found on his office floor, in a state of collapse after vomiting blood. Probably he was indeed – as his secretary certainly believed – near death at that moment, so it is difficult to blame Pamela for wondering what the next twenty-four hours will bring. But the effect of her fear is to push her oddly out of character. She is trying to control it in case he has not realised for himself how serious his condition is; yet at the same time she wants him to know that she is frightened for him, because otherwise he might wonder whether she loves him enough. The conflict of feelings has left her confused and indecisive.

This is not the woman Jarvis knows; not the woman to whom he has been married for twenty-eight years. Pamela Elliott is the editor of a magazine for women. In her office she is decisive and even ruthless when necessary and at home she is always well organised. It is an indication of just how bad things are that she can't get a grip on herself today. Jarvis himself, the one who ought to be receiving comfort, has to provide reassurance.

'I'm in good hands here,' he reminds her. He has almost certainly done himself a favour by collapsing within a ten-minute ambulance ride of a London teaching hospital instead of at home in the country. 'If Dr Brook thought I was likely to snuff it at any moment he'd have sent me off for an operation straight away instead of waiting for all those test results.'

This statement may not be entirely accurate. Although at the time he was not conscious of what was going on, he has been told in the course of the afternoon that the first priority was to stabilise his condition with intravenous fluids until such time as his blood could be matched for a transfusion. He knows also that the internal bleeding has been checked. What he doesn't know is whether the bleeding will start again before the specialist has had time to locate the cause of the trouble. Although no one has told him that it is necessary, he finds himself instinctively lying very still in the bed.

Nevertheless, the impression he is giving his wife is fair enough. Tomorrow he is to have an endoscopy. The procedure of insinuating an optical telescope through the complicated channels of his body has been explained to him, but he doesn't pretend to understand how it can be possible: he is content to accept it as magic. There will not necessarily prove to be any need for surgery. Jarvis strongly suspects that the purpose of the nil-by-mouth policy is to guard against the eventuality of the telescope taking a wrong turning at some point and causing sufficient damage itself to require an urgent operation. This is something he doesn't mention to Pamela.

By now the ward is noisy with the bustle of visitors who take the serving of the evening meal as a signal to depart.

'You really ought to have a room to yourself,' says Pamela, still unwilling to leave. The magazine company for which she works provides private health insurance not only for its employees but also for their spouses. Now that the immediate emergency of his admission is over, she wishes he would take advantage of it. Jarvis's own feelings on the subject are ambivalent. He is a socialist who believes passionately in the National Health Service – but what does 'believing in it' imply? That it should be there to cope with every emergency, certainly; and it is coping with his. But since he is entitled to call on the services of private medicine, it could be argued that he would serve the NHS better by leaving this bed free now for someone else.

In practice he has abandoned logic and settled for being selfish. He feels safest where he is.

He has had a scare, and he is not closing his eyes to the danger which still exists; but there is nothing that either he or Pamela can do at the moment. Except for one thing – the one thing that he doesn't

21

feel able to manage: a serious conversation. Pamela has been sitting at his bedside for two hours now, but he still hasn't managed to talk to her about more than trivialities.

How much simpler it would be if he knew for certain that he is about to die. He could tell her how much he loves her, how much she means to him, how grateful he is for the years of their life together. In spite of one or two wanderings on his part when he was in his forties, their marriage – perhaps because it is childless – has been an exceptionally close and happy one. How ridiculous it is that a kind of embarrassment should inhibit him from saying all these things that she would love to hear, just because there is a chance that after such a deathbed scene, he might find himself still living! He knows that it is crazy to be inhibited from what is not really sentimentality but sincerity; yet he still cannot force himself to do it. She knows how he feels, he tells himself; of course she must know. But he ought to try.

'Thank you,' he begins awkwardly.

Pamela looks at him curiously. 'Thank you for what?'

No, he can't say it. For one thing, if he does, it will confirm her fear that he is more seriously ill than he has been prepared to admit. Smoothly he changes tack.

'Thank you for not saying that you told me so.' For years she has been trying to persuade him that just because he has found a brand of tablet which eases the aches and pains of over-energetic games of tennis, it doesn't mean that it will act twice as well if he takes double the recommended dose. He has already confessed to receiving a ticking-off on this subject from the registrar, severe enough to convince him that his collapse must be considered a self-inflicted injury.

'They oughtn't to sell such things over the counter.' Pamela has made this comment often before. He cuts her off quickly before she can deliver another lecture.

'Off you go now, my darling,' he says affectionately instead. 'And remember, if they do have to operate tomorrow, I'd rather you didn't come in. I'll be far too woozy to know whether you're there or not, and it will only upset you to see me covered in tubes and drips and that sort of thing.' Some of these are in place already, but at least his nose and mouth are unobstructed for the moment.

Pamela bends over to kiss him. 'Love you,' she says, and manages to smile as she straightens herself. She, like him, is being careful not to give the impression that this is anything more than a temporary parting; putting a brave face on it in order not to alarm him. But Jarvis knows that she will cry as she drives home. In spite of her businesslike professional behaviour, she has always been a woman to whom tears come easily in private life.

22

After she leaves, it is time for Jarvis to get organised. Like Pamela in her normal state, he is a well-ordered man. He is a publisher. In an age when most book publishers have amalgamated into large conglomerates, he has managed to remain independent, still owning a business which he built up from nothing. The experience of running his own office almost single-handed in the early days has made him tidy-minded and efficient. He puts that tidiness to work now.

From the hospital shop trolley which was pushed round during the course of the afternoon he asked Pamela to buy him a notebook. It is not easy to write with one hand immobilised by the drip; he takes it slowly. Pamela knows where his will is lodged, but there are one or two small bequests that he would like to add – bequests which have never seemed worth the cost of incorporating in lawyer-drafted codicils, but which can be personally handed over as an assurance that the recipients have not been forgotten.

On another page he puts a suggestion which she can discuss with his stockbroker, about the best way to provide for her future if she should find herself alone; and he reminds her where to find the folder containing all his insurance policies. In an odd sort of way, the meticulous listing of such details manages to reduce the possibility of death to a matter-of-fact diary appointment with a question mark against it.

Not that he really believes for a moment that his life is in danger. Although, at fifty-five, he is not a young man, he is certainly not old. Silently he orders himself to remain optimistic. One of the books on his current publishing list argues that the best cure for a wide range of illnesses is a cheerful state of mind, and he finds the argument persuasive. Positive thinking is the thing!

Nevertheless he worries – he is bound to worry – about his wife's future life if the worst should happen. Pamela is successful in her career, but she has never had to come home to an empty house. And the life of an editor is not a secure one. They have laughed about that in the past, together visualising a time when, instead of overseeing each edition of *At Home*, Pamela will actually have to stay at home like most of her readers. But she would not find it so funny to do it alone. Would she be able to cope without his support?

On an impulse he reaches for the notebook again and begins to write a letter. He and Pamela are both professionally concerned with the written rather than the spoken word. He can write what he was unable to say, and she will understand his shyness. So she will after all learn in so many words how grateful he is for the happy years they have spent together. He will give her the notebook when everything

23

is under control and she comes to visit him in two days' time – and she will cry as she reads it. She is a real cry-baby, Pamela.

A nurse arrives to check on him yet again. He allows himself to relax back into the pillows. This is one of the many moments during this unusual day when he would have liked a cigarette. But the doctor has been specific in his orders. 'Not cut down, stop! Not one more, ever!' Jarvis has made a promise, and temptation has been thrown away.

The nurse makes her notes and hangs the clipboard back on the end of the bed. She outlines his timetable and promises that she will be back to check again before too long. He has no further responsibilities of his own. For the next few days other people will be in charge of his life.

Jarvis finds the prospect restful. After all, had he collapsed in the car while he was driving to work, instead of in his own office after an hour of smoking rage at the traffic hold-up which caused him to be late for his first appointment of the day, Pamela might be a widow already. There is no point in worrying about her future. She has never been the sort of 'little woman' who has to be fussed over and protected. She will manage if she has to.

Chapter Two

1

It is ten o'clock on the same evening. Candida has given Daniel his last feed a little earlier than usual so that she can go to sleep herself. It is usually Tom who picks him up and brings him to her in bed when the first faint whimper is heard at five in the morning, but for once she will need to be on the alert. She gives a luxuriant yawn and stretches herself, pressing her elbows back until her shoulder blades feel as though they are touching.

She and Tom have made a bedroom for themselves in what was once the hayloft of the stable. Two mattresses on top of each other make a comfortable bed; and a rail on wheels, of the kind used by charity shops to display cast-off clothing, acts as a wardrobe. A mirror is fastened to the wooden wall above two chests which Candida has covered with a sale-price remnant to serve as a dressing table. It is primitive, certainly, but adequate; and it will not be for long. She showers herself in one of the horse stalls and climbs the ladder up to the loft.

She has not been up there since Tom left that morning, so it comes as a surprise to find that there is a sealed envelope with her name on it lying on the pillow on Tom's side of the bed. For a moment her heart bumps with anxiety. This is the sort of envelope left by husbands or wives who are planning never to return. She has often feared that Tom may one day feel that he has been trapped into a relationship for which he is not really prepared. Is that fear coming true at last? It takes her a moment to screw up her courage and pull the folded sheet of paper out of its envelope.

Dearest Candy,
Will you marry me?
I hope you're going to have a thoroughly lonely and miserable
night without me and wake up in the morning seeing sense at last.
I shall ask you again as soon as I get home and this time I want a
proper answer: the right answer. I want to live happily ever after
with you and Daniel and his brother and two sisters.
WILL YOU MARRY ME? PLEASE.
I love you.
Tom

Candida gives a shriek of delight, not caring whether she wakes the baby. Only four hours have passed since she decided that it is time to stop sacrificing what she and Tom both want to some stupid principle, and here is the proof that she was right. She searches in the pockets of Tom's denim jacket, hanging on the rail, until she finds a ballpoint, and writes her answer in huge capitals at the bottom of the letter.

YES.

There is nothing lonely and miserable about her night. She is warm with happiness and falls asleep at once.

2

At ten o'clock on the same evening Helen smiles her thanks to the waiter and leads the way out of the restaurant. Her eyes are bright with more than the wine; the evening has gone well. As Derek unlocks the passenger door for her, his arm encircles her waist.

'How about a nightcap at my place?' he suggests.

'Why don't you come back to the Hall? Michael has some very special whisky. I forget quite how many years old, but a lot.'

'Are you sure that he –?' Derek has the appearance of a military man, but perhaps not the courage.

'Quite sure.'

This is not altogether true. Michael has mentioned the very slight possibility that the negotiations might collapse – although even then he would expect to stay on in London with the others. The truth is that just that whiff of danger increases Helen's excitement. In her heart she believes the danger is slight. If Michael were to return early he might indeed come to her bedroom door, but only to assure her that any sounds she hears are not made by a burglar. If, on opening the door, he finds only darkness and the silence of sleep, he will not intrude further. But she doesn't tell Derek this. Her only concession to the risk is to suggest that he should leave his car in the stable yard, where it will be out of sight, when together they return to Monckton Hall. She switches off the burglar alarm and leads the way inside.

'This is the malt whisky.' She shows him the label. 'But there's brandy or a liqueur if you prefer.'

Derek knows his lines to perfection; he has played this scene before.

'You don't think I've really come in just for a drink, do you?' Now his arms are around her. There is a question mark in his first kiss which does away with the need to say the words out loud: I am right, aren't I, in thinking that this is what you want? There have been so many cases of date rape reported in the papers recently, so much talk about the giving and receiving of wrong signals, that he needs to be sure.

Helen provides the response he is hoping for, pressing her body against him and opening her lips to his. Just such a prolonged embrace is the moment in any evening of this kind which gives her the most pleasure. The messy part which will come later is always more a gesture of appreciation on her part than a spontaneous seizing of pleasure.

For once, however, the messy part proves to be enjoyable. As their bodies move together in her darkened bedroom, Helen realises that it is not only the words of his seduction scene that Derek has practised to perfection. He is at the same time passionate and gentle, murmuring sounds which express emotion without necessarily making sense. Michael – even before giving up altogether – was for some years too quick and perfunctory, but in Derek's more skilful hands Helen finds herself first aroused and then satisfied; aroused and satisfied again.

It is well after midnight before she falls asleep; and when, some time later, she becomes aware that Derek is stirring beside her, she keeps her eyes shut. Once again he is doing everything right. She has no wish for him to see her, tousled, in the cold light of morning and she has left the burglar alarm off so that he can slip quietly away. No doubt he guesses that she is awake, for he bends over to touch each shoulder in turn with his lips. Then the bedroom door closes behind him and Helen, smiling, falls into a deep sleep.

3

By ten o'clock on the same evening Madge Manderson is feeling distinctly squiffy and rather sick. The combination of whisky, ginger wine and far too much sweet sherry is proving to be an unfortunate one. For the past half-hour the television screen has been presenting to her confused eyes the third instalment of a serial of which she has never seen the beginning. She tries and fails to work out what is going on and at last gives up.

What she ought to be thinking about is not someone else's plot but her own future. That casual comment about the catering at the bowls club has put the matter into her mind. For seventeen years of her life she has been Julie's mother: nothing else. Washing, dressing, exercising, carrying to the lavatory, lifting in and out of the wheelchair, waiting for the special school transport, being ready when it returns, talking with a sometimes forced brightness, straining to interpret the responses, lifting, lifting, lifting. It has been a life in itself.

But Julie is dead. Julie has been dead for three years and, although the days have often since then seemed empty and lonely, how could anyone have wished long life to someone so frustrated by her limitations? It would be ridiculous for Madge to pretend to herself that she has been in mourning for three years, but for all that time she has been standing still. Allowing time to pass: a moment, an hour, a day at a time. Pleasurably, for the most part, but in a manner which at this moment of introspection feels unproductive.

Playing bowls, cultivating the garden, feeding Harry: is this enough to fill the rest of her life? On this unusual evening – because she is for once alone – she feels as trapped in her home as Julie was in her wheelchair. Harry loves her; he loves her passionately. But his love and protectiveness are smothering her and she can see no way out. There are refuges for women who need to escape from bullying and abuse, but there is nowhere to take refuge from kindness.

Her thoughts are going round and round. Her head feels muzzy. It is clear – well, fairly clear – that she ought to make plans and find a way to assert herself without causing hurt. But this is the wrong moment for facing facts clearly and making objective decisions. And ten o'clock is in any case her usual time for starting to tidy up and move towards bed.

This process is not as smooth as usual. She drops her sherry glass. Luckily it falls on a soft hearthrug and doesn't break; she decides to leave it there in safety until morning, in case she should drop it again on the quarry tiles of the kitchen floor.

She is drunk; no point in denying it to herself. It is because she is drunk that she is attempting to formulate a problem where no problem has ever existed before, and it is because she is drunk that she is failing to solve it. The last – and first – time she was in this state was at least thirty years ago. She ought to be ashamed, but instead is

28

rather enjoying the giggly irresponsibility. Or rather, she would enjoy it if she didn't feel so sick. She makes her erratic way into the kitchen and finds a pudding basin to carry upstairs with her, just in case.

Gwen has been quite right in her comment. The cat is away and so the mouse has played. But only for one night. It won't ever happen again.

4

At ten o'clock on the same evening Penny Martin is studying the plans of the house which is to be built in the walled garden next door. The name on the planning application suggests that the owner of the land is not only the architect but proposes to live in it himself. She amuses herself by trying to create a mental picture of him with only the drawings as a guide. Although she once or twice met the old lady who lived in The Manor until her death, the grandson who has inherited is an unknown quantity.

It is easy to deduce that he is a fitness freak. Over the double garage there is to be an exercise room, a sauna and a plunge pool. He believes in cleanliness as well. The five bedrooms are served by three bathrooms and two shower rooms. Penny wonders idly how large his family is. Usually in a house of such a size she would expect to find something labelled playroom or rumpus room, but the only possible candidate says firmly 'study'.

Her musings are interrupted by the telephone, which she picks up before it has time to ring a second time. As she hopes, it is Clive – and Clive is in a high state of excitement.

'All settled!' he announces. 'Went like a breeze. A few days for the lawyers to draw up the legal stuff, and then we'll be up and running. Nothing more for the rest of us to talk about, so we're coming home tonight. Thought I'd better warn you in case you wake up and hear mysterious noises. It won't be till after midnight.'

Penny grins happily. He is not giving a warning at all. He is asking her not to go to sleep before he arrives.

'Roll on the mysterious noises!' she exclaims; and she continues to smile after the brief conversation. Has the time come, she wonders, when they could start a family? With a baby to bring up, she would no longer feel underemployed. Until now she has sympathised with Clive's caution in this respect, because although Margaret has a new man to support her, maintaining the two boys at boarding school will be an expensive business for several years to come. But she feels sure that he understands her need for a child of her own; and if today's discussions have had the results he hoped for, he will soon cease to be merely a salaried employee with little prospect of advancement and will be working for himself, with bonuses, share options or some other incentive to reward success.

To be wealthy would of course be pleasant, but Penny isn't greedy. All she wants is for Clive to feel secure enough to start a second family, and that moment may come very soon. Hugging herself with pleasure, she folds away the architect's plans.

Instead of picking up a book, she goes to look for her drawing pad. She has an idea. It has been brewing in her mind for some time already, ever since she first tasted Formula Four. The idea is for a bottle of distinctive shape, so different from anything else that setting up the machines to make it would certainly be expensive; but it is for exactly this sort of reason that financial backing has been sought.

Even more extravagant is her vision of having male and female versions of the bottle eventually, so that if there is ever a 'diet' version of the drink it can be differentiated from the start. Of course, she has no idea what the ingredients are, and there may not be any sugar to be removed. The details don't bother her as she makes her sketch, lightly at first before making a tracing in a sharp, clear pencil. This is the work she is trained for. She whistles tunelessly but happily as she draws.

At half past eleven she puts the pad away and goes upstairs. It won't matter if she is still in the bath when Clive returns; he loves to see her body wet and glistening. Only when the hot water has become almost cold does she pull out the plug and dry herself. It is half past twelve now; he ought not to be much longer.

She takes a book to bed and, propping herself up with Clive's pillow as well as her own, settles down to read. Every passing car interrupts her concentration, but none turns in to crunch over the gravel of the drive and after a while there are no traffic sounds at all. By now she is fighting to keep herself awake, and before long the battle is lost. Her head falls back on the pillow; the book falls from her hand. Clive will have to awaken her when he comes.

5

At ten o'clock on the same evening Pamela Elliott turns on the television for the news. But the headlines promise pictures of surgery: war victims waiting for aid, a little girl receiving a transplant. Blood and scalpels and men in masks are not Pamela's idea of entertainment at the best of times, and tonight they come too close to home. By this time tomorrow . . .

No, she mustn't think like that. The panic is over. The emergency has been controlled. By this time tomorrow Dr Brook will have discovered the source of the trouble and will have dealt with it. The most likely cause of the gastro-intestinal haemorrhage has been explained to her, and she has no reason to doubt the explanation. An ulcer, if that is what it is, is not in itself a killer.

But she has no reason to believe the explanation, either. No one has answered the question which she has not dared to ask. She is one of those people who find it difficult to speak the word 'cancer', but she has come near to doing so today. What stopped her was the fear of what she might be told, because if Jarvis puts the same question to her, she doesn't want to know what the answer is. She and Jarvis have always been honest with each other.

This is ridiculous. No one is talking about cancer because he hasn't got cancer. He's had a bad bleed, a bleed which was dangerous in itself, and it's obviously important to make sure that it never happens again. But that's what hospitals are for. Everything is going to be all right. She switches off the news and goes upstairs.

It is too early to sleep; and in any case how can she possibly sleep when she is so worried? But sleep she must, if tomorrow is to be endured, with its revelations about whatever the endoscopy may discover. She is not the sort of woman who regularly takes pills of any kind, but she has a few sleeping tablets left over from the period after her hysterectomy. She takes two of them and goes to bed.

She is awakened from a deep sleep by the telephone, which is on Jarvis's side of the bed. At first, struggling to pull herself out of unconsciousness, she waits for him to answer it. But it rings on and on, until she remembers.

The call is from the hospital, which thinks she ought to know that her husband's condition has deteriorated with such speed that it has been decided to take him to the operating theatre at once; an emergency team is already there. She is not to worry. Her husband has been under continuous observation and the crisis was recognised immediately. There will be no further news for several hours, but she is given a telephone extension to ring at eight o'clock in the morning.

At first she is terrified, and then she is angry. What is the point of frightening her by ringing in the middle of the night when there is absolutely nothing she can do except worry? Switching on the bedside light, she looks at the clock, preparing to be indignant about the time. But it is only just after eleven. In a hospital which never sleeps it may not have occurred to the night sister that some people go to bed before midnight.

Because she is awake she goes to the bathroom and because she has been to the bathroom she automatically begins to dress. Her head is fuddled from the sleeping pills, and the only thought that seems to have any coherence is that she would not have been informed of the change of plan unless she was expected to act on the information; to hurry to her husband's side.

Still on automatic pilot she goes downstairs, reverses the car out of the garage and sets off for the hospital: through the village, along a dark and narrow lane, towards the dual carriageway.

This is where she usually turns south. When she and Jarvis moved out of London a year earlier they chose their present house, not far from Marlow, because it gives equally good access to her office in Reading and to the motorway which leads Jarvis directly to Bloomsbury. On this occasion – because he collapsed on his own business premises and so was taken quickly to a London hospital – she takes his usual route and turns north towards the M40.

Above the motorway is a huge roundabout. During peak hours its six entrances are controlled by a series of traffic lights and approached by slow-moving queues; but at night the lights are switched off, allowing her to whizz round without a halt. This is not, of course, the first time she has approached this particular roundabout, but as a rule, when she is in her own car, she goes straight on, taking the road which leads to the supermarket. If she is on her way to London, it is almost always Jarvis who is driving.

Fighting her sleepiness, she tries to be efficient, noting from the approach sign that she needs to take the fifth exit. But she is crying as well as confused, and the unaccustomed speed with which she is able to enter the roundabout system causes her to forget, or not to notice, the first unobtrusive road. Tears are blurring her eyes. She switches on the windscreen wipers, which effect no improvement. As she reaches the number five in her count, she completely fails to see the No Entry sign as she turns down towards the motorway.

It is almost midnight by now and the roads are quiet. There is nothing coming up the curving hill. She is bemused to find, as she joins the main carriageway, that she seems to be driving on the right. Signalling meticulously, she moves over into the left-hand lane and continues on her way towards London at a steady seventy miles an hour.

32

6

At ten o'clock on the same evening the celebration dinner ends with a flurry of handshaking and high hopes for the future.

'Only ten o'clock,' says Clive. 'And nothing more to be discussed tomorrow. No need to stay in London and have to cope with the traffic in the morning. Why don't we get back tonight?' Although he has been married to Penny for almost three years, he is still a joyous honeymooner.

The four men all live in one or other of the three villages which make up 'the Moncktons', but not all the others are as anxious as Clive to return. Michael has a lady friend with a flat in St John's Wood and has alerted her to the fact that he will be spending the night in London. This is not, however, something he wants to confess in front of the others. As is often the case in family businesses which have built themselves up from small beginnings by hard work, Purefrew is rather a puritanical firm.

Tom, however, is just as eager as Clive to return to his own bed, and for much the same reason. As for Harry, he weighs up the situation with the care which he applies to any question. As guardian of Purefrew's money, it goes against his grain to pay the cancellation fee which the hotel will be entitled to charge; but that will be less than the full bill for staying for breakfast, and he certainly prefers to sleep in his own bed. Rufus Grant, their lawyer, will – unlike the others – be returning to Wright and King's offices next morning. In any case he is London-based and so is not involved in a travel decision. There is a majority for return.

'I'm afraid I'm over the limit,' Michael points out, making one last bid for a few hours with Delia; but the objection is overruled.

'Harry can drive.' Harry is a teetotaller who has been celebrating with tonic water and lemon; and this would not be the first time he has driven Michael's BMW, which is actually a company car.

'We'd better make some phone calls.' Clive is full of energy and excitement. 'Cancel the hotel. And let the girls know we're coming.' Although it will be after midnight before he has been dropped in the Purefrew car park to pick up his own car, Penny will stay awake for him if she is alerted. He is the only one to be carrying a mobile telephone, and he uses it now.

'Anyone else?' But there is no rush to follow his example. Tom knows that Candida will be giving Daniel his last feed of the day, and would not in any case wish to disturb her – but the question doesn't arise, because there is no telephone connection to the stable in which

33

they are camping out. Harry expects that, early as it is, Madge will already have gone to bed. Only Michael accepts the offer; and the number he dials is in fact Delia's. Choosing his words carefully, because the others are within earshot, he announces that his business has been completed earlier than expected and so he is making straight for home that night. He realises, as he switches off, that he will have to make another call as soon as possible to say that he is sorry.

As they have hoped, their route out of the city is, although not speedy, at least free from hold-ups. When they reach the M40 Harry increases his speed. He is a careful driver who never exceeds the speed limit; but there is no need to dawdle, either. There is not too much traffic on the road, so for the most part he stays in the middle lane, listening to the others as they discuss their own futures and the firm's, but not joining in the conversation.

There are always road works somewhere on the M40. A barrier of cones cuts off the inside lane, forcing a slow-moving articulated lorry over to the right. Harry, anticipating the movement, is already indicating that he is about to overtake in the outside lane. As soon as he has pulled out, he is startled to see a pair of headlights which seem to be coming straight towards him. He is dazzled and puzzled, but wastes a second or two in assuming that a contraflow system must be in operation. By the time he realises his mistake, the long bulk of the lorry on his left leaves him nowhere to go. He can brake and hope to fall in behind it, or he can accelerate and try to swerve in front. He chooses speed and almost succeeds, getting the bonnet of the car into the middle lane in front of the lorry; but the lights are too close now.

'Bloody maniac!' he yells – Harry, who never swears. The other three are shocked into silence. They have just time, a millionth of a second, to realise what is about to happen. Pamela Elliott's car hits one side of the swerving BMW; the articulated lorry hits the other. The lorry driver is sitting high and in a strengthened cab, but none of the four men in the car stands a chance. Nor, or course, does Pamela.

Chapter Three

1

Helen is awakened by the sound of a door quietly closing. It must be Derek departing downstairs – and yet she feels as though she has had a sound sleep for some hours since becoming aware that he was leaving. She is surprised, even confused, but still too sleepy to feel alarmed. Her eyes close again.

The sound is repeated. The door is not closing but banging. When it happens for a third time she leaves the bed so quickly that for a moment she is dizzy and almost falls. Pulling on a negligee and slippers, she hurries downstairs.

What she sees makes her physically sick with shock and disgust. Retching, she turns aside – but why should she try to spare the Persian carpet when it has already been defiled by excrement? All Michael's miniatures have disappeared. The larger pictures for the most part remain but have been left on the skew, perhaps by someone searching for a concealed safe. She hurries to the dining room, where the bulk of their silver is kept, and that too has been cleaned out. Her handbag has gone from the hall, as well, with its keys and credit cards and diary.

'God!' She is still shaking with the shock. What will Michael say when he gets back? Although she need not mention Derek, she will have to pretend that she forgot to set the alarm. Her husband will probably believe her, since as a rule this is something he does himself each night, but he will be justifiably furious. What an appalling coincidence that a burglar should try his luck on just this night when she has left their possessions at risk.

Or is it a coincidence? Ashamed of herself even for wondering, she tries another scenario. Could Derek himself be a thief, relying on the fact that she would not dare confess to having admitted him to the house? But she dismisses the thought almost before it has time to formulate itself. Derek is a decent, honest man.

Without thinking, she moves to pick things up, as though by tidying the rooms she can prevent Michael from learning what has happened. But no; she must leave them untouched. Sobbing, although dry-eyed, she moves to the telephone and calls the police.

The doorbell rings only five minutes later, while she is still in the process of dressing. Pulling on a jersey, she hurries downstairs and is surprised to find only a single woman police constable standing empty-handed on the doorstep. She has expected a whole squad, equipped with torches for searching the grounds and notebooks for taking details and plastic bags for picking up clues and puffers and sticky tape for taking fingerprints. No doubt she has been watching too much television.

'Come in. I'll show you.'

There was nothing in the large stone-floored central hall worth stealing, and so nothing looks out of the ordinary as they cross it on the way to the drawing room. Helen opens the door and the constable gasps.

'When did this happen? Have you reported it?'

'Of course I've reported it. Isn't that why you're here?'

The young women's face is very pale as she turns to face Helen.

'No, I'm afraid not, Mrs Cunningham. Is there another room we could go to? The kitchen, perhaps.'

Helen finds it extraordinary that anyone should call at such an hour and ask to be entertained in the kitchen. But she is too preoccupied by the burglary to give any thought to the possible reasons for this. She leads the way across the hall again and they both sit down at the kitchen table. It is here that she learns that she is now a widow.

There is a very long silence. Without asking permission, the policewoman gets up and switches on the electric kettle. Helen recognises that she is about to be offered a cup of tea, but makes no move to indicate where anything is to be found. She is still struggling to believe what she has been told.

No, she can't believe it. It is less than twenty-four hours since she said goodbye to Michael. He was fit and healthy and cheerful — exceptionally cheerful, in fact, because of the negotiations which were just coming to a head. How can it possibly be true that he doesn't exist any more? Had he been suffering from a long illness, perhaps she could have reconciled herself to watching him slip away, but to be there one moment, warm and solid, and then suddenly not to exist any more, to have disappeared from the earth . . .

'Excuse me.' She is going to be sick again, although on this occasion she manages to reach the kitchen sink in time. She leans over it, shuddering. The kettle clicks itself off and, by the time she has splashed her face with cold water in an attempt to bring herself under control, there is tea brewing in the pot.

Slowly she walks back to her seat at the table.

'He, my husband, wasn't due to be on the road last night. He was going to spend the night in London. I could phone the hotel. There must be some mistake. Someone else. How can you be sure?'

'I gather that it hasn't yet been possible to make positive identifications of the bodies, Mrs Cunningham. We shall have to ask you . . . But your husband's briefcase was found nearby, on the central reservation. It must have come out of one of the cars in the crash, before the fire.'

'Fire?' Helen groans at this new detail.

'Please don't be any more distressed, Mrs Cunningham. It was a head-on crash. All the five people in the two cars must have died instantly.' The policewoman pauses for as long as she can, but she has an important question to ask. 'Would you be able to tell us who might have been in the car with your husband?'

Helen finds it hard to answer. It is as though a milky, cloudy liquid is swirling around her brain, swamping any attempt to think clearly. An enormous effort of concentration is needed to produce a perfectly simple piece of information.

'They were all from the same firm. Four of them, at least. There was a lawyer, as well, but I don't think he travelled with them.'

'So who were the three besides Mr Cunningham?'

'Harry Manderson. Clive Martin. Tom . . . Tom something.' Tom is a comparatively new member of the staff. 'A brilliant chap,' Michael has told her, but if he mentioned the surname she has forgotten it, and they have never met. He would no doubt have come to the staff party which the Cunninghams give in Monckton Hall every Christmas. Or used to give.

The policewoman is writing this down.

'And can you give us any help with addresses, or the names of their wives?'

This is the first moment when Helen realises that she is not the only new widow. She has known Madge Manderson for more than twenty years. She will have to call and express as well as receive condolences. She gives the name and address. She knows Clive's address as well, and the name of his new wife, Penny, whom she has met on various social occasions.

'I can't help you about Tom, I'm afraid. The office will have details. But you can't really be sure . . .'

'Perhaps you'd like to phone up the hotel while I'm still here, Mrs Cunningham.'

Helen would if she could, but remembers now that Michael did not give her its name. 'Only for one night. Not likely to be any dramas, are there?' he said as he left. She also remembers wondering whether he was intending in fact to spend the night apart from the others. It has naturally often occurred to her that the reason for his loss of interest in his wife could be the existence of a mistress somewhere. It is not a question she has ever wanted to press, because she is perfectly content with the present state of their marriage.

Or rather, with its state twenty-four hours ago. Now she has no marriage, no husband. She is alone. For the first time since the news was broken to her, tears begin to run down her cheeks.

They are checked by another urgent question. It is the reminder of her suspicion that Michael has a lover somewhere that puts the thought into her mind. Almost fiercely, she turns towards the constable.

'What time did the accident happen?'

'I don't know the exact time. About midnight.'

'Oh, no!' Helen buries her head in her hands. At midnight she was lying in the arms of her own lover. At the moment of her husband's death, she was betraying him. She groans aloud, overcome by guilt.

'Mrs Cunningham.'

'Go away. Thank you for coming, but go away.'

'Have you got any children, Mrs Cunningham?'

'Not close at hand.' Her only daughter, Lucy, is married to an American and lives in Washington.

'Or a friend who could come round and keep you company for a little while?'

She shakes her head. This is not the sort of occasion to have a neighbour or fellow bridge-player fussing around.

'I'll be all right. Just go.'

Since she is not prepared to look up, she doesn't know whether or not she is alone in the house when the doorbell rings again. Sighing, she drags herself to the front door.

Two more police officers stand there, sent in response to the report of the burglary. Without speaking, Helen shows them into the desecrated drawing room. They know nothing about her recent bereavement and enquire about her husband. A weariness which goes almost as deep as grief and shame overwhelms her. She will never after all have to confess to Michael that she is responsible for the loss of his miniatures. But she will have to deal with the insurance company by herself. She will have to set the house to rights and change locks and replace credit cards by herself. Somehow or other, she will have to make a life for herself in this huge, empty house. She is on her own.

2

In the intensive care unit Jarvis Elliott slips in and out of consciousness. From time to time he is aware of rustlings nearby. Sometimes he is touched. Once or twice it seems that perhaps someone is speaking quietly. But all this is none of his business. His eyes remain closed and he drifts back into sleep again.

Time passes, and there is a second period of awareness. He becomes conscious of shadowy figures pausing at a little distance, approaching, bending over him. When they speak, he recognises that he is the one they are addressing, but something is obstructing his throat, preventing him from speaking. He lies on in silence. A needle pricks his arm and once again his eyelids become too heavy for him to keep open.

Another awakening. This time his eyes open wide. For the first time he is aware of his own body. The tube which earlier seemed to fill his throat has been removed, leaving only soreness. A mask has been placed over his face, causing a cool breeze to refresh his skin while the oxygen fills his lungs. There is an ache, a seriously deep ache, somewhere near his waist, but it stabs him with pain only if he moves, so he keeps very still. Somewhere down there, out of sight, a drainage tube has been inserted. One arm is rigid, with a drip leading into it. His other hand is untethered, but refuses to move when he orders it to explore. Either he has no strength at all or else he has been in some invisible way restrained: it's too complicated to work out which. His head is swimming and he feels as though he is going to be sick.

A nurse, who has been monitoring his progress on a screen, appears at the side of the bed. Almost before he has time to register her presence she moistens his mouth and cleans his nostrils with something soft and damp. 'Good,' she says, replacing the oxygen mask before moving out of sight again. Jarvis presumes her comment to refer to the fact that he is still alive.

The next person to arrive is the anaesthetist. Dr Craig is very thin and so tall that Jarvis, still unable to move his head, can't look at his face but only at the knot in his tie.

'The operation went very well,' Dr Craig tells him. 'I think you could do without the oxygen now.' As the nurse removes the mask he waits to make sure that his patient has not lost the knack of breathing. Jarvis is anxious to talk but finds it hard to force speech through the soreness of his throat. He needs three attempts before the tip of his tongue manages to push the words out. 'Told Pamela?'

The anaesthetist goes on speaking as though he has not heard the interruption.

'We'll carry on for a little longer with the injections to control any pain. They may leave you feeling a bit fuzzy, but that's normal. It'll be best if you have no visitors at all for a day or two more. And no stress. That means no phone calls. Even though you may think you're indispensable to your business. I want you to cut absolutely everything out of your mind except the thought that you're getting stronger with every moment that passes. You're doing very well. Very well indeed. Keep it up.'

The effort merely of listening has exhausted Jarvis. Once again he allows his eyes to close. It doesn't distress him that Pamela has been asked, apparently, to postpone her first visit; he doesn't want her to see him like this and he is still too woolly-headed to take part in a conversation. After all, he himself suggested that she should keep away for the first twenty-four hours. Has that much time passed already? Or more? He doesn't know. He doesn't really know anything. He is a passive object, happy to be looked after.

Only for a very short time indeed do the nursing staff indulge this laziness. They order him to cough, although coughing is painful. They announce – surely too soon – that he has slept for long enough and must take a little exercise. Naturally the exercise is to begin with gentle and controlled, but it is enough to exhaust him. Once again he lies back, sinking warmly into the pillows.

He continues to be injected with some kind of analgesic and accepts the process without objection even though, as he has been warned, it is probably responsible for the difficulty he has in clearing his mind. But a moment comes, in the middle of one night, when for the first time since the operation he feels wide awake and thinking straight.

To this newly cleared consciousness two thoughts present themselves. The first one is a craving for a cigarette. Fortunately he is in no position to indulge himself; but in any case his self-discipline is strong. He has given up smoking. It was a promise to the surgeon, and one which he intends to keep.

The second of his wishes could more easily be fulfilled. He wants to see Pamela. He can talk again by now. He can listen. He wants to be brought up to date with all her office gossip, with what is happening in the world, with the latest doings of the neighbours. But anyway, he just wants to see her, to hold her hand, to tell her he loves her now that this is no longer a dramatic statement heralding a possible parting but simply a repetition of what he murmurs every time they make love. It's something that he must remember to enquire before he is discharged: when it will be safe for him to make love again. In the meantime, when the surgeon comes round next morning to inspect his handiwork, Jarvis asks whether the time has come when his wife may start to visit.

The surgeon appears surprised by the question but promises to discuss it with Dr Brook, the physician who attended Jarvis in the emergency of his admission to hospital. This seems an unnecessarily high-level consultation for what must surely be a routine matter, but he awaits the answer without any feeling of anxiety. It is Dr Brook, sympathetic and approaching the subject carefully, who breaks the news that he will never see Pamela again.

3

This is not an easy day for Rufus Grant. As he prepares to make his fourth call of the afternoon, he feels a certain resentment about what he is being asked to do.

Because his law firm has for many years handled Purefrew's legal affairs, it will be perfectly in order for Helen Cunningham to ask him – when she gets round to thinking about it – to report on the situation regarding the deal which was agreed but unfortunately not signed. He will have to break it to her that Wright and King are unlikely to proceed in the absence of key members of Purefrew's staff. Since she will now inherit the business, she is obviously also entitled to ask his advice about its future structure – and, indeed, on anything else in the legal field.

But it's a bit much to be expected to call on four widows in one day: four women all poleaxed by what has happened to them, because they have only had twenty-four hours in which to absorb the news. He could have said no, because funeral arrangements are none of his business. But Helen, nervy and listless, is so clearly incapable at the moment of taking any decisions or making any arrangements that he hasn't had the heart to refuse her request.

So it is that at three o'clock in the afternoon he turns his car past a lopsided wooden notice which must once have said 'Orchard Farm', although by this time several of the letters are missing, and up a long

41

and potholed track. On either side there are indeed orchards at first, but after a time the lines of fruit trees come to an end and are replaced by a field thick with thistles and nettles and docks, all drooping now after the first frosts of the year.

Rufus is an urban man who finds the country uncongenial at the best of times, but this is unusually messy. He has heard of set-aside and presumes that is what is happening here, but surely farmers usually mow down the weeds from time to time to give an impression of tidiness? How grim it must have been for Tom Harding to drive past this wilderness every day on his way to and from work.

The drive ends in a farmyard, but there is no sign of any farmhouse. Most of the buildings which surround the yard seem to be derelict, housing only broken-down items of rusty machinery. The afternoon is damp and misty; he finds the whole atmosphere of the place unbearably depressing.

The address he has been given is The Stables, so he makes his way to the building that fits that description. There is no bell or knocker, but the top half of the stable door is pushed outwards. He leans inside and calls, 'Anyone in?'

There is a movement in one of the horse stalls. Someone is scrubbing the floor. She rises to her feet and steps out to face him.

She is a tall young woman, straight-backed and slender. Her neat, curly hair is black and her skin is brown. It is beautiful skin, enclosing a beautiful body whose shape is revealed rather than covered by her tight jeans and sweatshirt, which don't quite meet at the waist. The shabbiness of her clothes seems only to emphasise how stunning she could look were she to be smartly dressed, just as the sad dullness of her brown eyes convinces him that it would need only a little life to return to them for her to be a real beauty. In short, Rufus finds himself bowled over. He can't remember that any girl has ever before had quite such an immediate effect on him.

He reminds himself that this is not the time or occasion for trying to establish a personal relationship. What he needs to establish first of all is who she is. She is still holding a scrubbing brush, but it somehow doesn't seem likely that a young man like Tom would employ a cleaner. Helen Cunningham, while telling him that Tom had been given permission to camp out in an unused farm building as he waited to buy a house, has stated confidently that he was living there alone; but Penny Martin, later in the day, has dismissed that statement with a cry of 'Nonsense! He had Candida.' Rufus realises, too late, that he ought to have enquired more closely into the relationship. Is Candida a wife, now a widow, or was the relationship a less permanent one? Is this young woman Candida?

42

'My name's Rufus Grant,' he says now, holding out a hand. 'I'm a lawyer, and I've been advising Purefrew in their recent negotiations.'

'Oh, yes.' She wipes her hand down the side of her jeans before shaking his. 'Tom talked about you. I remember your name.'

Her voice comes as a surprise. Rufus likes to think that he is free of racial prejudice, but he does nevertheless rather expect a black girl to speak – well, like a black girl. But this is the voice of an educated young woman. In an era when rich girls try to speak like poor girls and television presenters are unable to sound their consonants, she is speaking standard English in cool, low tones which still further excite him. She has a beautiful voice.

'May I come in and talk to you for a moment, Mrs Harding?'

'Oh, of course come in.' She opens the door. 'But I'm not Mrs Harding. Candida Brown. We were sort of engaged, but . . .'

She leads the way inside. This part of the stable is divided into six stalls, spacious enough for the sturdy farm horses which no doubt were still pulling ploughs in the age when it was built. In one of these stalls, carpeted now, a padded seat has been constructed against one wall to look like a sofa. Facing it are two low chairs of the kind which are called TV chairs, although there is no television set in the cubicle. It is surprisingly comfortable; and although the air smells slightly of paraffin, it is warm.

'It's bit primitive,' she apologises. 'We were hoping to buy one of those houses being built on what used to be the school playing field. Living here rent-free was helping us to save for the deposit.'

'You've made a very nice home out of it.'

'No,' she says. 'I know what a home ought to be like. It was temporary, that's all. A stepping stone. Although now . . .' She turns her head away, struggling to prevent herself from breaking down in tears.

Rufus is reminded of his errand. He expresses formal condolences and makes a short speech about his own liking for Tom.

'There will have to be an inquest,' he tells her. 'Mrs Cunningham has already asked me to attend on behalf of all four of you. Do you agree to that?'

'Is it necessary?'

'Yes. The coroner's verdict could affect any insurance claim. I'm sure the inquest will be adjourned almost at once, but by opening quickly it allows you to get on with the funeral arrangements.'

'I don't think I have any rights,' Candida tells him unhappily. 'Tom's parents live in Yorkshire. They may want to have the funeral there. I'd like to have it here, because if *they* fix it they probably won't even let me know the date. But . . .'

'Then Mrs Cunningham's suggestion of a joint service may be

43

better for you. If it isn't arranged by you personally, Mr and Mrs Harding may be more willing to accept that it should take place where his friends and colleagues live. They could always arrange a memorial service in Yorkshire later if they chose. Will you leave it to me?'

'Thank you, yes. I'll get you their address.'

While she is away, Rufus becomes aware of a noise nearby. He stands up and looks over the shoulder-high partition into the next stall. A young baby is lying there, his lips opening and bubbling as he experiments with new sounds. His existence puts a new complexion on Candida's situation. How will she survive without Tom? By the time she returns, Rufus is feeling seriously worried on her behalf.

'Did Tom make a will, Miss Brown?'

'Call me Candida. No, he hadn't done that. He was only twenty-five. Oh, you don't need to tell me. I know about intestacy. Nothing for me. But Daniel is his son.'

'Acknowledged?'

'Yes, of course. Tom's name is on the birth certificate.'

'Did he have any insurance?'

'Not that he paid for himself. He did say something about being insured under this new deal that was going through.'

'That would have been what we call key-man insurance. It wouldn't have benefited him or his family in any way. It's a way in which a big firm recognises that a particular employee is of such value to them that his death will cause them loss. It gives them financial recompense for the loss. But anyway, I very much doubt whether Wright and King will proceed with the takeover. They'll want to see whether Purefrew can survive the accident.'

'It's still got the same products and markets as before.'

'Yes, but . . .' Rufus pauses. Does she really want to talk about business organisation at a time like this? But perhaps such a distraction may come as a relief, helping her to think about something other than her bereavement for a few minutes. He prepares to answer her point, but watches her expression closely to be sure that he does not go on for too long.

'There are three ways in which large corporations can approach takeovers,' he points out. 'They may intend to sell off part of what they've acquired at sufficient profit to pay for what they keep.'

'Asset stripping, you mean?' Candida has become surprisingly calm and businesslike. He has been correct in guessing that she needs distraction.

'Right. But that wouldn't have been the intention in this case, and it would be difficult for them to sell Purefrew now, without its management. Another possible motive is simply to absorb a competitor, but that didn't apply here either. Purefrew wasn't big enough to give them any trouble. I believe that their intention was quite straightforward. They could see that with access to more capital the company had the potential to become extremely profitable, but they were happy to let the existing management continue to run it, almost as a self-contained division. There was the potential for developing new ideas.'

'You mean Formula Four?'

Rufus is startled. Formula Four is strictly hush-hush and he would not have expected Tom to talk about it at home. Yet to mention a name, two words, would have given nothing away.

Formula Four is, as it happens, the only thing that might persuade Wright and King not to withdraw their bid. The problem is that the formula is nowhere to be found. Rufus has spent part of the morning searching Purefrew's lab and anywhere that Tom might have put the details for safekeeping, but without success, and has come to the conclusion that it may have been in Tom's briefcase and burned to ashes in the accident.

But perhaps all the time it has been somewhere in this stable. Tom always made it clear that he had not developed the new drink in his working hours and that Purefrew has no claim on the idea unless he should agree to give them one. Rufus knows this to be true, because Clive Martin has described to him how he was first offered a drink of this amazing liquid. It had, he said a taste like nothing he had ever known and a kick which sent him back on to the tennis court refreshed and with renewed energy. It was not until a week after that episode that Tom – on Clive's suggestion – applied for a job at Purefrew.

'You know about Formula Four?' Rufus enquires cautiously.

'Yes, of course. It's mine.'

'Yours!' Now she has really startled him. 'Tom said –'

'Tom could have had it, of course he could. But it was my recipe. I never even let him watch me make it. I used to tease him that it was my hold over him.'

'Have you ever let anyone take a sample out of your sight; anyone who might have analysed it?'

'No.'

'Have you taken out any kind of protection for the recipe?'

'You mean a patent? Not formally, no. As I said, I was going to let Tom have it, so everything would have been done in his name. Twenty-five. Only twenty-five. I never expected –'

For a second time she is on the verge of breaking down. Rufus longs to comfort her, but can tell that she doesn't want to be touched.

He waits until, with three deep breaths, she brings herself back under control.

'The thing I did do is this,' she says. Disappearing for a moment, she returns carrying a sealed envelope. It is addressed to Miss Candida Brown and has been delivered by registered post; but sealing wax and Post Office stamps across the fastenings show that it has never been opened.

'I wrote down the recipe and put it in here to establish the date, in case there was ever any fuss later on.'

For a second time Rufus is impressed. Although she would still have many health and legal hurdles to cross before an unquestionable right to market a product for public consumption could be established, this young mother has taken exactly the right first step to guard the copyright in her idea.

'Well done,' he congratulates her. 'Are you going to have a shot at marketing it commercially yourself?'

'I don't expect so. I haven't any experience.'

Rufus opens his month. He is just about to offer his support, even his partnership, if she chooses to proceed. But just in time he remembers that he is the representative of Purefrew's interests, which may conflict with hers. It is safer to talk about Candida herself.

'Candida, what about money? I take it Tom was supporting you. What are you going to live on now?'

'I get child benefit.'

'You can't keep two people on that. Look, why don't you let me drive you down to the social-security office now to see what else you're entitled to.' Not a widow's pension, presumably, but there must be other things. He has no expertise in the field of state benefits, but since there is currently a great debate going on about the manner in which unmarried mothers are allowed to sponge on society, it is reasonable to assume that someone like Candida will be helped to stay afloat. But it seems that he has hit a sensitive spot.

'No.' For the first time in the conversation her brown eyes lose the dull carapace of sadness and her expression becomes forceful. 'I don't approve of these girls who have babies just to get away from their homes, to get a home of their own. I'm not going to become one of those, living on the security. I didn't have to let Daniel be born. I know about terminations. I made a choice and it's my responsibility now. Nobody else's.'

'But your circumstances have changed. You're going to need money to bring up a baby, and because you have a baby it's going to be that much harder for you to earn it. Will your parents help you? Or Tom's?'

'Tom's parents know what they think about niggers. They don't want ever to meet me. And my mother, she's never going to forgive me for not being married.'

'Well, then. What *are* you going to do? You mustn't borrow, Candida. Whatever you do, you mustn't let any of these loan sharks try to lend you money.'

Candida smiles. There is still a trace of sadness in the smile, but the way in which her whole face changes its shape as her lips part shows Rufus how delightful she must look when she is able to express wholehearted happiness.

'It's very kind of you to be concerned on my behalf,' she tells him.

'Well, I *am* concerned. There must be something I can do to help you. You're going to need to buy food. You must let me –' He is pulling his wallet from his pocket as he speaks; but Candida lays her hand on his wrist, checking the movement.

'Wasn't it you who just told me not to borrow money?' She is almost laughing now.

'This is a gift, not a loan. Just to tide you over while you think what to do.'

'You're very kind.' Her voice is low and friendly. 'But I'll be all right for a month or two. We had a joint account. There is something you could do for me, though. The car. That day, Tom drove it to the Purefrew car park and then went on in Mr Cunningham's car. It's a long way for me to walk, with Daniel.'

'Yes, of course I'll drive you there.' He watches as she picks up the baby, changes his nappy and drops him into a baby-carrier.

Twenty minutes later he pulls up beside an elderly Ford Fiesta and waits while she unlocks the door and straps the baby-carrier in at the back. She turns back to thank him. By now she is holding herself very straight, as though her spirits have been to some extent restored by their conversation.

'Thank you very much, Rufus,' she says as they shake hands.

He holds on to her hand for a moment longer than the farewell requires.

'You will think about what I've said, won't you? It's a mistake to be proud if the baby's going to suffer for it.'

He can tell from her smile and the way she holds herself that she is never going to let the baby suffer.

'Yes,' she promises. 'You've given me a lot to think about.'

4

On the morning of the funeral Madge Manderson rises early. She has already done all the baking which she and Helen in consultation have decided to be sufficient; it is waiting in the pantries or refrigerators or freezers of Monckton Hall. But it may not be enough. How can they possibly know how many people will attend the service and how many will go on to the Hall afterwards. The factory is to be closed for the day as a mark of respect. No doubt some of Purefrew's employees will accept the day as a holiday; but every one of them knew at least one of the dead men. They may all attend the service. They may bring their husbands or wives. It would be disgraceful if the food were to run out. Still wearing her dressing gown, Madge adjusts the Aga and begins to make more pastry.

Helen has arranged to send a car to transport her to Monckton Hall, so that they can travel to the crematorium together. Before it arrives, however, Gwen rings the bell.

Gwen's friendship with Madge is entirely based on their joint passion for playing bowls, and her acquaintance with Harry was of the slightest. She would have attended the service in spite of that, to give her friend support, but Madge has asked a different favour. She knows, from reading the local paper, that there is a particularly nasty kind of thief who chooses to break into houses when he has learned that all the occupants are likely to be attending a funeral.

The three villages that make up the Moncktons are so close together that events in any one of them are local to the others, so naturally Madge knows by now that Monckton Hall was burgled on the night of the accident. The need to guard her own home against intruders is very much in her mind. It is not that there is anything particularly valuable to steal in College Farm but she has been shocked by the effect that the burglary has had on Helen Cunningham. Even her bereavement, unexpected and sad though it was, seems insufficient to explain her nervous collapse. It must be the invasion of her home that has left her not only vulnerable but completely unable to cope.

So Gwen has kindly agreed to bring along her German shepherd and act as house-sitter. Her eyes open at the sight of a hundred newly baked sausage rolls cooling on a wire rack.

'I should have thought Helen Cunningham could have afforded to hire a caterer.'

'Yes, of course she could. But I wanted to contribute. And now that I haven't got anyone to cook for . . .'

Her voice trails away. Since the moment when the police rang her

48

door bell, she has cried for Harry, of course she has. But in an odd way this is the first time that the feeling of being alone in the world has hit her. And she is only fifty. This is a loneliness which may continue for twenty years or more.

For seventeen years she cared for Julie. Julie's death left a gap in her life, but there was a sense in which it wasn't possible to feel sorry. To talk about a happy release would have been a cliché, but it was true. No truly loving mother could have wanted her child to endure such a restricted life for any longer.

And of course after Julie's death she still had Harry to look after. Well, it was true that in the main it was Harry who looked after her, but as far as food was concerned she was always in charge. Now, as she has just told Gwen, she has no one to cook for.

Gwen, although knowing that it is too soon to cheer her friend up, refuses to let her sink any further into depression.

'Nonsense. You'll still need to cook for yourself. And now you can choose the times that suit you.'

To be lonely is to be free? This aspect of loneliness has not previously occurred to Madge. But she ignores Gwen's other comment. Madge has never taken any pleasure in cooking only for herself. She isn't likely to start now.

5

As soon as she steps inside the chapel of the crematorium, Penny knows that she has made a mistake. She should never have agreed to this idea of a joint service. At the time when Rufus Grant called to make the suggestion she was still numb with shock and glad to be relieved of a task which she felt incompetent to undertake.

Now she feels guilty about the responsibility she has shirked, and the sight of the four coffins upsets her. She might just be able to endure it if she could think that the one which bears Clive's name actually contains the body she knew, the body she loved. But the police were honest with her when they called, and she realises that no one can be absolutely sure which pieces of burned flesh belong to whom.

Almost certainly the other bereaved women must have come to the same conclusion, for without needing any discussion they have each chosen cremation rather than burial. The thought of that fire makes her feel sick and she has to pause for a moment in the doorway. Someone puts a copy of the service sheet into the hand she has held out, but her fingers refuse to grip it; it flutters to the floor.

Helen and Madge are already sitting at the front, together with a younger woman who must be Helen's daughter. They turn now and Helen raises a hand, inviting her forward. They are both wearing hats. Helen, who is tall and always well-dressed, is given an Edwardian dignity by her hat, but Madge seems to disappear under hers.

Except for something woollen which she can pull down over her ears on wintery walks, Penny doesn't own a hat. To mark the solemnity of the occasion her long blonde hair, which usually swings about her shoulders, has been swept up and twisted into a neat coil on the top of her head. It is her party hairstyle; she was wearing it exactly like that on the evening she first met Clive. This is another thought to make her uneasy.

The two older women stand up as she approaches and kiss her, although she does not know them well. In the two and three-quarter years of her marriage she has met them only on infrequent social occasions. Probably they are both, unlike her, churchgoers. It must have seemed sensible to them that the vicar who serves all the three linked parishes in which the dead men lived should preside over a single service. But how can he make his remarks personal to each of the four? How can he offer Penny private comfort? She tells herself that she hasn't come for comfort. This is simply a ceremony which must be endured, a formal farewell; a necessary stage in the management of bereavement and grief.

As she is about to sit down, a movement in the back of the church takes her eye. She is better acquainted with Candida than with the other two. They have often chatted together as they watched Clive and Tom playing tennis, and it was Clive who was responsible for recruiting Tom to the firm. It seems that Candida is intending to remain at the back. Penny whispers across to Helen.

'That's Tom's Candida who's just come in. I'll go and get her to join us.'

What Helen Cunningham sees when she turns round again appears to startle her. 'The black girl?'

Penny is already moving down the aisle. 'Come and sit with us in the front,' she says to Candida, who shakes her head.

'Thanks, but I'd better stay near the door in case Daniel cries and I have to take him out.' The baby is pressed close to her breasts in a sling.

'He has the right to cry for his father if he wants to. Come on.'

She takes Candida by the hand and leads her forwards, introducing her to Helen and Madge before sitting down. A middle-aged man and woman sitting together on the other side of the aisle stare across with hostile expressions on their faces. If these are Tom's parents, it would seem that they are not prepared to forgive their grandson for being brown.

The organist's vague meanderings come to an end and the service begins. It is just as unendurable as Penny has expected, and seems to have nothing to do with the man she has known. She closes her mind and ears to it and instead listens to Daniel's bubbly breathing close beside her. The sleeping child makes it painfully clear to her that she has lost not only her husband but also the babies which will now never be born.

As they rise to sing the first hymn, Daniel's eyes open and he makes a sound to tell his mother that he is awake. It can hardly be called crying, but is enough to remind Penny of the remark she made to Candida, and to send her thoughts off in another direction. Clive's sons ought to be here. Margaret has had plenty of time to arrange it, but claimed, when Penny made her second phone call and told her the date and time, that they are too young to attend a funeral. That is ridiculous; they are thirteen and fifteen.

The second excuse was that they can't leave their boarding school during term. Penny doesn't believe that either. Probably they haven't even been asked whether or not they would like to attend. Later on they will be sorry, because formalities have their uses. Even this ludicrous occasion is better than nothing. Penny resolves that as soon as she gets home she will find two of Clive's possessions which the boys might value and send them off as a token of his love: a memento. It was no more their fault than his that the family broke up five years ago.

Using such mental distractions she manages to survive the service without tears – at least until the moment when each of the coffins moves slowly away on the rollers and disappears behind a curtain. The process takes too long and she comes close to screaming. But at last, thank God, it is over.

The congregation, standing, waits for the four bereaved women to leave the chapel first. Another woman follows them out immediately and touches Penny's arm with her hand. Although Clive's two wives have never met – because Clive was already divorced when Penny met him for the first time – she guesses at once who this is.

'You're Penny, aren't you?' says the stranger. 'I'm Margaret. I haven't any right to mourn him. I feel just as bad about that as I do about leaving him. I'm glad he found you. I just wanted to say how sorry I am.'

Uncertain how to deal with this unexpected meeting, Penny merely nods. Helen, in front of her, is issuing invitations to the whole con-

51

gregation to reassemble at Monckton Hall. Penny passes the invitation on to Margaret, but is relieved when it is refused.

It is almost two o'clock before Penny returns to The Old Rectory. Helen Cunningham has provided coffee, sherry and wine and a waitress to dispense them, while Madge Manderson has transported trays of home-baked savouries and gateaux to Monckton Hall. Although it seemed odd to Penny to make a funeral the occasion for a kind of party, she recognised herself to be in a sense one of the hostesses, who ought not to leave before the last of the guests.

She goes up to the bedroom which is only her bedroom now; nothing in the house is any longer 'ours'. As she prepares to change out of her funeral clothes she becomes conscious of an unusual noise coming from the walled garden next door. Curious, she goes up the second flight of stairs to her attic studio.

Work is about to begin on the new house. Two men are making a breach in the high stone wall. It is the sound of the huge, heavy lumps of stone being thrown on to a pile that she has heard.

Two other men stand in the centre of the plot, holding a large sheet of paper which must be the architect's plan. One of them is pointing; the other is nodding. Penny recognises the pointer as being the old lady's grandson: the man who once picked peaches.

At that very moment of recognition he looks up and sees her standing at the window. He says something to his companion and steps through the new breach in the wall. It comes as no surprise to Penny when she hears her doorbell ring.

'Mrs Martin?' The bearded man who stands on the door step has – now that she can see him close up – a pleasant, smiling face; and when he smiles, a deep dimple appears in his right cheek and his eyes are bright. Like a jolly pirate in a children's picture book, Penny thinks, and automatically her own expression loses a little of its grim unhappiness.

The stranger's smile changes character even before she has time to acknowledge who she is. There is admiration in his eyes. She has seen this look many times before in the days when she was a smart and unattached working woman. The formal style in which she has dressed her hair for the day was chosen in order that she should not appear frivolous or happy, but it has the unintended effect of increasing her height and helping her to look elegant. Her black suit is three years old, but it was expensive at the time and is well enough cut to be dateless, and the colour suits her fair skin. She is looking good, on a day when she doesn't care how she looks.

'Yes, that's me.'

'I'm Jonathan Verne. You knew my grandmother, I think, at The Manor.'

'Yes, of course. Won't you come in?'

He looks doubtfully down at his feet, on which he is wearing wellington boots.

'I don't mind seeing your socks.'

'Thanks, then.' He pulls the boots off and follows her into the drawing room. 'I called earlier, but you were out. The thing is, the men are just about to start work in the walled garden. There's bound, I'm afraid, to be a lot of noise to begin with. Dirt as well, probably. And perhaps a few temporary obstructions of the lane. I wanted to apologise in advance. And to give you my telephone number, so that if anything happens which particularly annoys you, you can give me a ring and get it off your chest at once. I'm very anxious to keep my new neighbours happy.'

'You're going to live here yourself, then?'

'Yes. I've always loved the place. That's why Grandmother left it directly to me, I think, instead of to my mother first. There wasn't any money to go with it, unfortunately, so I can't afford to maintain a house like The Manor in the style it deserves. But I've always been particularly fond of the walled garden. That marvellous wall!'

'I love it too,' says Penny. 'It came as a bit of a shock when I saw the men starting to pull it down.'

'There'll have to be enough of an opening to let cars directly on to the lane. It'll be wider than that to start with, to let lorries and bull-dozers in. But they'll restore as much as possible once the work's finished.'

'Good.' Penny, although anxious not to appear unfriendly, is not feeling chatty or sociable at the moment. She glances down at his card, on which he announces himself as an architect. He recognises this as a gesture of dismissal and rises to his feet.

'I really mean it, about complaining if anything upsets you. Presumably it won't affect Clive as much, since he's out all day. But tell him the same thing, will you? And tell him that I'm planning to have a tennis court, and I shall expect him to help me christen it.'

Startled, Penny looks up, into his eyes. But why should she be surprised that he doesn't know? The address on the card he has given her is a London one.

'Clive is dead,' she says simply. 'I've just come home from the funeral.' Her chin quivers and for a second time she stares down at the card. This time the words swim unreadably before her eyes.

'Clive? I don't believe it. I didn't know. Oh, God, how terrible! And he was only, what, forty-three?'

'Forty-five. It was in an accident. You knew him, then?'

'Our grandparents were great friends. Clive and I both used to spend holidays here as boys, and we often overlapped. He was older than me, of course, and was allowed to do all sorts of exciting things like shooting pigeons when I was still far too young to have a gun. A severe case of hero-worship, you might say. He was always terribly nice to me, letting me tag along.'

'I'm sorry you weren't told, then. I didn't realise.'

'Well, we haven't seen much of each other in the past six or seven years. I've been working on some big contracts in the Gulf. But some memories last. I really am tremendously sorry.'

He grasps both her hands and grips them tightly. She is glad of the comfort and gives a quick nod of thanks.

'Will you stay on here?' he asks. 'I do hope you will.'

'I don't know. I haven't had time to think yet.'

'No, of course not. Well, I'm sorry to have disturbed you at such a bad time.'

Outside the front door he tugs his boots on again. A moment later she sees him, from the attic again, resume his conversation with the builder. She feels depressed and flat. The cremation has provided something to be arranged, something to be endured, but now that it is over the future is empty.

Will she stay on here? She doesn't know. She hasn't had time to think.

But perhaps she doesn't need to think. Perhaps the thinking process has been going on inside her mind without her being aware of it, because the answer to the question is after all quite clear.

No, of course she won't stay. She has not had time to put down roots here, nor to make close friends. There was only Clive; and without Clive there is nothing. There is more of Margaret and her sons in The Old Rectory than there is of Penny. If she were to remain in the house, she would not even be alone with the memory of her husband. She has nowhere particular to go, but go she must.

Unlike Margaret, Penny has nothing to feel ashamed of in her marriage. The loss which overwhelms her contains no element of guilt. It is simply an emptiness. She has been happy, and now that happiness has ended. She will have to start again.

Chapter Four

1

Jarvis Elliott is not making good progress. He ought by this time to have been discharged from hospital, but perhaps Dr Brook is worried lest he should cease to do his exercises when there is no longer a physiotherapist at hand to insist on them – and that he might even begin to smoke again. This is not an unjustifiable fear. As a rule Jarvis prides himself on keeping promises, but this particular promise of abstinence has been made for the purpose of staying alive, and he no longer cares very much whether he lives or dies.

He is unable to come to terms with Pamela's death. What was she doing on the road at all at that hour? And how could it possibly have happened that someone who is – was – a good driver, someone who had been driving for thirty years, should have got herself into such a position? The whole situation is so improbable that it can't possibly be true. And yet of course it is true. As he lies in bed his thoughts go round and round, seeking an exit like a key too thick to be extracted from a key ring. None of the facts will ever alter. His mind seems to be trapped in that tiny circle of the past, making it impossible for him to consider the future.

And so he is reluctant to allow anything in the present to change. He is being looked after: nursed, fed and generally made comfortable. The nurses are sympathetic. They all know what has happened and one of them, Betty, has appointed herself as counsellor. 'Is there anything you'd like to talk about?' she asks regularly in the hour before the drugs trolley comes round: an hour when there is apparently time in her evening routine for a chat. But no, there is nothing he wants to talk about.

He is, however, a National Health Service patient. Perhaps in a pri-

55

vate hospital his wish to remain insulated from the rest of the world might have been indulged for a little longer, but here he gradually becomes aware of a subtle change in the atmosphere – as though a directive has gone out from above that he is to be jump-started back into life again. Nurses no longer run errands for him but suggest that he is well enough to manage for himself. Hints are dropped about emergency admissions and a shortage of beds and the annual attempt to close a ward or two over Christmas.

Christmas is still several weeks ahead, but the mention of it reminds him that he and Pamela – childless and hard-working – have regularly celebrated the festival by being pampered in a country hotel. Since he can't bear the thought of going alone, he ought to phone and cancel the booking.

That decision represents the first occasion since hearing of Pamela's death on which he has allowed himself to think of life without her. He has taken a step into the future. After that there is no going back. It is necessary to make some alternative arrangement. Pamela's sister, who in view of his incapacity made all the arrangements for the funeral, has already invited him to spend Christmas with her family in the country – and, in fact, not to wait for Christmas itself, but to come and convalesce as soon as he is ready. He makes a telephone call to accept.

The question of Christmas presents is the next to be faced: his sister-in-law has four children. He will not for some time be fit enough to plunge into crowded shops, so before leaving the telephone he asks his secretary to come to the hospital. When she arrives, he dictates a list of names and ages and general suggestions about what she might buy on his behalf. In return he himself is given a small present, in the shape of a new manuscript from one of the authors on his list. He begins to read it as soon as she has left.

There is no way in which the nurses can know exactly what has happened to him in the course of the afternoon but, as though he has run up a flag to mark some turning point in his recovery, the atmosphere in his cubicle changes. There is a new briskness in the voice of everyone who speaks to him. His supper is not, as usual, brought to him in bed but instead set out on the table in the middle of the ward. There are fewer tablets for him to take. It is like the moment in an office party when the lights are dimmed to indicate that it is time to leave. He is no longer an emergency; not even regarded as an invalid. The hospital can do nothing to ease the pain of bereavement, but it has dealt efficiently with everything else. The time has come for him to move on.

Rufus Grant's visit has given Candida a good deal to think about, and she does not shirk the task. Her conclusions bring her no joy, so she thinks the matter through again and comes to exactly the same decision. Because it is an uncomfortable decision, she allows herself to procrastinate – after the inquest, after the funeral, after Daniel's next visit to the clinic. At last she designates a day, but then the November morning proves foggy. If this goes on, her courage will seep away. On Sunday, she tells herself firmly: on Sunday she will drive to London.

She arrives in Shepherd's Bush at a quarter to four that afternoon and parks as close as she can to the house in which she was brought up. Her grandfather came from Barbados to drive London Transport buses. He was glad to be offered a house within walking distance of the depot. When he went back to the West Indies his son, Candida's father, took over the tenancy and eventually become the owner. It is an end-of-terrace house, made larger than any other in the row by a single-storey extension built on to the side. Mrs Brown became a registered child-minder while Candida herself was still young; she uses this room to keep the children's inevitable mess out of her own part of the house.

Candida does not remember her father clearly. There is a photograph in the house of a slim young man with the long legs and straight back which she has inherited. The photograph has formed whatever memory she has of him, although by the time he left home, when she was ten, he would have been fourteen or fifteen years older than the grinning youth in the baseball cap. He left to look for work. It was a long time before she realised that he was never coming back, and no one ever told her why not. All that her mother said, when the question was at last asked aloud, was that men are no good: that was why Candida must work hard at school and get on in the world and look after herself.

At this moment, Candida knows, her mother will be teaching Sunday school at the Baptist chapel. She lets herself in with the key whose hiding place has not changed in forty years and carries Daniel's cot upstairs to the bedroom that was once her own. Then she locks the door again and returns to the car. Ten minutes later she follows her mother to the front door.

Mrs Brown is a sturdy and stiffly corseted woman in her mid-forties, wearing sensible lace-up shoes, a sensible warm overcoat and a sensible brown felt hat. Her dark-rimmed spectacles give her a stern appearance, but even without them there would be no trace of welcome in her expression as she turns at the sound of footsteps behind her. She doesn't even allow herself to show surprise.

'What you doing here, girl? I told you before, I don't allow no wicked woman to set foot in this house.'

There is a moment in which Candida feels that she is looking at a stranger. Her own voice has been altered by education and by the strength of her own desire for self-improvement. She speaks like an educated white woman. From time to time a look in someone's eyes reminds her that her skin is differently pigmented from theirs, but beneath that skin she doesn't feel that she is any different from a white woman of her own age. It is impossible for her to believe that she may one day grow into the rigidly righteous matron who is confronting her now; it is even a little difficult to believe that this woman is her mother.

Mrs Brown takes advantage of the silence to repeat what Candida has heard before, when she first confessed to her pregnancy and was greeted not with sympathy but with expulsion.

'The Good Book says, I shall bewail many which have sinned already and have not repented of the uncleanness and fornication and lasciviousness which they have committed.'

'I repent,' says Candida simply. She has made this journey in the full knowledge of what she must do. There can be no half measures.

It is Mrs Brown now who is silenced, perhaps by surprise, and Candida who fills the gap.

'I have sinned. I have done amiss.' Seventeen years of long sermons and Sunday school and daily Bible study have left her well able to hold her own in the exchanging of texts.

Her mother, who has clearly not expected this, steps aside and nods that her daughter may enter. Candida goes into the front room. The life of the family has always taken place in the kitchen at the back, but she rightly judges that this cold and overornamented parlour is the right setting for a formal act of reconciliation.

'You think that's all it needs, a few words and everything's all right again?' Mrs Brown is not yet letting down her guard.

'Doesn't the Good Book say, if thy brother repent, forgive him? I say unto you, likewise, joy shall be in heaven over one sinner that repenteth, more than over ninety and nine just persons, which need no repentance.'

'There's no repentance without pain.'

'I have had the pain.' Candida's fists clench with the determination not to cry. She is not here to plead for sympathy.

Mrs Brown is softening, but still unsure. She goes down on her knees. Candida follows suit.

'God be merciful to me, a sinner.' It is Candida who speaks, but her mother's lips form the words in silence. 'God be merciful to me, a sinner.' She grips a chair and her head leans forwards on her wrists as she repeats the phrase over and over again. This, like the earlier quotations, is something she has rehearsed on the journey, as though she were an actress learning her part; but unexpectedly the words are coming not from her lips but from her heart. Yes, she has sinned. She doesn't repent about loving Tom and she doesn't repent about giving birth to Daniel, but as her body rocks forward with each repetition she truly repents of her sin.

'I wasn't drunk. I wasn't on drugs.' She wasn't even on the pill, because her mother had taught her that only loose girls went on the pill before marriage. That was her undoing. 'It was the first time. It was love. I loved him so much.'

'It was lust. The lust of the flesh.'

Perhaps that's true. Love could have waited. Perhaps that over-whelming need which tumbled two young people on to a narrow bed in a student's bedsitter was indeed lust. In accepting the correction Candida proves herself to be, after all, her mother's daughter. She has been expelled from the rigid religious community in which she was brought up, but it was not her own wish to escape from it.

She finds herself overcome now by a guilt which she did not feel at the time. In the past twelve months she has experienced the ecstasy of a love affair, the shock and shame of a pregnancy, the delight of realising that Tom still loved her, the joy of her baby's birth, the des-olation of bereavement. Now all these emotions are swept aside by guilt. She is being punished because punishment is what she deserves. She is a miserable sinner. And it is Daniel who will suffer. The sin of the mother will be visited on the child.

'I repent!' she cries again.

Mrs Brown is convinced. Rising to her feet, she stretches out a hand to help Candida up.

'I suppose by now that no-good man has run off and left you with the baby.'

For a second time Candida's fists clench as she fights for self-con-trol.

'He died. We were going to be married, but he died.' The written proposal of marriage and her scrawled acceptance of it have together formalised in her mind as though a wedding date had actually been fixed; she is not conscious of any exaggeration. 'I need your help, Mum.'

59

She goes out of the room and up the stairs. When she returns, she is carrying the cot in which Daniel is peacefully sleeping. As she sets it down on a table, he opens his eyes.

This is the first time Mrs Brown has seen her grandson. She steps up to the table and looks down. Daniel's lips part in a wide smile and his hands wave in the air, searching for a finger to clutch. His grandmother provides the finger, which he carries to his mouth, making contented gurgling noises. Candida, who knows how much her mother loves young children, has always been confident that Daniel will win her over if he is once allowed into her presence.

'I need to get a job.'

'You're asking me to look after your baby?'

'There's no one else I could trust.'

'That's one big thing you're expecting, girl.'

'I know.'

'You reckoning to come back and live here yourself?'

'I shall have to see what kind of work I can get, and where.' Now that she is a mother herself, to live as a daughter in her old home would be to take a step backwards. Yet if she moves anywhere else, or even stays in the stable, she will miss all the little landmarks of Daniel's life: first word, first tooth, first step. She will no longer be the most important person in his life; she will hardly be a mother at all.

Well, that will be her punishment, and to be punished is the only way in which she can endure her guilt. She waits anxiously for the verdict. 'Please.'

Mrs Brown is still looking down at Daniel, and for the first time that afternoon she gives the loving smile which Candida remembers from her own childhood. With one accord the two women move into each other's arms, hugging and kissing. Daniel, deprived of the finger he was sucking, makes a faint noise of protest. His grandmother picks him up and holds him with his white-coffee cheek next to her chestnut-brown one. Candida is not sure whether to laugh or cry: but she has achieved what she came to do.

'Now you believe me, what I told you before,' says Mrs Brown. 'Men are no good. Dying or running, all the same. Never there when you need them. Only way for a woman to survive is look after herself. You've had advantages. You're young; your life in front of you. You can make a life for yourself, on your own. Not depending on anyone.'

'Except my poor overworked mother!'

'That's what a mother's for. You make it worth my while, though, girl. Make something of yourself.'

60

'Yes,' says Candida. 'Yes, I will.'

3

Work has started in earnest inside the walled garden. Penny sits at her high attic window and watches the arrivals of men and machines. She spends much of her day upstairs. It is the only part of the house that is hers and only hers. She has not yet come to terms with the spaces in the rooms she once shared with Clive: the empty armchair in the drawing room, the empty seat at the dining table, the empty canister in the kitchen which once held his preferred blend of tea.

As well as that, the attic offers an escape from the ceaseless flow of correspondence which is pushing her into a state of panic. There are bills to be paid, forms to be filled in and certificates to be photo-copied and dispatched and questions, questions, questions to be answered. Penny has always thought of herself as someone who is able to cope with the practical needs of everyday life; but the feeling of being alone, of having no one with whom she can check her deci-sions, seems to be paralysing her. The panic is not just in her mind but is a physical reaction: she feels sick every time she hears the click and slither which means that the postman has called.

Taking refuge upstairs, she tries to concentrate on her painting, but it is not as easy as she had hoped to turn a pleasure into a kind of therapy. The talent needed to produce pictures for sale is something she knows herself not to possess, and without even a financial incen-tive to spur her on it is difficult to see what the point of the activity is. No one will ever see what she paints. There is no one to offer cheerful congratulations: 'I say, Penny, that's rather good!'

So for much of the day she is only pretending to paint. What really holds her attention is the noise and movement below her, which would be distracting even if her concentration were in better shape. The pergola has come down and the roses which clothed it have been uprooted. It would break the heart of the head gardener who first cre-ated the garden inside the walls if he could see what was happening now. The new tyrant of the plot is a bright yellow JCB.

At first Penny is horrified by the process of destruction, but little by little her distress is replaced by admiration for the skill of the JCB's operator. He sits high above the huge front wheel in a glass-walled cab, surrounded by levers and turning on a swivelling seat whenever his machine changes direction. Seen from this distance, his hands and feet hardly seem to move at all, and yet under his directions the heavy mechanical tools operate with an almost unbelievable delicacy.

The JCB has two strong yellow arms, one at each end of the cab. The larger one is being used today rather as a dinosaur might use its tail, to establish a firm balance for the machine and prevent it from tipping over into one of the foundation trenches it has itself dug. The smaller scoop – more like a neck than an arm, in fact — is applying itself to the removal of whatever topsoil remains near to the walls, calculating to within an inch how close it can go without damaging the roots of the fan-trained fruit trees.

This outstretched scoop, like the tail, brings to Penny's mind the image of some prehistoric monster. As though alive, the long neck extends itself, the greedy mouth opens wide, the strong steel teeth bite into the earth and lift their titbit into the air, poising it for a second before swinging to one side and gently spitting it out on the further side of the wall. It is good black loam which has been tilled and mulched for a century. Now it rises like a slag heap, but Penny is glad to think that it is being saved and will presumably be returned to the garden section of the site after the house has been completed.

She finds herself fascinated by the nonstop movement of the machine and begins to enjoy small touches. After each load is deposited outside the wall, the head of the scoop, with its smoothly curved top, gives a little shake to free itself of any remaining clods. Then – a dinosaur still – it raises itself again high enough to swoop back above the wall and turns very slightly from side to side as if to see where next it should dig. It is almost as though it has eyes, quite independent of those of the man in the cab. Penny pulls out a new painting pad from the rack beside her table and begins to sketch.

Her hand moves freely. This is the kind of subject for which her training has fitted her. Within only a short time she is considering three views of the JCB in bright yellow paint outlined in black. The temptation is irresistible. To each of the heads she adds an eye. The tiny black marks are enough to transform the machines into something alive and intelligent. They lead her on, demanding to be given character.

The real JCB has come to a halt for some reason, but although her ears register the fact, her eyes are concentrating on her own work. She begins to work on one of the sketches with touches of more black. A raised eyebrow above the eye gives a sardonic expression. A simple thin line above the jagged steel teeth provides an upper lip. The very slight hint of a curve in the upper part of the grab suggests a cheek. A clod of earth adhering to precisely the right spot shows her where to draw in a moustache. This is clearly a male bulldozer;

she wonders frivolously whether there is such a thing as a cowdozer. If there isn't, there ought to be. She looks down again into the walled garden with eyes half closed, trying to envisage some tiny detail which could be used to suggest femininity.

The operator is no longer in his cab; he has jumped down to the ground and is talking to someone. To Jonathan Verne, in fact, who has come to check that work has begun. As the conversation ends, Jonathan deliberately looks up towards the attic window at which he has seen Penny once before, and waves. Smiling, she waves back. Jonathan raises a clenched hand to his lips in a gesture which clearly requests a cup of tea. Penny puts up a thumb. Good idea. She is already downstairs, with the kettle about to boil, before he rings the bell.

'Coffee, if I may,' he says in answer to her first question. 'Lovely.' He cups his hands round the hot mug. 'I'm sorry about all the noise.'

'I'm enjoying it.' Penny's answer is a truthful one. The Old Rectory is too quiet these days.

'I've got an impertinent question to ask. What is it you do up in the skivvy's bedroom?'

'Would you like to see?'

Of course he would. He follows her upstairs.

The first thing to catch his eye is the painting of his own walled garden as it might have looked a hundred years earlier. This is the picture that was to have been Clive's Christmas present. Penny has finished and mounted it and it is now propped up on the small folding easel which she uses for outside work.

'Sad,' says Jonathan, even as he smiles in affectionate recognition. 'Sad, I mean, that a way of life is disappearing. And not just the life of the owner. There was a lot of satisfaction in being a gardener, I believe. Hard work, but something to show for it. When I look at these unemployment statistics and think how bored people must get with nothing to do, I can never understand why there isn't a great rush for allotments so that they could at least grow their own food, and enjoy the process.'

'Speaking as one of them, I suspect that the unemployed develop tunnel vision. You think you know what you can do, and only that, and you either don't want or don't dare to try anything new.'

'You don't count yourself as unemployed, surely?'

'Not in the sense of being on the dole or on the breadline, no. But in the sense of needing employment, yes, definitely. Even while Clive was alive, it made me uneasy, not doing anything. That was what he wanted, but it did make me feel a bit – well, not exactly useless, but lazy. I don't suppose older women feel like that, because at the time when they were young the expectation may have been that married women stayed at home. But people of my age expect to work and to keep on working, at least until they have children – and often after.'

'So are you job-hunting?'

'Not as energetically as I should. I wrote to my old firm, but they haven't got anything to offer at the moment and they were pretty gloomy about my chances. Everyone seems to be firing rather than hiring at the moment. I've decided to wait until I've moved back into London before I really get down to it. Living here, I'm out of the swim. I need to get my face back into people's memories.'

'You're going to move!' Jonathan makes no attempt to hide his dismay. 'Oh, but I want you for a neighbour, Penny.'

'Sorry. I shall go as soon as all the probate business is settled. Assuming I can sell the house, of course. I haven't really put down roots here, and I need to be where the work is.'

'But nowadays the work comes to the home. I intend to run my practice from the walled garden. I'm sure there must be something –'

He stops abruptly. For the whole of this conversation Penny has been sitting down, perched on the high stool which she often uses for still-life arrangements, while Jonathan has been on the prowl. This is the moment at which he arrives at her sloping table near the window.

'Oh!' he exclaims. He is looking down at the three JCB sketches. 'Brilliant! Are you a children's-book writer, then? Well, surely this is just the place –'

'Sorry.' Smilingly Penny shakes her head. 'Nothing like that. I did these simply to pass the time. To justify the hours I was spending just staring.'

'But you ought to do it. A book for children, I mean. These are marvellous characters. Mother, father and child. I can tell the difference just from these tiny touches. That one in the middle is the greedy one. All you need is to make up a story. You're obviously a born illustrator.'

'It's all very well to say "make up a story". I wouldn't have the faintest idea how to begin. And I'm not sure that I approve of anthropomorphism.'

'Children do, which is all that matters. Someone put faces on a handful of railway engines and made himself into a millionaire. And just think how much more attractive *your* machines would be, when you can suggest movement just by the way they extend all their various bits and pieces.'

'Well.' Penny is polite but unconvinced. 'On the day I *do* become a millionaire I'll remember that I owe it all to you.'

Jonathan doesn't press the point. His mug is empty and he is ready to leave.

'I must get off to keep a four o'clock appointment,' he tells her. 'But I shall have to call at the site quite often to make sure that everything's going to plan. Next time I fix a visit, may I give you a ring in advance and take you out to dinner?'

'You could have dinner here.' Penny speaks without thinking. What she really means to say is that she is not ready for evenings out with presumably unattached males; but instead of simply turning down his invitation she realises, too late, that she has substituted one of her own. It is, of course, immediately accepted.

Perhaps after all that is no bad thing. It will force her to dust the house, to clean the silver, to buy and cook something more elaborate than the convenience snacks on which she has been existing.

'I shall look forward to that,' she says in order to make her reaction sound less grudging.

'So shall I. This is a lonely time for you, must be. You need friends, you know.'

Penny has plenty of friends, although most of them live in London. She could pick up her old social life without any trouble if she chose; but she is not yet ready to start. What she needs at the moment is not friends but occupation.

Has Jonathan offered that as well? After he leaves, she returns to the attic and studies her drawings again. Yes, she can certainly see the possibilities purely from the picture point of view. One set of classes in her commercial-art course, as it happens, was devoted to book illustration. But the students were always issued with chapters of text which other people had already written. Thinking of an idea, writing a story, is a completely different kettle of fish. She continues to stare downwards until it is too dark to see. If thinking is an occupation, then she is occupied.

4

Madge Manderson has arrived at the Purefrew headquarters to pick up Harry's personal belongings from his office. Naturally Harry's secretary, Sharon, has offered to save her the journey and bring everything over herself, but Madge feels the need to pay what will almost certainly be a last visit. She wants to sit in her husband's office for a few moments and to say goodbye to some of the people with whom he spent his working hours.

Sharon, bless her heart, has recognised the need to make the visit into a small ceremony and has considerately given warning of this, allowing Madge to arrive tidily by taxi instead of turning up wet and windswept after a ninety-minute cycle ride. Tea is waiting. Various members of the staff have been invited and Robert Sharman, whom Helen Cunningham has hastily promoted to become managing director, is on hand to act as host and to deliver a short speech about Harry's value to the company.

He speaks fluently and gives the impression of being competently in control. Madge guesses that Harry may have been overprotective at work as much as in his home, and reluctant to grant too much responsibility to a younger man; whereas Robert probably reckoned that a degree in business administration was the equal of a lifetime's experience. Now, at the age of thirty-four, he is in charge and is revelling in the chance to show what he can do.

It is not a comfortable occasion, but Madge sits out the hour before thanking everyone and handing over a large Christmas cake which she has baked and decorated, as well as what would have been her husband's Christmas present to his secretary. In return she is shown a box which has been packed up to await her collection.

'I'll carry it out to the car,' Sharon offers. 'And here's the key.'

Madge is taken by surprise. She has not ordered a taxi to take her home, thinking it probable that one of the staff will offer her a lift. But that she should be expected to drive herself back comes as a shock.

'I thought . . .' But of course she remembers now. It has been established that Harry was in the driving seat at the time of the accident, and for that reason she has allowed herself to assume that the burned-out car was his. But witnesses at the inquest – the Wright and King representatives who had dined with the four dead men – gave evidence that Harry drank no alcohol at all in the course of the evening and almost certainly was asked by the others to take the wheel for that reason: the car, now she comes to think of it, was Michael Cunningham's.

Her second reaction is to explain that unfortunately she doesn't drive; but these words too she smothers before they are born. Being unable to drive is not exactly shameful, but there is something wimpish about it, making her reluctant to confess. After all, she *has* driven in the past. Somewhere at home she has a licence, and she knows that Harry's insurance allows other people to use the car. Or rather, it used to allow that. Will his death have made any difference? And even if it will not be illegal for her to take the wheel, will it be unwise?

Sharon notices her hesitation and mistakenly interprets it in terms of Madge's lack of inches.

'Shall I adjust the seat for you?' she asks helpfully.

Madge makes up her mind. Is she going to spend the rest of her life imprisoned in Lower Monckton or else perpetually dependent on friends? No, she is not. Loneliness is freedom. It would be idiotic to endure the one without taking advantage of the other. She is already doing her best to come to terms with the fact – as a generalisation – that from now on she will have to look after herself. This is the first test.

'That would be very kind,' she says.

Even with the seat as far forward as it will go and its back in the most upright position, she can hardly see over the long bonnet of the Jaguar. The car is far too large and powerful for her and her heart pounds with panic as she turns on the ignition, waves goodbye to Sharon in what she hopes is a carefree manner, and lets in the clutch. The Jaguar bounds forwards – but luckily has been waiting in an empty section of the car park, so there is nothing to damage. She brakes violently and stalls the engine.

Returning to neutral, she counts slowly to ten. As her heartbeat returns to something like normal, she tries again. This time she takes it more carefully. Not caring what Sharon may think, she experiments until she has discovered the controls for indicators and lights and then drives cautiously twice round the car park before turning into the public road.

Harry used to do the journey in ten minutes. She allows herself thirty. Only thirty minutes of danger. The greatest danger, she suspects, is that a powerful car being driven at twenty miles an hour may arouse the suspicions of a policeman. And in fact it refuses to stay at twenty. Her speed creeps up. Her muscles are tensed and she is gripping the wheel too tightly – but she is, nevertheless, in control.

Twenty minutes later she drives through the gates of College Farm and presses the gadget that, as Harry has demonstrated to her, will open the garage door as she approaches it. So unexpectedly long is the car that she bumps it into the sacks of water-softening salt which are stacked against the back wall. But although she tuts at herself for spoiling a run which has been smoother than she had any right to expect, there is no damage.

For a moment or two she sits without moving. That was a crazy thing to do. But she has done it. The Jaguar will have to be sold, certainly, but there is no reason why she shouldn't take to the road in something small. And then she will no longer be confined to bicycle range or imprisoned by other people's timetables.

Is she being disloyal to Harry in thinking like this? The question worries her slightly as she carries the box of his possessions into the house. It is true that for the whole of their married life he has regarded her solely as a homemaker, someone expected to leave major decisions, heavy physical tasks and financial affairs to him while she cooks and looks after the house and occasionally pursues gentle hobbies. But if he were to look down and see her now, he would surely want to be reassured that she could look after herself and be of use to other people? Wouldn't he? Madge is not actually quite sure. She gives herself the benefit of the doubt – but the question combines with the strain of the drive home to send her rushing to the lavatory.

She doesn't understand quite why bereavement should have had such an emptying effect on her body. For the first few days after hearing the news of Harry's death she was either sick or wanted to be whenever she thought about it. Well, there was a reason for that: her mental picture of his last few moments, trapped in a burning car. In that respect the inquest had proved helpful, making it clear that he must have died instantaneously at the moment of collision, before the fire began. So now she no longer vomits, but instead is afflicted with diarrhoea. Any kind of anxiety brings it on; any departure from the routines of her former life. And of course every day brings new such departures, as she takes to herself responsibilities which have always in the past been Harry's.

She tries to deal with the problem by fasting. If she can empty her body completely, then perhaps it will be possible to start again – and since she has no appetite at all, this decision requires no effort. But each time she thinks that the problem has been solved, and begins to take a little food, some new strain makes itself felt. On this occasion, without doubt, the Jaguar is to blame.

By the time she returns, exhausted, to the kitchen, the cat is waiting for her, indignantly indicating that she is late in providing tea.

'That's all you think I'm good for!' Since Harry's death Madge has begun to talk aloud to Charlie, because some kind of conversation is needed to break up the silence of the house. Charlie, rubbing against her leg, agrees with a sycophantic purr before leading the way, tail high, to his feeding corner. She is the opener of tins, the cooker of fish, the pourer of milk. From a cat's point of view, it *is* all she is good for.

Leaving Charlie to tuck in, she starts to unpack the box of Harry's possessions. Expecting to be distressed, she is relieved to discover that there are no intimate secrets to be discovered. Instead, it comes as a surprise that the first items to catch her eyes are half-empty bottles of whisky, gin and vodka.

Madge sets the bottles down on the kitchen table and stares at them. A suspicious woman might wonder whether her husband was less strictly teetotal than he has always led her to believe; but she wastes no time on such thoughts. The alcohol was almost certainly – no, absolutely certainly – for the entertainment of visitors, just like the sweet sherry which he kept at home. What has made her pause in the unpacking is her memory of the night he died.

She was drunk that night. At the time, she would have described herself only as a little tiddly; but because of what happened she has already faced up to a stricter truth. At the moment when her husband died she, Madge, was drunk. Ought she to feel guilty about that?

She has put the question to herself before, and the answer is still the same today: no. Nothing that she did or didn't do that evening had the slightest influence on the accident. She doesn't intend ever to let herself get drunk again, but that's a different matter.

And so she resists the gesture that comes instinctively to mind: that she should pour away the contents of the three bottles, removing not only temptation but a reminder of that tragic night. She will do exactly what Harry had been doing, and keep the whisky, the gin and the vodka for offering to visitors. She puts the bottles into a cupboard and makes a note on her shopping list to buy tonic and soda water.

In a good many respects Madge is still lost and lonely. She doesn't yet see clearly how she is going to spend the rest of her life. But the events of the afternoon have begun to send a new pulse of courage and independence throbbing through her veins. That cheerful, confident young woman who once ran her own business and dealt competently with daily emergencies has over the years become smothered by a daughter's dependence and a husband's protectiveness; but she has not completely given up the ghost. Madge tells herself that she has coped with life on her own once: she can cope with it again.

Glancing at her watch, she sees that it is not yet quite five o'clock, when offices may be expected to close. She looks in the Yellow Pages for the names of driving schools. Although there may be no legal requirement for her to take a new driving test, she recognises that it would be sensible for her to have supervised experience in today's traffic conditions and to be brought up to date with road signs and regulations.

The telephone is answered. She books herself in with a driver who specialises in bringing old skills back to life. And tomorrow, at the bowls club, she will start asking her friends about small cars and trade-in values. From what might have proved to be a harrowing afternoon, something positive has emerged.

5

Helen Cunningham wanders restlessly about her huge house. She picks things up apparently at random and moves them to other places in other rooms. The process is disorganised, slow and uncertain, but not as aimless as it appears at first sight. She has an aim. She is making collections.

These will have nothing in common with Michael's collections, which he built up with the expenditure of much time, money and enthusiasm. Helen is assembling objects for disposal. Why?

A large house filled with valuable items and with no close neighbours will always be a target for thieves, and it is true that since the burglary she has become nervous. She lies awake in bed listening to sounds. The nightly cooling-down of the central-heating system makes a noise exactly like someone coming cautiously up the stairs. The two owls – familiar and undoubtedly genuine owls – which screech across the whole width of the garden sound nowadays more like potential intruders signalling to each other. Even the trees outside the bedroom window conspire to upset her, dropping their crisp brown leaves with the rustle of a prowler.

All these disturbing noises are familiar and have never worried her before, even though she has not shared a bedroom for many years. It is simply the difference between being and not being completely alone in the house.

If nervousness were her only spur, she could find easier ways to deal with it: by hiring a live-in housekeeper instead of a daily one, say, or acquiring a large dog, or even taking a lodger for the sake of company rather than rent. But Helen's problem goes deeper than that. She cannot, must not stay on in Monckton Hall, where the very walls seem to scream out a reminder of her guilt.

It is the timing that she can't forget: the fact that she was lying in Derek Forsyth's arms at the very moment of her husband's death. Reason tells her that infidelity is infidelity regardless of what the clock may say, but on this point she is unable to be reasonable.

There is another aspect to consider as well. Had there been no accident, Michael would have arrived home without warning while Derek was still in the house. He might have noticed the car. The two men might even have met in the hall. For all Helen's brave words at the time, and her certainty that her husband would not turn on the light in her bedroom in the middle of the night, she is aware that she would have suffered a very nasty moment indeed had she heard his footsteps on the stairs. She was saved from that embarrassment by his death, but of course it would be unthinkable to feel relief.

The attempt to smother so many different emotions has brought her near to collapse. Over and over again she reminds herself how much and for how long she has loved Michael. Although one side of their relationship had come to an end, they remained intimate friends, enjoying each other's company and to some extent still sharing each other's lives. The fact that Michael could no longer make her feel that she was desirable ought to have been only a small matter, of no importance. To allow other men to feed her vanity was a despicable mistake. If she were given another chance, she would abandon all those efforts to appear younger than her age without a moment's regret. Indeed, she has already abandoned them; her hair is grey at the roots. But death offers no second chances.

And so she roams the house, making lists, picking up objects, always alone. Friends have written notes of condolence, but seem reluctant to call. Derek Forsyth has telephoned several times, but she has tried to make it clear, without being rude, that she doesn't want to see him again. She guesses from the telephone calls that he – like her – is suffering from a confusion of emotions, and it is not at all obvious whether he is seeking or fearing an invitation to visit.

No doubt he feels as guilty as she does; on top of that, he may be apprehensive that when she emerges from a period of mourning she will wish to embark on a more permanent relationship. He has always been straightforward about his preference for married women who have no desire to leave their husbands. On the other hand, it may have occurred to him that Helen Cunningham must now be a very wealthy widow. Helen deals with her own uncertainties and his by writing to end her membership of the bridge club of which he is secretary.

Her daughter Lucy flew over from Washington for the funeral and stayed for a week afterwards. Although she has by now returned home, it was arranged several months ago that she and Cliff and their two children would come to England for Christmas. The work involved in transforming Monckton Hall into the scene of merry Olde English jollity and feasting is something that Helen is not yet strong enough to contemplate, but about one matter she is clear. Nothing must be sold or given away that her daughter or grandchildren would like to own either now or in the future. Furniture that wouldn't suit an American house or would not be worth the cost of transportation can be put in storage if necessary, to wait indefinitely; but the time for making choices will be this December.

She has not yet warned Lucy of this. Lucy is in many ways a rather

71

distant daughter, but she is not greedy. She will protest that her mother should continue to live in her old style, surrounded by all her familiar possessions. This is an argument which Helen intends to win, and so she is making her preparations in a more businesslike manner than is apparent on the surface.

In one bedroom is being placed everything Helen intends to take with her when she moves. Into another one go what she thinks of as the heirlooms: old portraits, old glass, old porcelain, old books, old embroidery and a few – alas, only a very few – pieces of old silver which escaped the attention of the burglars.

Michael's collections pose a different problem. They are so personal to him that to sell them will feel in a way like a gesture of rejection of the man himself, or the memory of him, which is not at all what she intends. Yet, just because they are so personal, she has no real interest in the various items. She has often suspected that it was only the hunt that appealed to him. He liked to browse in antique shops and felt the need to have a motive, something special to ask for, something to fill a gap. A seventeenth-century truncheon, an Art Deco pince-nez, an Australian button hook. Over the years Helen has smiled her congratulations at each addition to what has always seemed to her to be a ragbag of enthusiasms, but what do they mean to her now, when the delight with which they were acquired is dead?

She would have kept the miniatures. The tiny portraits appealed to her and could be hung on the wall of even a small room. But the miniatures were one of the casualties of the burglary. She is unlikely to see them again and has already filled up the insurance claim.

The remaining collections she assembles in Michael's study, except for the coins, which have always been kept in the bank. Perhaps one of the grandchildren will like to take over one of them. Yet even as she lays the button hooks out in rows, something near to nausea overcomes her. What is – what ever was – the point of all these acquisitions? A man hunts and buys and gloats and arranges and catalogues and then he dies and what was it all for? But then, what is the point of doing anything when it all comes to nothing in the end? Although Helen is not thinking clearly enough to realise it, guilt has added such a weight to bereavement that she has sunk to the depths of depression.

She works on. The day and night nurseries became Lucy's bedroom and sitting room as she grew up, and these now are filled with the shabbier items of furniture and kitchen utensils which even a prosperous household tends to retain just because they have always been there. Lucy will not want any of this, so it can all go to charity.

It would have no value in an auction room, but is still sound enough to be of use to a refugee or homeless family.

A thought occurs to Helen as with some difficulty she carries a Windsor chair up two flights of stairs from the kitchen into this particular store: the thought of the black girl, Tom Harding's girl, whom she spoke to for the first time after the funeral. Candida, that was her name. Helen disapproves in principle of unmarried mothers, but this one seemed to be a polite and well-spoken young woman – although, still stunned on that occasion by her loss, she did not speak very much. Alone of the four bereaved women, it seems that Candida has no pension, no capital, no proper home. She might well be glad of help in furnishing wherever it is that she proposes to live.

Momentarily aroused from her mental lethargy by this positive idea, Helen phones Madge Manderson to find out how she can contact Candida.

'Harry told Tom he could camp out for a bit in the old Orchard Farm buildings,' Madge tells her. Helen knows that when four farms were amalgamated into the Purefrew holding, one of the farmhouses was sold off separately and another, already in poor repair, was demolished. 'I don't imagine that anyone was in too much of a hurry to inform the planning or health authorities, but he would have cleared it with Michael, I'm sure.'

'Oh yes, I'm not raising any objection.' Helen is now the owner and chairwoman of the company, but has not yet taken the reins into her hands, and probably never will. After promoting Robert Sharman to be managing director, because he already knows the business, she is leaving it to him to find a replacement for Clive and to take care of any other problems that may arise. 'I just wondered . . . I must say, she looked very clean and, well, respectable.'

'They weren't what you might think of as squatters. Not like these awful New Age travellers. They were hoping to buy one of those new houses in the school-fields development. It wasn't due to be finished until March. Living rent-free gave them the chance to save for the deposit. She won't be able to manage that now, of course. I don't know what she's planning to do.'

Helen feels a flicker of responsibility. Playing the role of chairman's wife has not for many years involved more than acting as a gracious hostess on occasions like the annual Christmas party. But a young woman with a baby needs support. Helen reproaches herself for not investigating the situation earlier.

There is no telephone number listed under Tom Harding's name, and it seems from what Madge has hinted that the postman is unlikely to call at what is generally believed to be a deserted farmyard. Helen, who has hardly left the house since the funeral, gets into her car.

Reaching her destination, she looks around in horror. There has been heavy rain during the night. Water drips from the corrugated iron roofs of sheds and forms puddles in the muddy yard. Something that looks suspiciously like a rat scuttles out of sight through an open barn entrance. The whole scene is unutterably lowering. This is no place in which to bring up a baby alone.

Before leaving the car, she takes time to put a straight question to herself. Would she be prepared to offer Candida a temporary home in Monckton Hall? There is so much surplus space there that the two women would hardly need to meet if they didn't want to; and it would reduce the feeling of isolation and vulnerability which Helen suffers from at night.

The idea ought to have everything going for it, but she turns it down. Loneliness is part of her punishment. She needs it. Besides, she intends to put the house on the market as soon after Christmas as she can find somewhere smaller to live. It would be unfair to disrupt Candida's present arrangements and then leave her even worse off after a short time.

This, at least, is what she tells herself. The truth is that she doesn't want to share her home with a stranger; but the very selfishness of that decision seems to put her under an obligation to help Candida in some other way if she can. Stepping with care, because she is wearing unsuitable shoes, Helen makes her way between puddles to the stable building. It looks locked up and deserted, and proves to be so. She knocks with her knuckles and calls out Candida's name, but it is almost a relief when no one answers.

Returning to the car, Helen scribbles a note. She addresses it simply to Candida, although she is not of the generation which takes for granted the use of Christian names among strangers, and she noted on the day of the funeral that Candida politely and properly addressed her as Mrs Cunningham. But she has forgotten Candida's surname and presumes that, in the modern manner, the girl would not have bothered to take Tom's.

Her message is brief. She has furniture to give away to anyone who would find it useful. If Candida would be willing to take any of it off her hands, this is the number to phone.

For a few moments, then, she has emerged from her mood of self-centred depression, but it returns as soon as she begins the journey home. She is not really interested in Candida. All they have in common is a motorway accident. It is not enough.

74

6

Candida is dressed to look businesslike. After more than a year of wearing the loose clothes suitable for pregnancy or breast-feeding or simply mucking around in the country, she finds her tight skirt, short though it is, constricting. The high collar of her blouse tickles her neck and she has lost the habit of wearing tights. Although her hips are as slim as they were before Daniel was born, her breasts are fuller, making her jacket uncomfortably close-fitting.

There is no choice, though. The suit she wears is the only one she possesses. She bought it three years earlier for the matriculation ceremony and kept it in readiness for graduation, never thinking that it might be required instead for a funeral. Black doesn't suit her, which is why she has chosen a high-necked blouse to bring colour near her face.

She is staying at her mother's house at least until she finds work, so that Daniel will accept the change from one carer to another gradually. Mrs Brown is a happy woman now. Her forgiveness of her daughter is as wholehearted as her earlier condemnation. She is delighted that she and Candida are friends again and already adores her grandson. Now, as she inspects her smart daughter, dressed for the City, she beams with approval. This is what all the education was for; it may not after all have been wasted.

An hour and a half later Candida is sitting in a secretary's office at Wright and King's headquarters. The quietness of the building makes it curiously remote from the firm's spheres of activity. Wright and King, originally a wholesaler for provisions, has over the years expanded to develop its own transport business and a packaging company which supplies 'own brand' goods to many of its retail customers. It has also more recently adopted an aggressive policy of buying some of the smaller companies whose products it distributes. But here, in the heart of the City, there are no fork-lift trucks moving loads of goods and no lorry engines revving up. Every footstep is subdued by the deep pile of the carpet, telephones flash rather than ring and there is not even the clatter of typewriters now that computers and word processors are standard equipment.

Two hours later she is still waiting, and she is still there two hours after that. The letter she prepared has proved sufficient to get her past the ground-floor receptionist, but Mr Price's secretary has made it clear that he sees nobody without an appointment and there is no likelihood that he will have even five minutes free in the course of the day. Candida is prepared to wait.

75

At ten to one there is a window in his day and perhaps he is curious. Candida is invited into his office. She does her best to look cool and businesslike as she goes in, but nervousness makes her stand even straighter than usual.

It is from Tom that she has heard Mr Price's name, and she has used Tom's name in the letter which he is reading at this moment with a puzzled expression on his face. He is the director in charge of new projects and acquisitions. The Purefrew project has fallen through, thanks to the death of its senior staff, but while it was still alive it was Mr Price who was both knowledgeable and enthusiastic. He is not enthusiastic now, but merely polite.

'What can I do for you, Miss Brown?'

'You've read my letter?'

'Yes. Naturally I was extremely sorry when I heard about the death of your fiancé and his colleagues. Please accept my sympathy for you personally. But . . .'

'I've come to ask whether you will offer me a place on your management-trainee scheme.'

Mr Price's puzzlement turns to surprise, but he is still polite.

'Won't you sit down?'

'Thank you.'

'You've come to the wrong person, I'm afraid, Miss Brown. Our personnel manager deals with all that sort of thing.'

'Yours was the only name I knew. And Tom told me how helpful you'd been, and how impressed he was with the research you did into the project.'

'Well, if it's a name you want, I can tell you who you should see. In fact, I'll ring through now if you like and make an appointment for you. There may be something going; I don't know. But our trainee scheme, I'm afraid, is only for graduates.'

Candida gives him a long look before speaking. To make him uncomfortable is her best chance of success.

'Are you taking it for granted that I'm not a graduate, Mr Price?' There is no need to accuse him in so many words of making a judgement on the grounds of colour; he will know what she thinks.

'Ah.' She has succeeded in unsettling him sufficiently to push him into making amends. 'Well, I wasn't asking questions myself because, as I say, this isn't my sphere. But by all means tell me if you wish.' He draws a pad towards him. 'You were at university, then?'

'Yes. At Oxford. A scholar in my second and third years.'

'What did you read?'

'Law.'

'And did you go on to qualify?' He knows as well as Candida does

76

that a law degree is of little vocational value in itself but must be followed by years of training to be either a barrister or a solicitor.

'No. I can't afford to. I have to earn a living.'

'This isn't a legal firm. There's not much scope –'

'You must take on history graduates, say, without expecting them to work as historians. When you ask for a graduate, aren't you simply looking for a certain kind of trained mind?'

He makes no comment on that. 'What class did you get?'

This is the tricky one. 'I wasn't able to complete my Finals. I was taken ill in the middle.' To describe Daniel's birth, ten days earlier than expected, as an illness goes against the grain, but is the only way to explain her results. 'I got alphas in four out of my first five papers. I have a letter from my tutor saying that I would certainly have earned a 2:1 and had a good chance of a First. What I was actually given was an aegrotat.'

'Won't Oxford give you a second chance of getting a degree? You could try again next summer.'

'An aegrotat *is* a degree. I can put BA Oxon after my name. And now, as I said, I have to earn a living.'

One of the two telephones on Mr Price's desk buzzes and he answers it briefly. It is one o'clock, and perhaps a lunch guest has arrived. Or, more probably, he has instructed his secretary to ring and give him an excuse to bring the interview to an end. If that is the case, it seems that he is going to ignore it. The conversation is not yet at an end.

'What have you got to offer us, Miss Brown? Apart from an Oxford education, which you share with hundreds of other applicants.'

Candida looks him straight in the eye. 'I'm female. I'm black. And I'm disadvantaged. You could use one person to put three ticks against your minorities-employment record.'

'You approve of positive discrimination, do you?'

'No. Not at all. I reckon that I'm as well qualified as anyone else to make use of your training. I'm just pointing out the advantage from your point of view.'

Mr Price tries and fails to control a smile, but his next question expresses only curiosity.

'What do you mean by disadvantaged? Are you, um, disabled?'

'Oh, no. Fit as a fiddle. I mean that I come from a broken home in a run-down area and I got to Oxford from an ordinary comprehensive school.' This statement is unfair both to her mother, who was determined that Candida should never suffer as a result of her father's disappearance, and to Holland Park Comprehensive School, which

77

taught her how to study and think and argue and equipped her with the three A-levels at Grade A which won her a place at Oxford. But it seems fair to make the point that she has always had to work hard, with no money or privilege to help her.

'And what else can you offer? You've come here to sell yourself. What else is on sale?'

'I could bring you Formula Four.'

'What? I don't understand.'

'Didn't Tom tell you about the new drink which he was hoping would make everyone's fortune? Including your firm's.'

'Yes, he did mention it. But when we were investigating the changed situation after that most unfortunate accident, we were unable to discover anyone who knew the recipe for Formula Four.'

'That's because nobody asked *me*. It's mine.'

'Do you mean that you've appropriated it after your fiancé's death? I remember quite clearly that Mr Harding claimed that the new drink was his particular baby. If it evolved during the course of his employment –'

'It didn't. I gave him permission to take all the credit, because if it did him good it would be good for both of us. And anyway, I wouldn't know how to develop it commercially, so I didn't mind it being used as one of the selling points in the negotiations. If the deal had gone through, I'd have told Tom everything he needed to know. But it didn't, and so the formula is still mine. And I've taken out protection.'

'And that's what you're saying is on sale?'

Candida licks her lips nervously. She is out of her depth here.

'As I said, Mr Price, I wouldn't know how to put something like this into production. Tom and the others said it could be really big if it had the proper backing. Like Coca-Cola, one day. But that would need a firm like yours to build it up. I might ask for a kind of royalty, I suppose. But all I'm looking for now is work. Not just a job; a career. You could offer me that, if you chose, and I'd be happy to offer something in return.'

There is a long silence. Candida has nothing more to add and nor, it seems, has Mr Price.

'Well,' he says at last, looking down at the letter on his desk. 'As I said before, this is not my field. My secretary will take you down to the personnel department. I'll ring through to say you're on the way. There are some application forms you'll have to fill in. They'll want to see the letter from your tutor which you mentioned, and the names of a couple of other referees. I don't imagine there are any vacancies at the moment, but you can get yourself on the file.'

'Thank you, Mr Price.'

'I'm not doing anything. Just sending you to the right place.'

Candida doesn't believe him. When he phones down, she feels certain, he is going to say something in her favour. She gives him such a happy, wholehearted smile that he is seduced into smiling back.

'And the Formula Four thing?' she asks.

His face becomes businesslike again. 'Hold on to it,' he advises. 'It's not our line, developing something from scratch. Get yourself a little business going – like Purefrew but different – and approach us again when you're ready to move it up a notch.'

'But –'

'Weekend work,' he suggests. 'If you're going to make a businesswoman of yourself, that could prove a useful little exercise.' He stands up, already overdue for lunch. Candida stands as well and holds out her hand.

'Just one thing,' he says as he shakes it. 'Strictly off the record. Something we're definitely not allowed to ask. But if I'm going to put in a word for you, it will do me no favours if you start asking for maternity leave before you've had time to make yourself useful. Don't answer that question, because it isn't a question.'

The smile fades from Candida's face. It hasn't occurred to him to ask whether she already has a baby, and Daniel's existence is none of his business; but she can meet his point as specifically as he has made it. If Tom had lived, it would be different – but then, if Tom were alive she wouldn't be here now.

Her determination to prove herself a responsible employee, if she is given the opportunity, lifts her chin as she stares into Mr Price's eyes. She has accepted the guilt of loving too much as well as the guilt of not loving enough, and she has accepted her responsibility for Daniel. Now she is about to make a life for herself, and she will do it on her own.

'You needn't worry about that, Mr Price,' she promises.

Chapter Five

1

Candida's hope that Mr Price will somehow whisk her immediately on to the staff of Wright and King has proved to be overoptimistic. She has filled in all the application forms, has provided names of referees and photocopies of certificates and has returned for a more formal interview and aptitude test. But the letter which arrives at her mother's address is the printed form letter which is presumably designed primarily for undergraduates applying for work in their final year. The interviewing process will continue until the end of March; short-listed candidates will be re-interviewed in April; and those successful will be expected to start work in October. There is a system, a timetable: why should she expect that anyone would vary it for her?

The only ray of hope lies in a handwritten scribble at the bottom, suggesting that if she proposes to look for temporary employment while awaiting the verdict, to work in a supermarket might provide relevant experience.

Candida's first reaction to this suggestion is disdainful. She has not spent all these years passing examinations just to end up as a shop assistant. Surprisingly, it is her mother who makes her see the point of the suggestion. If she is to work for a firm like Wright and King, which owns and supplies grocers' shops and supermarkets all over the country, she needs to know what shoppers buy and why, and how to attract them to one product rather than another.

'You study, study, study and that's good, that's right. But you don't know what things cost. You don't know what makes people choose. You don't know why I buy this brand and Mrs Furlong next door, she

80

chooses a different brand.' They are washing up at the time and Mrs Brown is pointing to the washing-up liquid.

'You tell me why, then.'

'I buy this own brand because it's cheapest. Mrs Furlong, she pays more because there's a competition. You send in three caps and a slogan and perhaps you win a holiday.'

'Her chances of winning must be a million to one against.'

'Maybe so. But people like her, no family at home, every day the same as every other day, only her pension, not enough for holidays – what she wants is something to look forward to. A surprise. Postman coming to the door. A million to one, okay, but that one person's going to be happy. That's what's worth that little bit of extra money to her, thinking she might be the one.'

Candida is surprised by the note of acceptance, even approval, in her mother's voice. To pay over the odds for three washing-up-liquid caps as a stake in a competition must come quite near to gambling, and gambling is one of the many things which Mrs Brown regards as sinful. It would seem that there has recently been some softening of attitude.

'You work in a supermarket, Candy, you'll see people choosing. Some taking the first thing they see, straight in front of their eyes. Some working out which is cheapest. Special offers. Free gifts. And some like Mrs Furlong, not seeing washing-up liquid at all, but an air ticket or whatever. Sort of thing you need to know if you want to work for someone who sells these things.'

Candida allows herself to be convinced. The thought that her mother would be disappointed and disapproving to see her working as a shelf-filler or check-out girl was one of the reasons for her instinctive reluctance. But the conversation lowers her spirits as she realises that she is not genuinely interested in people and their motivations. There were two reasons why she chose to study law and one of them was the pleasure she takes in ferreting out the exact meanings of words and phrases and contracts and laws. Is Wright and King the sort of firm for which she really wants to work? Certainly marketing does not attract her. But there must be other departments. Contracts have presumably to be negotiated with both suppliers and retail outlets. The drafting of contracts would suit her very well. Yes, she has something to offer.

So it is not because of any doubts of this kind that she postpones for the time being an approach to the nearest supermarket. Christmas is coming, and she can earn more by taking a temporary job during the Christmas rush and the sales which follow. She catches a bus to

Oxford Street and within two hours has been signed up to sell stockings and tights, starting the next Tuesday.

Once she starts, she will have to work on Saturdays, so this is her last long weekend for some time. Without the matter having been further discussed, she has come to realise that she will have to live with her mother for the time being. And there will be no sense in travelling to the country every Sunday to spend the day in a building which is bound to become damp now that it is no longer heated. The time has come to close the stables up for the winter.

She may not be able to afford the renewal of the car tax and MOT on Tom's car when the time comes, but they still have several months to run. She drives to the country on a Saturday morning and opens the stable door. A smell of must and mould assaults her nose and she decides to leave Daniel in the car for the time being, until the paraffin stove has had time to heat the air.

There are two notes lying just inside the door. The first that she opens is from Penny Martin.

'Where are you, Candy? Please don't just disappear. Come and stay for a week or a weekend. Give me a ring.'

Candida nods a private acceptance and self-rebuke. Penny must be as lost and lonely as she is herself, and doesn't even have a baby for company. Although the two women have known each other for less than two years, that has been long enough to make them friends. Penny is quite right. They ought not to lose touch.

The second note is not in an envelope but scribbled on a crumpled piece of paper. Helen Cunningham has furniture to give away. Candida's immediate reaction is that she doesn't need anything. Second thoughts tell her that this is a kind offer which must be answered with politeness and gratitude. Third thoughts repeat the first. She has nowhere to put any furniture. It is all too clear that the stables are not really fit for habitation.

She turns at the sound of a car bumping down the long drive. It comes to a halt behind her own and she recognises the driver as Rufus Grant, the lawyer.

'Caught you at last,' he says cheerfully, coming over to shake hands. 'You shouldn't have just disappeared like that. I need an address for you.'

'Why?'

'In the first place, so that I can give you some money. A thousand pounds. Insurance.'

'I didn't think Tom –'

'Tom didn't have any proper insurance, no. But a few months ago it appears that his bank offered to insure him free against accidental death for a twelve-month period. He used Purefrew's address for all his correspondence, which was why it was passed to me. I take it that no postman realised anyone was living out here.'

She considers this piece of news suspiciously. Out of the kindness of his heart Rufus Grant has offered her money once before. Is he trying again, still feeling sorry for her but finding a way to disguise a personal interest?

Candida is not insensitive. She is too close to Tom's death to be interested in any other man and Rufus must realise this. But she can tell that he finds her attractive and that he is having to make a deliberate effort to keep his distance.

'Why should anyone give Tom free insurance?'

'Oh, quite a lot of this sort of thing goes on. The firm, or the bank in this case, does its best during the twelve months to persuade the client to take out a larger policy – and the correspondence shows that Tom was actually in the process of investigating that. In the meantime, he accepted the free offer and named you as beneficiary. So. You've become a bloated capitalist. Where are you living now?'

'With my mother.' Candida writes down the address and hands it to him. 'I don't know how long for, but she'll know where I am if I have to move on when I get a job.'

'You could get yourself on the top of the council list here simply by showing the housing officer these stables. I'm quite sure they'd condemn them and rank you and the baby as homeless straightaway.'

'And put us into bed-and-breakfast? No, thank you.'

'What I was thinking of was a council flat.'

'I may not be able to get a job in this area. And even if I could, I wouldn't be able to afford rent and childcare. And don't talk to me about housing benefit or income support, because I told you before that I want to stand on my own feet.' As soon as the words emerge she is appalled by the aggressiveness she is showing to someone who is only trying to be helpful. 'Sorry, Rufus. I didn't mean to sound snappy.' Although she may be claiming that she means to be independent, she is actually reliant on her mother, and even a short period of living at home has already put her under strain.

'You'd better prove that you're truly sorry by letting me take you and Daniel out to lunch. You need to let this place air properly if you're going to sleep here tonight.'

Taking a country route, he drives them towards Oxford and draws up in the car park of The Trout. It is not the happiest of choices because, as an undergraduate, Candida has been here often before. The terrace beside the river reminds her of the time when she had few worries and many friends. Some of her male friends fell away when she become so closely involved with Tom. And she has lost touch with many of her female friends simply because her life is so different from theirs. Those who have found jobs are working hard by day and partying by night. Others have temporarily given up the search for employment and are travelling round the world for a year. Neither group has anything in common with the mother of a young baby. Without meaning to, she has drifted away from the main stream of post-university life.

It is all her own fault if she is in danger of losing friendships which ought to last her for life. For a whole year Tom was all that she wanted. She makes a mental resolution to start writing letters to make contact again and then keep in touch.

While she and Rufus have a drink before lunch, she gives Daniel a bottle. She is weaning him off the breast in preparation for the time when she will be out all day. Rufus begins to tell her about The Trout and the nunnery which used to exist just across the river, and about Port Meadow and how it floods and freezes to become a skating rink in winter. All these things she knows already and needs a chance to make that clear without letting it sound like a snub.

'You were at Oxford, then?' she says casually.

'Yes. New College.'

'So was I. At Oxford, I mean, not New College. Keble.'

He stares at her with an astonishment which he tries desperately to disguise. This is exactly the same reaction as Mr Price's, and Candida laughs aloud.

'It's an odd thing. Nobody's too surprised to see a black man at Oxford. And there are plenty of Asian girls, from Indian families here or Hong Kong Chinese. But a black woman seems to make everyone do a double take.'

'What did you read?' Rufus has obviously worked out that to apologise for his surprise may make matters worse.

'Law.'

'Are you going to go on with it?'

'No. I didn't even apply for the Legal Practice Course. I'd have had to put my name down before December, and I already knew by then that Daniel was on the way.'

'You could apply for next year. It wouldn't be too late.'

Candida shakes her head. 'I've given up that idea. When I chose to do law, it was because I was ambitious. I don't very often think of myself as black – not aggressively black, I mean; black as different. But that did come into it a bit in this case. I wanted to be a high-flyer. One of the top black lawyers, given time. I liked the idea of having a professional career. But now I think that between a baby and a profession, something has to be sacrificed, and it's not going to be Daniel.'

'It seems a pity to say goodbye to your ambitions.'

'That's my punishment,' Candida tells him simply. Her Baptist upbringing has enclosed her in a cage of rules and penalties from which she will never be completely free.

'You're only twenty-one.' Rufus leans forward earnestly. 'Plenty of time to start again. Work towards a career.'

'Yes, I intend to do that. But a nine-to-five career, with no work to bring home. I know that means that I shan't ever get to the top of anything, but that's okay.' She has arranged to call at the university appointments board on Monday, and before that she intends to consult the directory of graduate opportunities which will be available at her old college. It has not taken her long to realise how foolish it would be to rely on the slim chance of finding employment with Wright and King. As she emerges from the first stage of shock and grief she is becoming once more well-organised and forward-looking, just as she was eighteen months ago.

Daniel has finished his bottle. Candida puts him up to her shoulder and pats him gently.

'Ready for lunch, then?' asks Rufus.

'Yes, indeed.' But for a moment longer she doesn't move. 'Did you realise, Rufus, you're talking to me in a different voice? Since you found out I was at Oxford. As though I were a different person.'

'No, that's not true. The same person, but you've given me a short cut to knowing you a little better. Because I was there myself, I know without having to root it out that you're clever and determined and hard-working.'

'Just like you, you mean?'

'That's right. Two of a kind. And both hungry, yes?'

His hand closes over hers as Candida smiles without putting an answer into words. She is hungry for food, yes, and hungry for security. But she is not hungry for Rufus. She hopes he realises that.

2

The giving and receiving of Christmas presents has played little part in Madge Manderson's life since the death of her daughter. Naturally Madge and Harry themselves used to exchange gifts, after each ascertaining what would be welcome, and something has always been provided for Harry's secretary; but that is about all. Madge's few relatives, all elderly, neither expect nor send anything more than

Christmas cards. Nor do her village or bowling friends, although it is Madge's custom to make an extra Christmas pudding and cake each year for Gwen in thanks for her generosity in the matter of lifts.

Five weeks after Harry's death, however, an unexpected letter arrives. Madge's Aunt Isabel is a wealthy widow who lives in Manchester. She did not come to the funeral, claiming to find it too upsetting when people younger than herself died. But three weeks later she hired a car and chauffeur to drive her down for a day's visit. She made no secret at the time of the shock caused by her niece's appearance. The letter repeats now what she said then face to face.

Of course you're upset, dear, but that's no excuse for not eating. If you're not careful you'll simply fade away, and goodness knows what damage you're doing to your body by starving yourself. I order you to accept and use the Christmas present enclosed here, and I shall expect a report on your visit. If you don't go, you may consider yourself disinherited!

This is a regular tease, since Madge has long ago been made aware that almost the whole of her aunt's fortune is bequeathed to a rest home for horses. She unfolds the first of the two pieces of paper enclosed in the envelope with curiosity but without excitement.

It is a voucher entitling her to spend any two weeks before 31 December at a health farm called Cossets. Madge stares at it in bemusement. Surely people go to health farms in order to slim, and she has no need to do that. But the second enclosure proves to be a brochure detailing the treatments and diets available. From this she learns that one speciality of Cossets is a regime designed for convalescents and those who need to build up strength and appetite.

Madge's first reaction is to reject the idea out of hand and throw the brochure away. But she pauses for just long enough to have second thoughts. The voucher has already been paid for, and her aunt will reasonably feel hurt if her money is wasted. Besides, there is the whole business of Christmas to be considered.

Christmas without Harry is bound to be a lonely time. Even on a superficial social level the contrast with past years will be depressing. Madge and Harry could never in any general sense have been described as party people, but December always brings a modest flurry of invitations. It is unlikely that Helen Cunningham will host her usual gathering this year, but the bowls club will organise its usual jolly social evening and half a dozen friends in the village are likely to hope for the pleasure of Madge's company. Drinks before lunch with Robert and Jane, and again with Gwen and Graham, mulled wine and mince pies with Patsy and Kate, wine and cheese with Fred, a carol singsong with the church organist and her husband, a buffet of home-made patés with Dorothy: neither the menus nor the guest lists are ever changed.

Madge is not in the mood to go to any parties at all, but if her would-be hosts discover that she is simply sitting at home alone they will be either hurt or worried. And what about Christmas Day itself? There can be no question of preparing the usual meal, but how can she pass the time without feeling sorry for herself? Perhaps there is after all something to be said for spending a couple of weeks away from home. She reads through the brochure again.

On 14 December she drives herself to Cossets. Six lessons on the road and an evening devoted to the study of the Highway Code have restored her confidence in herself as a driver, and her instructor has helped her to find a more suitable car than the Jaguar: a hatchback which will be roomy enough to carry supplies to the bowls club if she should decide to volunteer her services as caterer in the autumn. She has not yet mentioned this possibility to anyone, because in the shock of bereavement she has warned herself not to take any decisions about possible changes in her life at least until the new year.

This is her longest journey since acquiring the car and its smoothness increases her self-confidence. Before leaving the house she has done all the checks which in the past have always been left to Harry. The water is turned off at the mains and all pipes at risk of freezing have been drained. The central heating will turn itself on if the temperature drops too low, all doors and windows are locked, milk and newspapers have been cancelled, and Gwen has promised to feed the cat every day. Although Madge doesn't admit it in so many words, there is a certain pleasure in looking after herself and knowing that she is being efficient.

Above everything else, it is a pleasure to drive herself. She doesn't worry – as Harry always worried – about whether she is getting the maximum number of miles to the gallon. Nor does she grumble to herself about other drivers. She simply enjoys being in control and feeling competent.

The sight of Cossets increases her satisfaction in the day. In advance, she has thought of this fortnight as something to be endured rather than enjoyed. But as she draws to a halt in front of an imposing Georgian mansion whose snow-dusted lawn slopes down to a frozen serpentine lake, her spirits soar. No one can force her to take part in any activities or to eat any food if she doesn't choose to. She can use the institution simply as a comfortable hotel, and go out, if she wishes, for a country drive each day, or else read the books she has brought with her. She can do anything she likes. She is account-able to nobody at all.

A few days earlier that thought might have made her miserable, but her mood has changed. Her undernourished body may be lacking in strength, but she is beginning to recover some of the brisk efficiency which makes her such a good skip on the bowling green and which once upon a time helped her to cope with Julie's helplessness. This is a side of her nature that Harry rarely saw, but it was never banished; merely suppressed.

Such a mood does not fit altogether smoothly into the Cossets ambience. Within two hours of being welcomed and shown to her room Madge has been weighed and measured, tested for pulse and lung capacity and questioned in detail about her general health and possible allergies. It is then made clear by her personal supervisor that she is expected to put herself unquestioningly into the hands of experts and simply do whatever she is told. We'll see about that, Madge thinks to herself, but she does not speak the words aloud. Instead she smilingly accepts the invitation to join her fellow guests for a cup of tea in the drawing room.

Even before the introductions have been completed it becomes clear that she is going to be the outsider in the group. A brief silence falls as eighteen pairs of eyes register the sight of two chocolate digestive biscuits nestling on her saucer. Madge herself is the last to realise the significance of this. She drinks her tea, ignoring the biscuits, as she asks and answers the usual first questions between strangers who are about to become more closely acquainted. At last her neighbour on the sofa can bear it no longer.

'Do please eat up your nice bikkies and put us all out of our agony.'

Madge blinks in surprise at both the request and the baby talk.

'We're all here to lose weight. Except you, obviously. So it's unkind to put temptation in our way.'

Laughing, Madge eats both the biscuits. 'Am I the only skinny one, then?' she asks.

'There's a man as well. Like me, he's been here for a week already. Last week there were four other males, but he seems to be the only one left. No wonder he daren't face teatime with all of us fatties.'

'You don't look as though you need to lose any weight.' Madge's comment is sincere as well as polite, but proves to be a mistake as she is then forced to endure a ten-minute rundown of the pounds her new friend has gained and lost over the past five years. She escapes as soon as it is polite to do so.

Her timetable prescribes exercise before dinner. Ignoring the aerobics class, Madge makes her way to the heated swimming pool. She considers herself a strong swimmer, but it is not long before she realises that her aunt's warning is well justified. She is losing her strength. After only half the usual number of lengths she is forced to stop and rest. There is nothing wrong with her breathing; it is just that her arm muscles have suddenly refused to work any longer.

She thinks of herself as someone who is never ill; but weakness is an illness. Aunt Isabel has been right to give her the necessary prod. Madge promises herself that she will deal with the strength problem as competently as she has already dealt with the driving problem. Even though it may appear feeble to hand her body over to other people for the next two weeks, it will all be part of the process of becoming solely responsible for herself again.

In any case, as she discovers when she is shown to her table in the dining room that evening, it is easier to eat food that has been prepared by someone else. In her own kitchen, the act of cooking has somehow in itself become the meal, obliterating all enticement to appetite because there can be no surprises. She enjoys the vegetable soup and makes a valiant attempt to finish her helping of roast pork, balking only at the syrup pudding which should have followed.

The dining room is L-shaped. In the larger section the menu consists of a half grapefruit followed by a salad bar selection. Madge's table has been placed tactfully out of sight of the slimmers. The only other diner in her part of the room is a man who was already seated, with his back to her, when she arrived. Finishing before her now, he comes towards her to introduce himself.

'Peter Bright. How do you do? I'm glad I'm not going to be the only one being stuffed this week.'

'Madge Manderson.' They shake hands. 'Does the system work?'

It is a reasonable question. Peter Bright, who may be of any age from thirty-five to fifty, is not so much thin as cadaverous. He is very tall, but stooped as though his spine is unable to carry the weight of his head. His clothes hang on him loosely and his face seems to be almost without flesh, its skin stretching tightly over the bone structure beneath to give the impression of a skull.

'I started from a low base,' he tells her. 'I expect it will work in the end. If I can stand the boredom of the chatter.'

It doesn't take Madge long, next day, to realise what he means. The only topic of conversation appears to be weight and dress sizes and the headaches which follow a lemon-juice diet. She is glad of the session in which she and Peter alone are put through their paces on a variety of exercise machines, because Peter is not a talker.

So silent is he, in fact, that it comes as a surprise when he approaches her before dinner that evening.

'I was wondering whether I might join you at your table? Not if you'd rather be alone, of course. But I'd be glad of company – and none of the others can bear to see me pigging it while they starve.'

Madge, not caring whether she has company or not, says politely that she would be delighted. It puzzles her, though, to find that in spite of his request he shows no wish to chat and whenever Madge herself initiates a topic of conversation he often seems to know nothing about it.

'Look, I'm sorry about this,' he says at last, after admitting to ignorance on the current affairs of the royal family. 'I'm being dull. I've got to get used to talking to people again. And there's a lot of catching up I need to do. I shouldn't have inflicted myself –'

'Where have you been?' asks Madge.

'Imprisoned in China.' For the first time she has asked a question which he is able to answer. 'I'm a journalist. Or was. Three years ago I dug up a lot of dirt about corruption in Chinese politics. Right at the top. Unfortunately some of it leaked out while I was still in the country, and it was decided that I'd better not be allowed to leave. So I spent three years imprisoned in Inner Mongolia. The Chinese prisoners seemed able to survive on a diet of rice soup, but I didn't do so well.'

'I don't remember reading anything about that in the papers.'

'There wasn't anything for you to read. No trial. No publicity in China itself. And silence in England.'

'Didn't the Foreign Office –?'

'The Foreign Office had its hands full with negotiations over Hong Kong and didn't feel inclined to rock the boat. I shall have something to say about that later on, when I get back to the typewriter.'

'So how did you get out in the end?'

'All the scandals are four years old now. And the main crook has died. Probably the others will be quite glad to shunt everything I discovered on to his shoulders. I suddenly became more of an embarrassment as a prisoner than as an exposer. So I was shovelled out. No job, no girlfriend, no energy; but still just about alive. I'm sorry, Madge – may I call you Madge? I seem to have lost the knack of making social small talk.'

'I'm not surprised.' Madge is horrified by his story. 'It must have been awful, not knowing how long it might go on.'

'You've put your finger right on it. Being starved was bad. Having no one to talk to was bad. But wondering if I'd be there until I died was hell. Still. Over now. Time to cheer up. This place is a strictly fruit-juice establishment. Will you come down to the pub and have a drink with me?'

'Are we allowed . . . ?'

'*They* aren't allowed.' He nods towards the other section of the dining room, now almost empty. 'But I reckon it's necessary for my mental health that I shouldn't think of Cossets as a prison.' His face, as he grins, looks even more skull-like than before. 'Will you come?'

'Thank you.' It is thirty years or more since Madge was last inside a pub, because Harry didn't drink and if he wanted good food he could always find it at home. This will be a little adventure.

'How did you keep yourself sane?' she asks half an hour later as they sip their drinks in front of a log fire.

'Poetry,' says Peter simply.

'Writing it, do you mean?'

'No. Remembering it. I took a degree in English once, a long time ago. There must have been hundreds of poems that I'd read. I tried to reconstruct them all. Sometimes I only had one line to start me off. I expect that quite often I finished up with an original poem. But mostly I could work out anything that rhymed and scanned and that I'd ever learned or studied, given time – and time was the only thing I had.'

'What sort of poems?'

'Started with Shakespeare's sonnets and the other Elizabethans. Drayton, Marvell, that sort of thing. Then I decided to concentrate on poems about death. In the hope that they would make me realise I was lucky to be alive.' He smiles to himself and begins to quote.

'When I am dead, my dearest,
Sing no sad songs for me . . . '

His voice is deep and attractive. As he continues to recite the poem, Madge finds herself charmed by the sound of it but upset by the content. She turns away, staring into the glowing fire, so that he can't see her face. For a moment after reaching the end he is silent, but then reveals that he is sensitive to her mood.

'I'm sorry, Madge. Have I . . . ?'

She shakes her head in an effort to control her voice.

'I sometimes think that poets are a bit too romantic about death. It's messier than they seem to think. And the people left behind are more likely to be settling bills than singing sad songs.'

'Have I touched a raw nerve? Is there something . . . ?'

'My husband died two months ago.' This is the first time that Madge has ever had to speak the words: everyone else of her acquaintance has known without needing to be told. She can feel tears flooding her eyes and clenches her fists in a grim effort to prevent them from falling.

'Oh, God! How selfish of me to feel sorry for myself without thinking that other people might have worse things to face.' His fingers, long and bony, clasp her hand for a moment.

'Let's talk about something else.' Taking a deep breath, Madge turns back to face him again, forcing a smile on to her face. After a moment's hesitation he accepts the suggestion. Just like all the slimmers whom they both find so boring, they talk of weight and exercise and food. Madge reveals her own training as a cook and dietician, acknowledging that she is perfectly capable of providing the right food for herself and needs only an incentive to make her eat it.

'In my case the incentive is on view in the looking glass,' Peter points out. 'With you, of course, it doesn't show.'

Doesn't it? After they have left the cosy bar and walked briskly back through the crisp night, Madge takes a good look at herself in her bedroom mirror. She has never been a beauty, nor does she very often try to improve her appearance with make-up. But just as she always in the past felt herself to be strong, so too she has always looked healthy – until now. It is extraordinary that such a short period should not only have weakened her muscles but should somehow have removed the padding from her face, making her look much older than her fifty years.

It occurs to her suddenly that with Peter for company at her table that evening she ate everything put before her for dinner without noticing it. And she is looking forward to other conversations. Perhaps he will recite more poetry, this time on a more cheerful subject.

Peter also, it transpires next day, has enjoyed the time they shared. Not only does he now join her for every meal, but suggests that they should go for walks together in one of the periods allocated to the taking of exercise. They must look an odd couple, Madge thinks: one so tall and the other so small. But although the effort to keep up with his long stride makes her breathless, she can feel colour returning to her cheeks and strength to her legs with each day that passes.

So Christmas Day is not after all a lonely affair. As always, Madge spends a little time after she wakes remembering Julie, who was never able to enjoy the balls and bicycles which parents love to give their children. She tries to remember Harry as well, but Harry in a curious way is fading. He has become a shadowy figure; and because he would undoubtedly disapprove of the confidence with which she is managing her own affairs, she makes no effort to summon him out of the shadows. While he was alive she became used to his presence and dominance and now, although no doubt after such a very short time she ought to feel ashamed, she is becoming used to his absence. By the time she leaves her room and goes downstairs, she has resolved not to spoil the day for her new friend by retreating into mourning.

While the few remaining miserable slimmers console themselves with paper hats and crackers for the sprouts and thin slices of turkey which are all they are allowed, the two body-builders are plied in addition with stuffing and roast potatoes and Christmas pudding with brandy butter. They wash it all down with champagne and join merrily in the party games that follow.

The satisfaction of this new friendship lies in their instinctive care not to carry it too far. Peter takes it for granted that Madge can manage her own life, and Madge's burgeoning confidence is increased by that assumption. When, in the course of the evening, she learns that her new friend has nowhere to live after leaving Cossets, she invites him to lodge with her temporarily; and he, recognising that she is professionally competent to continue his body-building diet, is delighted to accept.

3

'Just look at yourself, Mother!' exclaims Lucy in dismay. It is the second day of her Christmas visit. 'You've let yourself go!'

'I've no doubt that to let oneself go rates as a heinous social crime in Washington, DC,' Helen comments mildly, not disagreeing with her daughter's accusation. 'It's hardly rated as a capital offence in the Moncktons.'

She does, nevertheless, attempt to see herself through Lucy's eyes as she stares into the cheval mirror. There is no doubt that the woman she sees there bears little resemblance to the Helen Cunningham of even two months earlier. At the time of Lucy's previous visit, for the funeral, Helen wore black for mourning and her black clothes happened to be new and smart. The same cannot be said of the beige jumper and skirt she has on at the moment, but they are perfectly suitable wear for domestic country life. It is true that the length of her skirt is temporarily unfashionable, but in a year or two it will almost certainly find itself just the thing once again. In the meantime, it is warm and comfortable.

'Your hair,' says Lucy, in a tone of voice which suggests that she intends to start at the top and work her way down.

In October Helen's hair was light brown and well cut to make the most of the remains of a perm. Now it is grey and straight and too long. To prevent it from falling over her face, she has held it back with a comb behind each ear.

'I'm letting it grow,' she says without apology. 'I can't be bothered with continually going to hairdressers.'

'And what will you do with it once it's long?'

'Put it in a bun. Neat and tidy. I do agree that this is rather an in-between stage. Come back again in three months.'

'Buns are for little old ladies. If you really want it long you could put it up and look smart again. Or have a french pleat at the back.' A comb appears in Lucy's hand and she begins to illustrate what she means.

'Don't do that, dear.' Helen finds herself choking with protest. As a mother she for years brushed and combed Lucy's own fair hair. The time has not yet come when she is prepared to accept a reversal of roles – even though her next remark might seem to be moving her in that direction. 'I *am* a little old lady. A grandmother, as your visit reminds me.'

'You're sixty,' Lucy reminds her briskly. 'Only sixty. That's nothing. You seem to be talking yourself into feeling old when there's no need for it. You used to be taller than me. Look at you now.'

She moves closer to her mother's side so that the long narrow mirror will reflect them both. Her comment proves to be justified. Helen has always been a tall woman who holds herself well. Now, incredibly, she sees that she has shrunk, making Lucy the taller of the two by more than the ebullient curls on the top of her head. Instinctively she straightens her back for a few seconds. But it is an effort. Why should she bother? Her shoulders beginning to round again.

'I've had enough of this conversation,' she says, moving to sit on one of the two armchairs in her bedroom and motioning Lucy to the other. 'The reason I wanted you to stay behind was that I have things to ask you.' Cliff, her son-in-law, has taken the two boys for a walk in the wood. 'I realise that they're questions which you'll want to discuss with Cliff, but if I put them to you first, you'll have time to think about them.'

'What sort of questions?'

'I don't intend to go on living here,' Helen tells her. 'That's definite. One way or another I shall dispose of this house. So the first question is, are you ever likely to want it yourself? If you are, I'd be very happy to make it over to you straight away and you could rent it out until you need it. If you aren't, I don't imagine that you'd want the hassle. But I don't want just to whisk it away from you without any consultation.'

There is a long silence, which confirms Helen's belief that this has been a matter best raised in private. Lucy is not an impulsive woman and she is neither sentimental nor greedy: she is thinking the question through.

Monckton Hall can in no sense be described as the Cunninghams' family seat. Helen and Michael bought it, in a run-down condition, thirty-four years ago. But it is the only home that Lucy, before her marriage, ever knew. She is being asked whether she is ready to move her memories of childhood into a different compartment of her life. She is being asked to consider seriously a choice which she has already made once, when she married Cliff, and to reaffirm – or not – her intention to spend the rest of her life in the United States.

In addition to this, she must be wondering whether to respect the decision her mother has made, or to challenge it. But Helen feels confident that they will agree on this point. It would be quite ridiculous for a lone widow to rattle around in a house as large as this.

After some moments have passed, Lucy comes to sit on the arm of Helen's chair and puts a hand on her shoulder.

'This must be tough for you, to think of leaving. Isn't it too soon? Shouldn't you wait a bit before you make such a big decision?'

Helen shakes her head. 'I've made the decision. And in a sense . . . When I move around the house, I see your father. It's upsetting in a manner I can't exactly explain. When I move to a new home, I shall be able to take my memories of him with me, but they'll be more under my control. Anyway, that's not something to influence your decision. I shall no longer live in the house. All you have to consider is whether *you* will ever want to. No need to answer now. Before you leave, that's all.'

She knows what the answer will be. Lucy's marriage is a happy one and her two sons are young Americans. There is no likelihood at all that she will wish to preserve her link with Monckton Hall. It has been necessary, nevertheless, for the offer to be made, so that its rejection will be by her own choice and will not leave her feeling that she has been deprived of something she wants.

'I wish very much that we could all come and live near you, to be company,' Lucy says slowly. 'So that you could watch the boys growing up. But Cliff's career isn't exportable.' Cliff is a lawyer. The fees he earns seem astronomical to Helen, but he cannot easily move even from one state to another and is certainly not qualified to practise outside the United States. 'You could come and live near us, though. Why don't you think about that, if you're set on leaving here?'

Helen laughs affectionately. 'That's definitely an invitation which you ought to have discussed first with Cliff, my darling! It's kind of you to suggest it, but no thanks. To move to a place where I didn't know anyone except you wouldn't be a good idea. And anyway, I'm far too old to undertake such an upheaval.'

'A bit less of this "far too old" business, if you please.'

Helen ignores the criticism, but it does persuade her to postpone her second offer for a day or two. It is on Boxing Day that she announces a kind of treasure hunt.

'I shall need to dispose of a lot of the contents of this house,' she says after lunch. 'The best things have been stolen, of course. But of the rest, it would give me pleasure to know that anything I don't need is still in the family and being appreciated, so I'd like to ship as much as possible over to you. But obviously, only objects that you'd want to have. I've done a lot of sorting already. There are three rooms – I'll show you – from which everything can go. But furniture was too heavy to move. If you go round the rooms, you'll find a label with a red spot on every piece that I'm not going to keep. I'm going to give each of you some sticky stars.'

She hands out the different colours. Blue for Lucy, green for Cliff, brown for Lenny, yellow for Vince.

'Anything you'd like, put your own star next to the red spot. Cliff and Lucy, why don't you start in the drawing room? Boys, come with me to the study.'

Michael's surviving collections are laid out there. The thimbles are dismissed as being for girls and neither of the boys can imagine what the purpose of a button hook was. But they are both delighted by the collection of old truncheons and it seems for a moment that these will be put into use as they fight to find the label on which to put a star.

The disturbance is quelled by their mother, who comes into the room looking upset.

'Quiet!' she orders. 'I won't have you grabbing for everything you see. I'm going to change the treasure hunt rules somewhat, if you don't mind, Mother. Lenny and Vince, you can each choose just one of the labelled objects to take back with you. Once you've put your star on the label, that's it. No second thoughts. So the first thing for you to do, before you decide, is to go right through the house and see what's on offer. Start at the top, but don't make up your mind till you've seen everything. Off you go.'

'I don't know that you have any right to change my rules, dear,' Helen suggests mildly as the two boys dash for the stairs.

'You can change them back afterwards. That would be okay. I just wanted a bit of time to talk.'

'To talk about what?' But Helen knows what the answer will be.

'There are labels everywhere,' says Lucy. 'What are you keeping for yourself?'

'I've collected most of what I shall need in the billiards room.'

'But you can't possibly know, Mother, not till you've found a new house.'

'I intend to look for something small. All the bigger pieces of furniture would be quite inappropriate. And I don't want anything valuable, either. Nothing that might attract burglars.'

'Well, I know how much that break-in upset you. But all the same . . . You need to have the things you love around you. And you won't want *too* small a place, not after being used to all this space.'

'There are some very attractive developments being built these days for older people. One of them's not far away, in fact; in Greater Monckton. If I moved there, I'd still be near all the people I know. I've seen the plans. There's just enough living space, and a maintenance arrangement for a communal garden so that there's no upkeep to worry about. I should be very happy in something like that.'

'With a warden to ring your bell every morning to find out whether you're still alive? Mother, that sort of thing is for *old* people.'

'I *am* old.'

'You're talking yourself into being old, but that's all wrong. People who retire from work at sixty look forward to beginning a new life, with new interests, for years and years ahead. You can make a new life for yourself, just as they do. I know it's too soon after Father's death, and maybe you don't see your way forward just yet, but it's really important to keep all the possibilities open. If you get rid of everything that ties you to your old life and simply pull yourself inside a tiny shell and close the door, you're not giving the new life a chance.'

Lucy doesn't know the half of it. What Helen would like more than anything else at this time in her life is to be told that she is ill. Not in pain, but ill enough for nothing to be expected of her. Someone would look after her. Someone would make arrangements. Compared with this scenario, she considers herself to be behaving in an extraordinarily businesslike manner in investigating the advantages of retirement housing.

'You're a dear girl to worry about me, but I've made up my mind. Go and choose what you want.'

They take their time about it, and it is soon clear to Helen that Lucy has been laying down the law. Lenny has found a toy theatre which was once his mother's; Vince is sticking with the truncheons; Cliff is delighted by the thought of possessing some of the

97

beautifully bound books from Michael's study and Lucy herself has chosen an eighteenth-century desk delicately inlaid with a pattern of scrolls and flowers. Almost every other labelled piece of furniture they have marked to go into store in England.

'We'll send for them when we move house and have room for them,' says Lucy, her tone of voice not pretending for a moment that they are doing anything but waiting for Helen to change her mind. Helen doesn't argue the unspoken point.

While Lucy continues to worry about her mother's own future, Cliff has a different question to ask on the last day of the visit.

'What are you doing about the business, Helen?'

'I've promoted someone to take Harry Manderson's place as managing director. He's dealing with any other appointments that are necessary. I don't propose to interfere. The business can look after itself.'

'That won't be true for ever. Michael was a hands-on chairman. And it's lost two other experienced executives. It doesn't take long for a small firm with unimaginative leadership to slide downhill. That will affect your income.'

Helen shrugs her shoulders. It is too late for her to start playing an active part in the business again.

She hasn't always been so remote from it. When she was young and newly married, her enthusiasm for the new project was as great as Michael's. Although not a chartered accountant, she was a trained bookkeeper and perfectly capable of keeping the accounts of the fledgling company until it was sufficiently prosperous to afford a finance director. She remained on the board herself, and continued to read the company reports and accounts with interest; but for years now she has given Michael her proxy vote to use. Although the business now belongs to her, and presumably she will have to take the chair at board meetings, she has no wish to become directly involved in running it. Even were it to collapse, she would have enough to live on.

'I have investments,' she tells Cliff. Although she brought no capital of her own to the marriage, Michael over the years bought shares in her name, to keep their joint tax bill low; and now of course she has inherited most of his holdings as well. 'And from the sale of the house. . .'

'There's another side to it,' Cliff says earnestly. 'Your employees. Their future is your responsibility. It's understandable that you may not want to run the firm yourself, but maybe in that case you should think about selling it, for their sakes. And you'll get a better price if you put it on the market in good heart. This isn't my line of business, so I can't give you practical advice: just that you do need advice.'

'Thank you, Cliff dear.' As the hour of farewell approaches, Helen is already sinking back into the depression from which the family reunion has aroused her. Lucy wants her to start a new life, but she has no hopes, no ambitions, no expectations. Perhaps it is true that she is not yet really old, but she soon will be. All she wants is to cross that threshold as quickly as possible: then she will never need to think about the future again.

4

There are a good many reasons why Penny so much enjoys what, since Christmas, have become Candida's regular Sunday visits. The main one is that they so obviously give pleasure to Candida herself.

'It's not just Mum I'm escaping from,' Candida explains on a Sunday in February, as they wash up together. 'It's the whole Baptist Sunday: two services and quite often the minister for lunch as well. Besides, I reckon Mum needs a rest from me and Daniel. It's awfully good of you, Penny.'

'Idiot! You know I need the company.'

Of course Candida must know. That is one of the other pleasures. Because the two women are in exactly the same boat, emerging very gradually from the first shock and grief of their bereavement and struggling to chart their way ahead, they can discuss their feelings without reserve. There is no need to conceal any loneliness – but no need, either, to feel ashamed when they are happy.

Penny's third delight is in Daniel. Sometimes, as she cradles him on her lap, she can hardly bear the knowledge that she has no rights to him. Her longing for a child of her own has become almost a physical pain – and even this she can confess honestly to her friend.

'The only thing that makes it bearable is that it was Clive who wanted to wait,' she says. 'If I'd been the one who'd said "Not yet", I don't think I'd ever forgive myself. No guilt. Just so much regret.'

'You're only thirty-two. Plenty of time. Once you move back to London and get into the swim of things again, you'll meet someone else. That's not a possibility to feel guilt about, either. Just natural. The right thing to do.'

Penny finds that particular kind of 'meeting someone' impossible to envisage. During her years in the agency there was an almost continuous party atmosphere even in working hours. Without ever needing to behave flirtatiously, it was easy for her as a young woman

99

to send out signals that she was looking for company, love, marriage. It was part of a dance whose steps were familiar. Young men approached, hovered, changed their minds or pressed their attentions and she knew how to reveal her feelings without hurting theirs; while at the same time she might be giving to other men the same subtle indications of her own interest. It was only when she met Clive that there was no longer any need for subtlety or consideration. They were right for each other, and knew it from the first moment.

So after that first moment she turned off all the signals and now it is impossibly difficult to imagine ever being able to take part in the courting dance again.

'Can you see yourself doing that?' she asks.

Candida shakes her head. 'It's different for me. Not only because of Daniel. I didn't have time to get started in a job, like you. I don't known yet what I can do, so I have to prove myself. I've decided, I'm going to give it ten years. Ten years working hard, to see where I can get. Ten years not being married. Ten years standing alone. At the end of that I'll be thirty-one, nearly thirty-two. Time enough to think again.'

Penny looks wonderingly at Candida. Does she not realise how seductive she is? The straightness of her back, the slimness of her hips, the length of her legs and, above all, the smoothness of the skin in which the whole slender package is enclosed tempts Penny herself to stretch out a finger and stroke. However hard Candida may try to signal that she is unavailable, she will find herself under siege.

'Ten years without sex?' she asks.

There is a long pause before Candida answers.

'I didn't say that. Missing Tom so much, I can't imagine anyone else in my bed. But if I try to look at those ten years straight, I don't know. No commitment, that's what I'm saying.' She rubs vigorously at a vegetable dish which is already dry as she moves to stare out of a window. 'Not a good day for a walk today, I guess.' February Filldyke is living up to its name. 'How's the house next door getting on?'

'Not as fast as I'd like,' Penny tells her. 'I had an estate agent round to measure up The Old Rectory. I thought the best time to put it on the market would be when the daffodils are in flower. But she told me that really I ought to wait a bit. Buyers don't like to have a building site next door. Once the house is finished and the garden is landscaped and it all looks as though it has been there for ever, it won't make any difference, but at the moment . . . ' She leaves the sentence unfinished, because she has not yet decided whether or not to accept the advice.

'Talking of building sites, though,' she continues, 'yesterday I was walking round the part of the park where they're going to build the sheltered housing.' Jonathan, as the architect responsible for designing the development of his own inherited estate, visits the site regularly and often takes the opportunity to drop in at The Old Rectory for a meal. On this Saturday he took her after lunch to see how the conversion of The Manor was going and to inspect the pegged-out area destined for a warden's house and a group of bungalows. 'Who should be there, snooping round, but Helen Cunningham? And not just out for a casual walk. Apparently she's seriously looking for a retirement home. I assumed that it must be one of The Manor flats that she'd have in mind. They're going to be quite grand, with each of them having at least one of the big rooms. But no; she seems to want something tiny and fitted with panic buttons and hand grips and all that sort of thing. And yet she doesn't look ill and she must be rolling in money.'

'Certainly must.' Candida hangs up the tea towel to dry and turns to lean with her back against the worktop. 'What's going to happen to Purefrew, Penny? Do you know?'

'Haven't got the faintest idea. There's no reason, really, for anyone to tell me. Why do you ask?'

'I was thinking about Formula Four. I called in at the stables on my way here this morning. As well as the original drink that you've all tasted, I started last summer seeing whether I could turn some of it into wine, so I wanted to check that the air locks were all clear. It really is a good drink. It seems a pity not to do something about it. I just wondered whether we, all of us . . .' There is a pause while Candida continues to wonder. 'Mrs Cunningham offered to let me have some furniture. I asked if I could leave it for a bit, until I knew how I was placed. It would give me an excuse to call on her again; next Sunday, maybe.'

'Are you suggesting that we should try to develop the drink ourselves?'

'Not suggesting, exactly. Just playing with the idea. I could contribute the formula. I wondered whether Helen Cunningham might put up some cash.'

'You could ask Madge Manderson to make the stuff,' Penny suggests, attaching herself to Candida's fantasy. 'She's a wizard in the kitchen.'

'Then what would you like to contribute?'

Penny doesn't answer at once. As it happens, she has from time to time indulged in a daydream very similar to the one to which Candida has just confessed. But after three years of exile from the world of work, she is uncertain of her ability to transform an idea into action.

'I could work on a marketing campaign,' she volunteers at last. 'Small-scale to start with. Just one television area.' The tentative note disappears from her voice, to be replaced by enthusiasm. 'Say, for example, that the only way you can drink Formula Four is to visit Devon and Cornwall. Publicity would build up. We might even get their tourist boards to back us.'

Candida claps her hands in approval, but then sobers down again. 'It's not something to be played at,' she points out. 'It's an all or nothing affair – and cash by itself wouldn't be enough. Nor even Mrs Manderson's kitchen. To turn out a few gallons a year would be no use. There'd have to be a proper manufacturing capacity; and bottling and labelling and selling and keeping accounts. It would be more than a spare-time hobby for amateurs.'

'So why the visit to Mrs Cunningham?'

'It could still be developed through Purefrew, just as the original plan was.'

'The original plan relied on new capital investment.'

'Well, on a smaller scale, then. And it could be done indirectly. You and I – and Mrs Cunningham and Mrs Manderson as well, if they wanted to be involved – could form ourselves into a small company and then license Purefrew to manufacture on our behalf. Well, perhaps. I don't really know. I could ask Rufus Grant.'

'I could have a word with Jonathan Verne, if you like,' says Penny. 'He's the chap who's building the house next door. He pops in here quite often.'

'Is he an accountant?' Candida asks hopefully. 'What we'd need most would be an accountant.'

Penny shakes her head. 'No. An architect.' Why has she mentioned Jonathan's name, when there is no reason to suppose that he would be knowledgeable on the subject of soft drinks? 'The agency I used to work for would be more practical use, I suppose. I've still got friends there. I could ask . . . But they'd chatter. No, perhaps that wouldn't be such a good idea.'

She is speaking more slowly than before as she thinks aloud. Earlier, she has been sharing in a fantasy; now she is considering a possibility. But it is not very likely that anything will come of it. She shakes her head once more, dismissing the idea. All the same . . .

'Something I'd like to show you,' she says, 'Come up to the studio.' They look down to check that Daniel is asleep.

At the top of the house Penny opens a portfolio. 'A frivol,' she says. 'My designs for the Formula Four bottle. Plastic, not glass.

Male and female versions. This is the Gaiety Girl, with nipped-in waist and generous bust and bum. Whereas the Gladiator, as you see, starts from broad shoulders and huge biceps and tapers down to slightly slimmer hips. The top seal would be that sort of ring-top pull thing that they put on bottles of cooking oil nowadays and over that there'd be a little round screw-on head. The faces printed on the heads could be changed from time to time to encourage people to collect them. And the real stroke of genius – Are you concentrating, Candy?'

Candida is concentrating so hard that she is almost hysterical with laughter. 'Go on,' she says.

'The real stroke of genius is that when you've drunk half the bottle you can pinch the waist very tightly and a sort of snap fastening in the plastic will seal it up to keep the air from the drink and stop it spilling.'

'Genius, as you say,' gasps Candida, trying to control her laughter. 'Do you know anything about plastic bottles to make you believe that might work?'

'Nothing at all. But doesn't the current philosophy of scientific thought say that first you put up a proposition and then you do everything you can to disprove it? If it refuses to be disproved, it's true. Or, in this case, practical.'

'I certainly don't see stolid little Purefrew investing in a machine to make Gaiety Girls. But . . . '

There is a long silence while Penny waits with interest to hear what Candida is going to say. Yes, the drawings are only a frivol. But there is something behind the frivolity: the need to get her brain moving again. The need to have something, anything, that can be thought of as a plan for the future.

Candida is ready to finish her sentence.

'I haven't got any capital,' she reminds Penny. 'None at all. And I've got to earn a living. I couldn't afford to give my working time free, even as an investment. What I could put into any arrangement we might make is the taste, that's all.'

'Well, that's the main thing.'

'I agree. I wouldn't value it lightly. But it does mean – well, there'd have to be an awful lot of hard thinking. Perhaps my visit to Mrs Cunningham had better wait until we've both scrounged a little free professional advice.' She turns to stare out of the window. 'The rain seems to have stopped. We could go out for a little fresh air.'

'Right.' But Penny does not move immediately. 'Just one more thing. I thought of a name for it, for Formula Four. Two names actually, because there could be a still version and a fizzy one – or the wine version that you were talking about.'

'So what are they?'

Penny walks across the studio and unlocks the Victorian watercolour cabinet which Clive gave her for her thirtieth birthday. The mere fact that she keeps it locked is a confession that all this is more than the whimsy she has just claimed it to be. She pulls out one of the wide shallow drawers and waits for Candida to look over her shoulder.

She has drawn the two bottles again, with the same shapes, but this time has imposed on each a flash of solid colour which slants upwards from left to right and tapers towards the top. The name on one bottle is printed in green on red; on the other, red on green.

'There you are,' she says. 'Phitta. And Phizz.'

It is not a joke. She has given considerable thought to the choice of words which could be registered as trademarks, and which would express the sense of refreshment and energy and, yes, fitness which Clive described to her after his first taste of the drink. And yet as she speaks the two names and looks down at her artwork she can't stop herself giggling.

In the past four months there have been periods – especially while she was working on her story about the JCBs – when she has temporarily ceased to be conscious that she is lonely. But this is her first experience of light-heartedness since Clive's death; the first moment of feeling young and carefree once more.

Perhaps it is the first moment for Candida as well, for she too begins to laugh again as wholeheartedly as when she was shown the earlier bottle designs. The high spirits which have been subdued in them both for so long bring tears to their eyes. Penny holds out her arms and Candida, still gasping with laughter, moves to embrace her. Together they are emerging from the tunnel of grief.

Chapter Six

1

'There's a man wants to talk to you.' Mrs Brown's voice is disapproving. 'Came at six o'clock, thinking you'd be home. Coming back at eight. Business to discuss, he say.'

Candida sighs. On Fridays and Saturdays she works until seven, and by the time she arrives home from the supermarket she is too tired to be sociable. In any case, she doesn't know any men, and is not aware that she has any business to be discussed.

'Did he tell you who he was?' she asks.

Her mother produces a card and hands it over. Rufus Grant.

Mrs Brown puts the question back at her. 'Who?'

'He's a lawyer who does some work for the company Tom used to be with.' In her first months of living at home Candida was never able to mention Tom's name and her mother never wanted to hear it. But little by little Mrs Brown has been able to accept his role in her daughter's past, and by now, in March, Candida herself can talk about him without wanting to cry.

'You better dress yourself up a bit, then.'

'To talk business? No need.'

'He going to take you out, he say.' The note of disapproval seems to have vanished. Does Mrs Brown imagine that in some way the company of a lawyer will help to draw Candida herself back to the law?

Candida wastes little time on that question, because there is another one to put to herself. She knows – she can hardly have failed to notice – that Rufus finds her attractive. The very restraint of his behaviour reveals consideration for her feelings. He obviously realises that it is too soon for her to move into any new relationship, but almost certainly he wants to be on the spot when the moment eventually arrives.

To think along these lines may seem conceited, but she is trying to be realistic. In telling Penny that she intends to preserve her independence for ten years, she has spoken the truth. How can she stop Rufus wasting his time on her? To reject something that he has been too considerate to offer will be embarrassing if she happens to have guessed wrong, and rude and hurtful if she is right. Thinking about it earlier, she has decided that the best way will be simply to refuse any social invitations. But he is claiming this one to be business. Smart move, Rufus.

Candida is decisive by nature and she makes her decision quickly now. This is an opportunity to follow up the suggestion she has mentioned to Penny and to discuss whether the development of Formula Four might be a commercial possibility. So whether Rufus really plans it as such or not, this can be a business discussion.

With that point settled in her mind, there is no reason why she should let him down by looking tired and shabby. After a quick visit to smile down at her sleeping baby, she showers and changes into an outfit that is suitable for anything he may offer.

'I've been prowling around Shepherd's Bush,' he says smilingly when he presents himself at eight o'clock. 'It doesn't seem to offer much in the way of gourmet delight, so I've booked a table at Chez Moi. I hope that's all right.'

That is very much all right. Candida has often walked past the Holland Park restaurant and knows it to be expensive and highly rated. It is flattering of Rufus to treat her to the very best that the neighbourhood has to offer.

In such a setting, talking about her supermarket job seems incongruous. Rufus already knows that she originally applied for the work on the suggestion of a graduate-trainee supervisor, but is surprised to find her still there.

'April 15 is my limit,' Candida tells him. March is almost at an end, so there is not too much further to go. 'I set myself a date before I even started. So that I wouldn't be tempted to duck out too soon, but at the same time I'd know that it wasn't going to last for ever.'

'Aren't you bored out of your mind?'

'Not as much as I'd expected. Doing a dull job leaves it possible to think about something else. I treat the shop as a kind of seminar room. Set myself a little essay to write every week on the different aspects of appealing to customers. Shelf position, product design, price, special offers, advertisements, all that sort of thing. It helps me to feel that I've still got a mind. I sent the first six off to Wright and

106

King at the beginning of March, to show them how keen I was – just at the time when I knew they'd be making up their short list for the traineeships.'

'Did it work?'

Candida nods. 'I'm to go for a second interview next month.' She speaks more enthusiastically than she feels, and accepts his congratulations without expressing any doubts. In truth her doubts are considerable. She is not at all sure that she wants to make a career for herself in any of the activities covered by Wright and King's business interests. For the moment, however, there is nothing better in view, so it is necessary to act positively.

'There's something I need to discuss with you,' says Rufus when this subject has been exhausted. 'Legal business. I could have invited you to my office for an hour, but then you'd have had to get off work, and anyway . . .' He hesitates for a moment as though uncertain how to approach the subject. 'Does it upset you to talk about the accident?'

'Talk about it in what way?'

'Well, the cause of it, to begin with. There's never been any doubt that Tom's death, like the others', was caused by Mrs Pamela Elliott. She was comprehensively insured, and claims for compensation are bound to succeed in principle, although there may be disputes over the actual amounts to be paid out. I've already been asked to prepare a claim. What I want to find out is whether you'd like to be joined in the same proceedings.'

Candida gives him a quizzical look, wondering whether it is ethical of him to approach her so directly in a way which savours of ambulance-chasing. Rufus understands exactly what is going through her mind.

'A case like this, where four people were directly affected by the same accident, is considerably strengthened if all four act together,' he points out. 'As a matter of fact, the person who first raised the subject with me was Mrs Cunningham. Not on her own behalf: I gather she's been left very well off. But she was anxious about the future of Mrs Manderson. She originally said that she would cover my fees for pursuing just that claim, since she wasn't in any need of money herself. I persuaded her, as I'm trying to persuade you, that you would all do best to act together. So you don't have to worry about expense, Candida. Mrs Cunningham has made herself responsible for all that – but in fact the costs will be covered in any settlement.'

'What sort of settlement?'

'There are two things we have to look at. First of all we have to make a guess at what the victim of the accident would have been

107

expected to earn in the rest of a natural life, if it hadn't been cut off; and secondly how much of that would have supported his dependants. Tom was a young man with a whole career in front of him. Not earning a fortune at the time of his death, but with first-rate qualifications and brilliant references: every expectation of success. There are actuarial rules on which we can work all that out. As for the second point –'

'The other three have all been widowed,' says Candida slowly. 'It's a bit different for me.'

'Not different at all. Except that there are two of you to be supported, so your claim would be larger than the others. Daniel has been deprived of the father who would have paid for his upbringing and education and you have lost the man whom you expected to provide you with a home and income. It would be necessary to prove that Tom had been supporting you both with regular payments and that he showed every sign of intending to continue doing that in the future. I remember you telling me that you had a joint account; and didn't you say something about buying a house?'

Candida nods.

'Any documents to support that – bank statements, mortgage applications, correspondence with the estate agent – would be very helpful.'

'But the fact that we weren't married –'

'Isn't necessarily relevant. Although it would be a considerable advantage if you could produce anything more personal to show that you were both envisaging a permanent relationship. Assuming that that was the case.'

Candida is silent for a moment. Then, slowly, she reaches down to pick her handbag off the floor beside her chair. Out of her wallet she produces the folded piece of paper which was still lying on Tom's pillow at the moment when she learned of his death. It is the letter in which, not for the first time, he begged her to marry him. It is the letter across which she joyfully scrawled in huge capitals YES.

She hands the paper across the table. As she watches Rufus unfold and read it her eyes flood with tears. If only Tom had lived for one more day, so that he could have known; or if only she had been stubborn and selfish for one day less. The regret which she thought she had conquered sweeps over her once again.

Sensitive to her feelings, Rufus stretches out a hand to grip hers tightly.

'This is upsetting for you, I know. I'm sorry.'

Candida swallows the lump in her throat and manages to smile.

'No, it's very good of you to look after my interests in this way.'

'May I keep this paper, just for a day? I'll get a photocopy made and certify it.'

'Yes, of course.'

There is an awkward silence. This is the time when Candida could raise the question of licensing Formula Four, but the matter seems somehow inappropriate. Just for the moment she is trapped in her memories, and before she can control her emotions sufficiently to discuss plans for the future, Rufus makes his own choice of a new topic of conversation. He begins to talk about himself: his family, the games he plays, the kind of holidays he enjoys. Although it might seem to be self-centred, Candida recognises that he is deliberately trying to take her mind off thoughts of the past and there is no polite way in which she can interrupt him. Formula Four will have to wait for another day. The evening ends, as it began, as merely a pleasant social occasion.

2

Helen has been a widow for only five months when Derek Forsyth pays his second visit to Monckton Hall. He wrote a letter of condolence at the time of Michael's death but has apparently accepted her resignation from the bridge club as exactly what she intended: an indication that their personal relationship is at an end. So why is he now, without warning, coming to call?

The daily housekeeper who worked for the Cunninghams for twenty-seven years gave in her notice after Christmas – claiming to have reached retirement age but more probably feeling that there was too little to do in a house which has become lifeless. It is Helen herself who, on her way to answer the doorbell, looks down through the wide window of the upper hall and recognises her lover's car.

For a moment she hesitates, unsure whether she can face him. But if she pretends not to be at home, and if he has something he wants to say, he will presumably call again; it may be better to get it over.

There is something else, though, to give her pause. Lucy was right, three months earlier, to accuse her of letting herself go, but the warning has had no effect. Helen knows that she looks a mess. Dressed for the gardening she intends to do later in the day, she is wearing a bulky sweater over trousers which have seen better days. How different she must look from the woman whose hair, scent, make-up and dress were prepared with such care on that evening in October.

Shrugging her shoulders, she tells herself that she doesn't care. Five months ago she wanted to seem desirable, and now she doesn't.

Five months earlier she would always have looked at least neat and respectable at morning-coffee time, when friends might call, but now she doesn't bother about that either. The bell rings for a second time. Not hurrying, but no longer delaying, Helen goes down the wide stairs to open the door.

She has forgotten how handsome Derek is. He is wearing a navy-blue blazer above his cavalry-twill trousers, with a white shirt and regimental tie. She can tell, as they stare at each other in silence, that he is unsure of his welcome.

'I've come,' he says at last, after licking his lips nervously, 'as a kind of one-man deputation. From all your friends at the bridge club.'

The bridge-players are not really friends. They are merely people with whom Helen once played bridge. But it is easy to guess what his message is going to be, and he might as well be allowed to deliver it. She stands aside and nods to him to come in. 'Would you like a cup of coffee?' she asks. He has chosen eleven o'clock for the time of his call.

'Thank you very much.'

She leaves him to wait in the drawing room while she goes to put the kettle on: instant coffee will do. It is tempting to put a comb through her hair but she shrugs the temptation aside. If Derek sees her as a wreck, that is just as well.

He stands up politely as she carries the tray into the drawing room, and remains standing as he begins to speak.

'There's something I want to say before I come to the point of this call.' His voice is nervous; he is speaking too fast. 'That night I spent with you here. I don't want to pretend that it never happened. I left before the burglary and before you heard the news of your husband's death, so I had no reason at that moment to feel anything but – oh, happy is far too weak a word. It was marvellous being with you. If things had been different, I would have hoped –'

'I don't want to talk about it,' says Helen, setting the tray down on a coffee table. 'Black or white?'

'Black, please. I think it's necessary to talk, Helen, just once. I understand absolutely how appalled you must have been that Michael died on that particular night, just as I can understand that you probably hoped never to see me again. I expect you've tried to put the whole thing out of your mind. But Michael never knew. That's the important thing to remember.'

'No,' says Helen. 'The only important thing is that I behaved badly and that's something I shall never be able to put out of my mind. Sugar?'

110

'Please.' He accepts the cup and saucer and they both sit down. But –'

'I said I don't want to discuss it.' Helen speaks more sharply this time. 'You were free and I was willing. You have nothing to reproach yourself with. But I have, and it's not something that can be talked out of existence. You said you were acting as a deputation?'

'Yes.' He needs another moment to decide whether or not to press on with the topic which she finds so unwelcome; but her will is the stronger. 'I have a message from the members of the bridge club. A unanimous request, passed at the AGM yesterday, that you should withdraw your resignation from the club. Of course the others, the members, all assume that you decided to leave while you were still in a state of shock after the accident, perhaps because you felt there was something frivolous about playing cards. They hope that now you may feel ready for company again – and I know from speaking to one or two of them individually that they're worried on your behalf and think it's actually important that you should have something like your regular afternoons with friends to look forward to.'

Helen gives a mirthless laugh. 'And you don't want to confess to them that my real reason for leaving was that I might be reluctant to bump into you again?'

'Naturally I hoped that your feelings on that point might change as well, given time. But now that I've delivered the official message, I can go further. Like the members, I hope that you'll reconsider your decision. And if you do, I make you a promise that I'll never do anything to cause you embarrassment. Speaking here, privately, I can admit that my feelings are unchanged. I can't suddenly cease to regard you as a very attractive woman. But I do understand that our relationship has been spoiled by what happened that night. Unless and until you give me some hint that you would like the situation to change, I will guarantee to treat you exactly like any other member of the club.'

'I'll think about it.' Helen sets down her cup and stands up, forcing Derek to swallow the rest of his own coffee at unwanted speed. 'And please thank the members on my behalf for their kind thoughts. I'm very grateful.' She leads the way to the front door.

After he has left, she pulls on an anorak and begins to walk round the garden, ostensibly to list in her head the jobs to be done that afternoon. There is buddleia to be cut back, and clematis, and more roses to be pruned. But although her eyes judge what is necessary, her thoughts are elsewhere.

With Derek, to start with. He has played his hand quite well. There is not much doubt in Helen's mind that he has reached an age when

111

he would be prepared to surrender independence in return for security. A widow with a large house which automatically confers social status in the local community, a portfolio of stocks and shares, a family business and an insurance claim is worth a few sacrifices. Although she is looking at the situation in the coldest light, she doesn't hold it against Derek that he may be a fortune-hunter. He would undoubtedly intend to play fair, offering considerate companionship.

Will he still be interested in her, she wonders, once he learns that Monckton Hall is now on the market? There will not be much room for two people in the kind of sheltered housing which Helen has in mind for her next home. No doubt he, like Lucy, will try to persuade her that she is too young for that.

The whole question of whether or not she wants company in what is left of her life is a confusing one, but her walk round the garden is long enough to bring her firmly to one conclusion. She doesn't want sex. Not ever again. What she feels about her body is not so much disgust as complete indifference. She doesn't want to have to think about it or to wonder how anyone else sees it; and time is unlikely to change that attitude. So that disposes of Derek.

But there is the other kind of companionship to consider: the bridge-club kind of company. For the past few months she has been kept busy answering letters from solicitors and accountants in the aftermath of Michael's death, and since the new year has done her own housework. But in a retirement home, with everything settled, she will have little to occupy her and may find herself sitting for hours simply reading or watching television. Should she perhaps . . .?

Impulsively she turns back towards the house. She has decided to pay another visit to Madge Manderson. Madge also has been left alone, but Madge will have no weight of guilt to influence her decisions. Helen is on the point of driving straight off when she checks herself. It is one thing to be caught badly dressed when she is not expecting company, but to pay a call in her gardening clothes would be impolite. When, ten minutes later, she finally sets off for Lower Monckton, she is wearing a neat cardigan suit and her hair – as grey now as Madge's has been for years already – is tidy.

There is no answer when she rings the bell at College Farm, but she can hear a faint sound of typing, so there must be someone at home. She rings again.

A long delay follows before the door at last opens a little way. The man who stands there, holding on to the handle as though fearing that the caller might be intending to charge inside, is very tall and very thin. This must be Madge's lodger. Everyone in the Moncktons knows that Madge has a lodger, but no one has ever spoken to him or even seen him except at a distance, striding out on his daily walk. He stands in the doorway, his shoulders stooping as though he expects to hit his head on beams and doorframes, waiting for Helen to speak.

'My name's Helen Cunningham. I'm a friend of Madge's. Is she in?'

'I'm afraid not.'

'When are you expecting her back?'

'At about twelve. Or half past. She can never be sure.'

Helen looks at her watch. It is ten to twelve. 'Perhaps I could come in and wait?'

He hesitates before opening the door wider, and follows her into the sitting room.

'Don't let me keep you from your work,' Helen says. 'I promise I'm not a burglar.' But it seems that he is not prepared to take the responsibility of believing her, for he sits down, smiling apologetically.

'I've finished for the morning.' For a moment he is silent. 'My name's Peter Bright, by the way.' Another moment passes in silence. Making conversation seems to require an effort on his part, but at last he screws himself up to it. 'Madge is on one of her hospital runs. Did she tell you? She volunteered to act as a driver for taking people to the outpatient clinics and bringing them home again. That's why she can't be sure about times. But I think I hear her now.'

He springs to his feet, glad to be relieved of the chore of entertaining a stranger, as Madge comes briskly into the room.

'Helen! How very nice to see you! Will you excuse me for a second while I just put something into the oven! I'll be right back.'

The cheerfulness of her voice causes Helen such surprise that it must show on her face, leading Peter to offer an explanation.

'She loves driving. She's like a child with a new toy in that car of hers.'

Helen nods in acknowledgement, but it is something other than that which she has noticed for the first time. In the weeks immediately following the accident Madge looked withdrawn and ill – and that was natural enough. Now she looks brisk and healthy again. But that is not the only change.

Even while Harry was alive Madge was always reserved in Helen's presence, as though their husbands' respective positions in the company must determine their social relationship. It didn't have anything to do with class or money. Although Michael Cunningham built up a small fortune over the years, he was only a farmer's son when Helen first met him, and she herself came from a very ordinary suburban family. Remembering one or two comments which Madge made

113

when she first came to live in the Moncktons, before her life was narrowed by the tragedy of her daughter's disability, Helen knows that she was sent to an expensive boarding school and that she is well read and was, at least until her marriage, interested in the arts. It has been almost as though Harry in the past instructed her to behave unobtrusively in Helen's company, like a junior officer's wife in the presence of his commanding officer's. The difference now is that she has regained her self-confidence. There is no longer any difference of rank, so she can talk to Helen simply as one woman to another.

The change delights Helen. She has known Madge for more than twenty years, but they have never achieved a true friendship. Now, cheered by the change of attitude, she has no hesitation in following her hostess into the kitchen and sitting down companionably on a Windsor chair to watch while saucepans are filled and placed on hobs.

'Your lodger tells me you've been driving people to hospital. That's very noble of you.'

'I can't tell you how many hours I wasted when Julie was alive, hanging around for hospital transport which never came at the time we expected and then having to wait for half a dozen people to finish their clinics before it could bring us back. Anything I can do to give a few people a less frustrating day is well worth while. And when they tell me all about whatever's wrong with them it reminds me how lucky I am to be healthy. I suppose I ought to come home sympathetically depressed on their behalf, but in fact it cheers me up no end. You'll stay for lunch, won't you, Helen?'

'Oh no, I couldn't possibly.'

'Yes, you could,' says Madge easily. 'I always cook for four and Peter only eats for two.'

'Well, thank you very much. I didn't intend – but yes, thank you. It's the first time I've actually spoken to your lodger. What made him choose to stay in a village like this?'

'My cooking,' says Madge. 'He needed feeding up.' She tells Helen the story of his imprisonment in China. 'He'd be well enough to leave now, if he wanted to. But he's writing a book about it all and it suits him to stay on. No distractions. It suits me, as well. He refuses to eat unless I do. I was getting into bad habits before. I feel a lot better now I'm having proper meals again.'

'How have you managed it?' asks Helen abruptly. 'I know it hit you as hard as it hit me, the accident. But you seem to have come through, in some way.'

'I keep busy,' Madge explains, sitting down to face her across the kitchen table. 'I play a lot of bowls. More than I used to before, now that I've got a car. And there's Peter. I don't mean . . . He's only a lodger. But there's more point to the cooking and the cleaning, that sort of thing, when there are two of us. And it's someone to talk to. I think that's why I stopped eating for a bit. Sitting down to a meal on one's own is so dismal, isn't it? You must find the same. As well as that, he reads poetry to me after dinner every night. It's a marvellous thing, listening to poetry. I've always enjoyed reading it to myself, but the sound of it is different, somehow. And of course there's the hospital driving.'

In all the years they have known each other, Helen has never before heard Madge speak so fluently. 'It's all so very well worth while,' she says admiringly; but Madge shakes her head.

'There's nothing worthwhile about playing bowls. It's something I like doing, that's all. It helps to pass the time. When Peter leaves, I shall look for work. Catering of some kind, perhaps, since I don't suppose anyone offers jobs to fifty-year-olds these days.' For the first time in the conversation she hesitates, as though there is something she is uncertain of confessing. 'I think perhaps I ought to have asserted myself more when Harry was alive,' she says slowly. 'But he was such a worrier. It seemed unkind to stand up and say, "I want to do this and this and I want to do it on my own." And while Julie was alive I couldn't anyway.'

'Harry was very lucky to have you.'

'Well, I don't feel that there's anything I need regret, from his point of view,' Madge agrees. 'Perhaps it's making it easier for me now to take charge of my own life. Even though there's nothing particular that I want to do with it. So yes, to use your phrase, I suppose I have come through. I miss Harry, but –'

'I think I shall have to borrow Peter from you some time,' says Helen. 'Listening to poetry is obviously good medicine.'

'Why not take up bowls? I'd be glad to sponsor you to join my club.'

Helen shakes her head. 'I've never been that sort of games player. Bridge is my only time-waster.'

'Play more of that, then. Why not? There's no virtue in being unhappy. And you haven't got anything to regret in your marriage either, I'm sure.'

Helen makes no comment. But in that, of course, Madge is wrong.

From the report of the inquest on Pamela Elliott it has been easy for Candida to discover where her widower lives. The address is in a village which consists mainly of picturesque stone cottages; but number 3 Kiln Close proves to be one of a cluster of modern executive-type houses built unsympathetically in dark-red brick.

Presumably Jarvis Elliott is an executive type and likes this sort of thing. His front garden, which has no boundary fence or hedge to divide it from the lawns of his neighbours, has been elaborately landscaped on a miniature scale, with circular and scroll patterns laid out in different colours of stone. There are small, trim junipers in three of the smaller circles and a statue in the largest. One of the others contains the frost-blackened skeletons of bedding plants whose flowering season must have ended in the previous October. Candida, hesitating on the pavement on a Sunday afternoon in April, considers these dead plants with interest. The fact that nobody has bothered to plant anything new or even to throw the dead plants away tells her something about the owner of the house.

She is nervous now. Perhaps it has been a mistake to come. Mr Elliott will think her impertinent and intrusive. But since she has made the journey, she steels herself to go through with it. He can't eat her. She steps up to the front door and rings the bell. Ding-dong.

Although it is still only spring, the day is warm and she is wearing a simple cotton dress with a full but very short skirt. It is light blue. White people, she has learned, find black people threatening when they dress in dark colours, and because the reason for her call will be a difficult one to explain, it is especially important that she should look unthreatening. When Jarvis Elliott opens the door he will see a friendly, summery young woman.

And now he does open the door. He is a man in his fifties with a crumpled face and crumpled clothes; he has not bothered to shave that day. Tiredness, it seems, makes it hard for him to smile or even express interest in what she wants, but he speaks politely enough.

'If you're selling religion, I'm afraid I'm not in the market.'

Obviously he has mistaken her for a Jehovah's Witness. Smiling, Candida shakes her head.

'Nothing like that. I'm looking for Mr Jarvis Elliott. Is that you?'

'Yes.'

'I wonder if you could spare me a moment. To talk.'

'What about?'

His abruptness makes her nervous; but why should she have expected this to be easy?

'It's about the accident in which your wife was involved.'

'Are you a reporter?' he demands.

'No. My fiancé, Tom Harding, died in the same accident.'

Mr Elliott's face hardens and he is no longer prepared to meet her eyes.

'I'm sorry about that; of course I am. But it has nothing, really, to do with me, and I'm afraid –'

'I know it hasn't!' Candida's exclamation is anxious and urgent, because she can see that he is about to close the door. 'But there's something I need to talk about. It's very important, and –' To her disgust she finds that she is crying, and gropes in her handbag for a tissue to dab at her eyes.

'Another of those!' Candida doesn't know what he means, but his expression is softening. 'My wife used to cry on every possible occasion.'

'I don't as a rule,' she protests. 'Hardly ever. It's just this one thing.' By now she has regained control of herself.

'Well, you'd better come in.' Although ungracious, it is an invitation. He holds open the door and she steps into the hall.

Just as the front garden has been landscaped, so the house has obviously been delivered into the hands of an interior designer. There is something dead about its atmosphere. It is not so much unlived in as unlivable in. The drawing room into which he leads her is clean and tidy because no one cares enough about it to make it littered and dirty. The air is stale, and she is glad when he slides open the glass patio doors as he gestures her to a sofa. He himself remains standing.

'What's your name?' he asks.

'Candida Brown.'

'And what are we to talk about, Miss Brown?'

His use of her surname in an age when almost everyone addresses complete strangers by Christian names is a sign that he has not yet let down his guard.

'It's about the accident. Obviously, nobody deliberately – well, I know that some people do decide to kill themselves and are so upset that they don't consider the consequences for other people, but – oh, shit, I'm starting this all wrong.' She looks down at her knees for a moment, pulling herself together, and starts again.

'I know that what happened to Tom on the motorway that night was an accident. But it was an accident with a cause.'

'And you're reminding me that my wife was the cause.'

'Yes.' She looks up into his eyes, from which the earlier wary

117

expression has disappeared. He is accepting her need to have a serious conversation.

'A lawyer came to see me the other day,' she continues. 'He's representing the widows of the other three men who were killed, in a claim for compensation. He offered to add my name to the claim. It's all the same case.'

'Although I suppose a fiancé isn't in precisely the same position as a widow.'

'We, I, have a baby.'

He nods, accepting the statement without making judgements, at least out aloud.

'I shall need the money for Daniel, my baby,' she tells him. 'And the lawyer said that it was all a matter of insurance companies. Not any individual who would have to pay. Not you, for example.'

'The lawyer was quite right. So why have you in fact come to me?'

It seems that he is still suspicious. Perhaps he thinks that she hopes for some extra compensation from him personally, on his wife's behalf.

'When the insurance claim goes in, our lawyer will be arguing that Tom and the others were killed as a direct result of your wife's actions that night. There's no other way he can put it, and an insurance company isn't likely to get upset about it. But it must be terrible for you, thinking about the consequences of what your wife did. What I wanted to say was that although for the claim I shall have to say that I blame Mrs Elliott, I do realise of course that she never meant it. I can't help being unhappy, but I don't feel any sort of bitterness.'

There is a very long silence. Has she failed to make herself clear? Does he still believe that she is trying to exert some kind of moral blackmail? She can't think of any other way of explaining why she has come. It is his turn to say something now.

When he does speak, it is not in the way she expects.

'Would you like something to drink? Cup of tea? Coffee? Orange juice?'

'Orange juice would be lovely. Thank you very much.'

'Come into the kitchen, then.'

Candida, who, before returning to her mother's home, used to cook in what was once the stall of a shire horse called Billy, opens her eyes wide as she stands in the doorway of the kitchen. Once or twice she has seen a room like this on television, but it has never occurred to her that anything of the sort existed in real life. In the centre of the room a huge copper hood is suspended over an island work station with a black ceramic hob. Copper saucepans hang from overhead racks; copper jelly moulds decorate high shelves on the wall. How can anyone possibly need six jelly moulds? On other shelves stand electric mixers, grinders, whisks, tin openers – and an orange squeezer which Mr Elliott now ignores, instead opening a large and almost empty refrigerator and taking out a plastic flask. As he pours out the contents, he looks up and notes her amazement.

'My wife used to edit a women's magazine. *At Home*. Perhaps you know it. When we moved into this house she thought it would be a good opportunity to practise what the magazine preached. Let designers and suppliers have their head, one room each. It provided the magazine with some good feature articles and photographs. We were going to put the house back to our own taste afterwards. But it seemed a pity not to leave everything for a bit, while it was all so new and clean. And now . . .'

Now it is clear enough that he doesn't care what his house looks like. Although tins and packets may have been opened, nothing has been cooked in this kitchen for months. The reason it gleams with a pristine brightness is almost certainly because he employs a cleaner who has nothing to wash up except an occasional coffee cup. Almost any woman, thinks Candida as she sits at the breakfast bar, sipping the chilled drink, knows how to transform a house into a home, even if she is left alone. This man obviously has no such talent, and no wish to acquire it. But perhaps it is too soon. She has to remind herself that he, like her, has been bereaved and may not yet have recovered from the shock.

'Tell me something about yourself,' he says, leaning against a speckled black and white worktop which looks as though it is made of granite. 'Were you living with your fiancé? Was he maintaining you and the baby?'

'Yes.'

'So how are you coping now? I could probably find you a job of some kind.'

'I'm fixed up, thanks.' By now she has in fact escaped with relief from the supermarket and is in the middle of a crash course in typing and word-processing, which she hopes will increase her value to potential employers. When it ends she will be unemployed again; but if she were to reveal even the slightest interest in his suggestion, he will assume that it is the real reason for her visit, and she doesn't want that. A small voice in the back of her mind tells her that this is exactly the sort of stupid pride which prevented her from agreeing to marry Tom until it was too late; but it's her nature and she can't change it. 'I didn't come here for that.'

'I'm sure you didn't.' All the aggression has gone out of his voice.

He is sympathetic and trying to be friendly, although something is inhibiting him from saying anything important. For her own part, she has to control her surprise that he has made no comment on what she has already explained to be the real purpose of her call.

There is another silence, and then the comment at last emerges. He begins to walk up and down the kitchen.

'You said a few minutes ago, Miss Brown, that I must feel terrible when I think about the consequences of what my wife did. Well, I'm feeling terrible now, just because I haven't been allowing myself to think about those consequences at all for all this time. It had nothing to do with me, you see. I was in hospital, about to undergo an operation. I didn't ask or expect my wife to visit me that night. By the time she set out I was already under the anaesthetic. I've had all the grief of her death, but I haven't felt any of the guilt of responsibility.'

Candida is not going to argue with that. 'Well, that's quite right.'

'But it's not right that I should have forbidden my imagination to dwell on what happened. I read the report of the inquest. I heard the names of those men. I shall never forget them. Harry Manderson, Michael Cunningham, Clive Martin, Tom Harding. I was sorry about them, deeply sorry; but they were dead. There was nothing I could do for them. I seem to have simply blotted out of my mind any thought that there were terrible consequences for other people as well. You, and the others. Perhaps because I couldn't do anything for them either. I mean, nothing to alter the fact that their men were dead.'

He turns away from her, leaning with both hands on the edge of one of the three sinks.

'You've made me very much ashamed. I was too busy mourning Pamela to remember that other people were in mourning as well. I loved her so much, and without her –'

He is weeping now, at first trying to conceal the fact but suddenly giving a gasp of misery and burying his face in his hands.

Candida stands up, uncertain what to do. She has never seen a man cry before and would like to comfort him, but knows from her own life that words have nothing to offer. Her high heels clatter on the quarry tiles as she walks across to stand near to him; but he may not want to be touched.

Yes, he does. The warmth of a human body is what has been missing in that antiseptic house. He reaches out to clasp her shoulders and pull her close and for a few minutes they weep silently in each other's arms. There is nothing sexual about the embrace. They are two unhappy people; strangers who wish that the paths of their lives had never had cause to cross.

120

After a little while they break apart. For a second time that after-noon Candida dries her eyes; she is ready to leave.

'I'm sorry to have upset you, Mr Elliott,' she says. 'This was the other thing I wanted to say, besides the bit about the compensation claim. I do realise that this is as rotten for you as for the rest of us.'

He nods, still not altogether in control of himself. Candida lets her-self out of the executive-type house. She does not expect ever to see Jarvis Elliott again.

4

On the night after Candida's visit, Jarvis sleeps badly. There is no need to look far for a reason. No sooner had the front door closed behind her than he poured himself a generous tot of whisky, and con-tinued to fill his glass for the rest of the evening. It is hardly surprising that he is lying awake with his mouth dry and his head aching. In the old days, before his collapse, he would have reached out for a couple of the pills which relieve headaches as effectively as muscular pains; but he has learned his lesson in that respect.

He knows, in any case, that the whisky is not solely to blame for his restlessness. What he has confessed to Candida is the truth. Until this time he has given no thought at all to the families of the men who died as a result of Pamela's aberration. What must have been a self-protecting lack of imagination he sees now as callousness. It is equally true that he has had no cause to feel any personal guilt; but responsibility is another matter. If he had smoked less, if he had been more sparing with the painkillers, if he had left home an hour earlier that morning and so avoided the traffic hold-up . . .

'No,' he says aloud at three o'clock in the morning. He is not in any way to blame for the accident. But it is right that he should shoulder blame for not caring about its consequences. Next morning, he promises himself, he will see if there is anything practical he can do to help the four victims, and not leave everything to the lawyers and insurers. Once that is settled in his mind, he is at last able to sleep.

Monday morning is one of Jarvis's favourite times of the week. He enjoys his work at the Elliott Press so much that even when Pamela was alive, when weekends were happy, he always looked forward to the beginning of a new week. Now that his home is empty, it is only in the working week that he feels himself to come alive.

He is not the only one to start the week with enthusiasm. Girl Friday is waiting in his secretary's office to accost him.

'I've got something for you, Mr Elliott. Something off the slush pile!'

'Goodness!' The slush pile is made up of unsolicited manuscripts written by authors unknown to the firm. A large proportion of them are novels submitted by writers who have not taken the trouble to discover that his firm publishes no fiction for adults whatsoever. Almost all the rest, although possibly more suitable in subject for his imprint, bear the telltale signs of many previous rejections: dog-eared corners and the rings of coffee cups. It is unusual indeed for any uncommissioned piece of work to arouse excitement. 'Eleven o'clock, then.'

'Thank you, Mr Elliott.' Bubbling with her find, Girl Friday disappears. Her real name is Eirwen, but she has become tired of always having to repeat it or spell it out and answers cheerfully to her job title instead.

She has created the job for herself, arriving on the doorstep of his offices in the previous September and announcing that she wants to get into publishing. She would be happy to live at home with Mummy, she said, and accept an allowance from Daddy, and act as a Girl Friday for the firm, doing anything she is asked if at the same time she can be given a kind of apprenticeship. Instead of telling her, as he ought to have done, that publishing is an overcrowded and underpaid profession, it occurred to Jarvis that an unpaid relief to answer the telephone in the lunch hour would certainly come in useful, and he allowed himself to be persuaded by her cheerful willingness to post parcels and run any kind of errand.

He plays fair by attaching her for several weeks to each member of his staff in turn for at least four hours of every day. So far Louise has reported that she is much too slapdash ever to deal successfully with rights and contracts, while Pat is equally scathing about her inability to understand accounts. Azil, whose responsibility it is to see that each book keeps to its timetable for printing, binding and distribution, has applied himself conscientiously to educating her, but the best he can say is that she has worked hard at trying to understand all the various processes.

In her most recent assignment, however, it seems that she has found her métier. She may make a good editor one day. She has awarded herself the title of Keeper of the Slush Pile and in this capacity records the arrival of every unsolicited manuscript. Once a week she presents Jarvis with a brief precis of each, to which she is allowed to add her own opinion. Naturally she is not trusted to take any decisions, but Jarvis is quite impressed by the number of times that her assessments prove to match his own. It seems that on this occasion she can't bear to wait until the regular time to report.

At eleven o'clock precisely she sets the manuscript down on his desk. 'It's called *Party Cookery for the Single Man* and don't tell me, the title's hopeless, but the rest of it's absolutely brilliant. It's great on things you can make in advance and freeze or whatever and it's got this marvellous section on cooking for the kids on access Sundays and a screamingly funny bit on preparing a midnight feast at boarding school but the big thing is that although a lot of the dishes are really fancy, the text always starts from the assumption that you've never as much as boiled an egg before, so every recipe explains everything from basics and tells you what might go wrong and what to do if it does. And right at the end there's a "more money than time" chapter which reminds you that you can buy things, oh, like vol-au-vent cases, so the place where you were told how to make them yourself has got a splash of colour over it to key in with that chapter.'

'You're allowed to breathe, Friday.' Jarvis smiles at her enthusiasm.

'Yes, well, the other great thing is the style, because it's quite simple and straightforward and jokey but it isn't patronising. She's got it exactly right. I was reading it all Saturday and I can't cook for toffee nuts but I made one of the puddings and Mummy put it on the table for her dinner party that night and everyone who had it said it was simply fab so then all the others tried it for second helpings.'

'And what do you reckon would be a better title, then?'

'Oh well, gosh, I haven't thought, but something like *Let's Party, Guys*. No one exactly wants to think of himself as a single man, does he?'

'No. Well, thank you very much. I'd obviously better read it. Now then, I've got an errand for you. You'll have time before you go on the switchboard.'

It is a personal errand: but then, it is his own firm. The decision he has reached in the small hours – the decision that allowed him at last to sleep – is that he is going to call on each of the four women who were bereaved in the accident. If there is anything he can do to help any of them to improve her circumstances, he will do it. If there isn't, the mere fact of saying how sorry he is will release him from the feeling that he has been in some way cowardly about facing the situation.

So, as he was driving to work that morning, he cursed himself for not asking Candida for her address. Briefly he has wondered whether to ask Pamela's insurers, who also provide cover for his own car, to put him in touch with the women; but he knows what the answer will

123

be. Any driver involved in an accident is always warned against apologising to the victims, and that will probably apply even to a driver's husband. But it shouldn't be too difficult to track the four down.

He writes down the names which are fixed in his memory: Michael Cunningham, Harry Manderson, Clive Martin, Tom Harding.

'I want the address or telephone number of any one of the widows of these men,' he tells Friday. A single contact should be enough to help him trace them all. 'This is the name and address of the place where the men all worked. You may be able to get the information directly from Purefrew. If they refuse to give out personal details, you'll have to track them down at the public library through the relevant telephone directories. Presumably they all lived fairly near their work.'

'They're not very unusual names,' Friday warns him.

'If you have to do it the directory way, concentrate on Cunningham. He was well off. You should be able to recognise a posh sort of address.'

Friday goes off cheerfully, leaving the print-out of the cookery book on his desk. Jarvis turns over the pages, getting an idea of the contents rather than reading the text. He finds it easier to do serious reading at home, away from the inevitable interruptions of the office.

His firm specialises in illustrated books. Since cookery books in general have been the non-fiction bestsellers of the past few years, he is prepared to take Friday's recommendation seriously. One small problem occurs to him at once. Pamela has always in the past allowed him to use the kitchen facilities of her magazine to do the necessary testing and photography of the recipes in any book he proposed to publish: in return *At Home* was allowed to use them in its cookery columns. The cookery editor hasn't changed and may perhaps be prepared to continue the arrangement; but with a new editor in charge it will doubtless be necessary to be more formal about fees and rights.

Fleetingly he wonders whether he might do some of the testing himself. He doesn't think of himself as a 'guy', but he is undoubtedly now a single man. The idea lingers for as long as it takes him to read one of the recipes through, and is then abandoned. He has no interest in learning to cook, he is in no mood to throw parties and, even if he decides to do so in the future, he certainly won't do the catering himself.

The thought of cooking makes him aware that he is hungry. His eating habits have changed since he left hospital. Now he has a good lunch each working day in a restaurant or his club, and doesn't

124

bother with more than a snack in the evening. He is just about to leave when Friday returns.

'No one suitable under Harding,' she reports, 'and there are millions of Martins. But I've found an M. C. Cunningham who lives at Monckton Hall: does that sound posh enough for you? And then there's an H. G. Manderson whose address is in Lower Monckton, which can't be too far away.'

'Thank you very much, Friday.' Jarvis takes the paper she holds out to him and returns to his desk. He decides to start at the top, with Mrs Cunningham, and for perhaps ten minutes he sits without moving, trying to decide how best to play it. It isn't easy to get into the mind of a complete stranger and to judge how she will react to this unexpected approach. Nor is he completely clear in his own mind what he is hoping to achieve, other than a lightening of his own conscience. Well, perhaps an honest admission of that will prove to be sufficient explanation. He pulls the telephone towards him.

Chapter Seven

1

Even as he raises his finger to ring the bell of College Farm, Jarvis is having his doubts about the wisdom of this call. It has been bad enough trying to make conversation with Mrs Cunningham, and at least in her case the visit was made by appointment, so that there was no need to explain who he was. Can he bear to go through the whole painful process for a second time in one day?

The same argument, though, can work the other way. Because that first visit has achieved nothing, it is tempting to think that the whole idea of calling on the bereaved women is a mistake. Once he returns home, he may feel that it will be too much trouble to drive out here for a second time in order to endure another bleak hour. But Monckton and Lower Monckton are very close together; it has proved tempting to drop in on Mrs Manderson without warning and ease his conscience without committing himself to a special journey. What he *ought* to have done, of course, is to make two separate advance appointments for the same afternoon, but he didn't, and so . . . He rings the bell.

There is a long pause. Just as he is wondering whether to ring again, the door is opened by a small woman wearing an apron and with a smudge of something white on one cheek. It is easy to tell that he has interrupted something and that she is impatient to return to it.

'Mrs Manderson?'

'Yes.'

'I'm sorry to disturb you without warning like this, Mrs Manderson, but –'

She is not prepared to let him finish but does not, as a Londoner might have done, close the door in his face.

"Would you mind very much coming into the kitchen if there's something you want to talk about? I need to get on with what I'm doing.'

'Oh yes, certainly.' She must have a trusting nature; but as he follows her into her large country kitchen he can hear the sound of a typewriter not far away, so she is not alone in the house.

The kitchen is full of warm baking aromas which make his mouth water. Mrs Cunningham offered him only a cup of tea and a biscuit long past its sell-by date. He sits down in the chair to which he is pointed and waits as Mrs Manderson bends down to take something carefully out of an oven. 'Goodness! What's that?'

'It will be a swan when I've finished. Part of a pudding for my lodger's dinner tonight. It's his birthday.'

'Lucky lodger!' He watches, fascinated, as she builds up the shape by adding more of the meringue mixture she has been whisking and sets it back in the oven to dry.

'I shall have to stay here so that I can do that a couple of times more, I'm afraid,' she tells him. 'Now, how can I help you?'

'My name is Jarvis Elliott.' Her eyes are bright and prepared to be interested, but he can tell from the lack of change in their expression that his name means nothing to her. Explaining himself is harder than he expected. He approaches the problem sideways. 'I've just spent an hour with Mrs Cunningham. By appointment. I ought to have made an appointment to call here as well, really, instead of just turning up on your doorstep. But I wasn't sure about your address until she confirmed it to me. When I realised how close I was, I –'

'Elliott, you said?' The mention of Mrs Cunningham's name must have given her the necessary context within which she can identify him. She sits down and stares at him across the table. 'Was it your wife . . . ?'

'Yes. Yes, I'm afraid it was.'

'I'm so sorry,' she says. 'Please accept my condolences. Ridiculous phrase. I mean, I do sympathise. You were in hospital at the time, weren't you? It must have been a terrible shock.'

'You're speaking my lines!' After the stilted conversation with Mrs Cunningham, he is amazed at the ease with which he can talk to this woman. '*You* were the victim; one of the victims. It's why I've come, although very late in the day, I'm afraid; to say how sorry I am, and to see –'

'We're both victims,' she says crisply. 'If you're trying to apologise on your wife's behalf, please don't. I found the shock of what happened bad enough without being angry as well. And I'm sure it must have hit you as hard as it hit me. I hope you've come through it by now.'

'Not really,' he confesses honestly. 'Have you?'

She cups her chin in her hands for a moment as she stares at him, considering what to say.

'It almost seems shameful to admit it,' she tells him at last. 'It's only, what, six months? I get lonely sometimes, of course I do. But what may be the important thing is that there's nothing I have to regret about my life with Harry. Not from Harry's point of view, I mean. I don't now sit around wishing I'd done this or that differently. That seems to make it easier to close the door on that chapter of my life and live with the good memories of it. And at the same time to start a new chapter. I'm fifty-one years old. Not young enough to start anything very new and exciting. But I may have to live for a good many years, all the same. I can't just sit still and pine.'

'Mrs Cunningham –'

'Oh, yes.' She obviously guesses what comment he is about to make. 'Helen's taken it very badly. I don't quite understand why she's reacted in that particular way. She used to be very self-assured. But now she seems to have given up trying. Excuse me.'

It is time for her to add another layer to the swan. She strokes its wings with a fork to suggest feathers. Once it is back in the oven she resumes her seat.

'Was your marriage a happy one, Mr Elliott?'

'Oh, yes. Won't you call me Jarvis?' He wanted to escape from Mrs Cunningham's presence as soon as he decently could, but Mrs Manderson's company is so congenial that even after such a short time he feels the wish to prolong the visit.

'If you like. My name's Madge.'

'Madge. Thank you. Yes, we were very happy. Like you, no regrets, except the big one that it was cut short too soon. I think perhaps . . . Pamela was a marvellous organiser. And although she held down a very important job herself, I suppose you could say that she was the opposite of a feminist. She recognised the need to work, either for money or for job satisfaction, and in the magazine she edited she was always going on about the importance of being able to make genuine choices. But she believed that in a perfect world most women were most likely to be happy looking after their own homes and families.'

'And she demonstrated that by looking after you?'

'Yes. I had my working life; but she was in charge at home. We both liked it that way. So with her death, I lost all my support systems, you might say.'

Madge nods sympathetically. 'Did Helen give you tea?' she asks abruptly.

'Well . . .'

'Have some scones,' she offers, guessing the answer. 'Still warm from the oven.' The wire rack on which they have been placed to cool is only a few inches away from him, and their aroma has been tantalising his nostrils ever since he sat down. Madge pushes across a bowl of cream and a jar of home-made raspberry jam. 'Help yourself.'

'You're very kind.' He begins to cut and spread. 'You like cooking?'

'I'm good at it,' she says simply. 'And I like doing things that have to be done again. I imagine a lot of people don't. When an artist paints a picture, I suppose one of his satisfactions is the knowledge that it will exist unchanged for ever. But I really enjoy watching someone demolish what I've just prepared, so that I shall have to make something else the next day. It keeps me busy.'

'Do you cook just for yourself now?' The scone is light and delicious and he reaches for another; there are still nine or ten left on the rack.

Madge guesses his thoughts. 'I shall freeze those for another day. No, I never cook for myself. My lodger, the birthday boy, needed feeding up when he first came here.' She describes how he was imprisoned and almost starved to death in China.

'There's a book which he might find helpful – or which might help you to get him back into normal life,' Jarvis suggests. A copy was given him by a friend, concerned about his state of apathy after his discharge from hospital. 'The subject is post-traumatic stress disorder. I'd be happy to lend it to you.'

Madge shakes her head, laughing.

'I don't see myself as any sort of counsellor. Where personality problems are concerned, I rather believe that if you behave as though everything's normal, then sooner or later it will in fact become normal. Very old-fashioned and unprofessional; I realise that. Bodies are different. My job has been to build up Peter's health, and I've pretty well finished that. That's why he can be treated to a meringue swan tonight, after months of milk puddings and treacle sponges and fruit crumbles. I think he's looking after his mind on his own, by writing a book about his experiences. A kind of therapy in itself. He often looks drained in the evening, but I'm sure it's the poison which is gradually draining out. Anyway, your book sounds rather tough reading.'

'What sort of books *do* you like to read? I'm a publisher myself, so I'm always curious. Market research.' Madge is so obviously a homebody that he expects her to confess to buying only magazines; she is probably part of the readership for which Pamela catered.

So her answer surprises him. Poetry heads her list. 'And novels, mainly. Most non-fiction prose is too heavy for me.'

'What kind of novels?'

'The Victorians are my favourites. Dickens, Thackeray, Trollope. But anything with a good plot, really. Can't stand romances, though. I don't like to see the ending too far ahead.'

'What about cookery books?'

'Ah, they're a different category. Cookery books I love, yes. Trying out new things. And then seeing how I can improve on them. I'm trying a new recipe for dinner tonight, in fact. You must stay and be one of my guinea pigs.'

She stands up to take the meringue swan out of the oven again. By now she has reached its head.

'Tricky bit,' she says, drawing up a support which she has already prepared before adding the stiff mixture a little at a time. Jarvis springs to his feet to open the oven door when she is ready to return her work of art.

'I couldn't possibly –'

'It would be very selfish of you to refuse,' she says. 'You say you're a publisher. Well, here I have a lodger who's going to be looking for a publisher very soon. You could tell him where to start.'

'What a nice person you are!' Jarvis exclaims. It is odd how quickly he has begun to feel at ease with her. 'Bribing me to do what I long to do anyway by telling me that it's my duty. Yes, I'd love to stay. Thank you.'

'In that case I'm going to banish you from the kitchen for an hour or two, if you don't mind. Make yourself at home in the sitting room. Or go for a walk round the village. Peter bought a bottle of champagne as a birthday present to himself. We shall open it at seven o'clock.'

It proves to be the most pleasant evening that Jarvis has enjoyed since Pamela's death, although he finds it difficult to understand quite why. Peter, friendly and clearly intelligent, is nevertheless no great conversationalist. He becomes more fluent, though, when asked to describe the contents of his book. It is not the sort of work that Jarvis publishes himself, but he is able to suggest two or three more appropriate firms and to give the names of the individuals to be approached at them. It's the best he can do in the way of a birthday present.

As for Madge, she has changed out of her kitchen clothes and is now neatly dressed, but in no way can she be called glamorous or even smart. Neither in London nor at any of his neighbours' houses would he ever have met a woman like this at a dinner party. She has not seen any of the plays currently on in London, although she is familiar with those which are classics. She ventures a literary opinion only if she has actually read the book, and not on the strength of a review. But she appears to be genuinely interested in hearing her guest describe his work and the publishing scene in general. He suspects that there is even an element of wistfulness in her attitude, as if she might have enjoyed a wider society than a village can offer. Probably he is talking too much, but she seems to enjoy listening.

And the meal is delicious. Although the swan, floating in a lake of ice-cream water lilies, is the visual highlight, each course in turn is as good to taste as to look at. It comes as no surprise to learn that his hostess has been professionally trained, and the discovery prompts a question which has been brewing in his mind throughout the evening.

'I don't suppose you'd have time to do a job for me?' he asks tentatively as he is on the point of leaving. He tells her about the cookery book which has sent Girl Friday into raptures. 'Naturally, I have to get all the recipes tested, to make sure that I'm not going to poison anyone by publishing them. My wife always used to arrange that for me, through her magazine. I'd been wondering how to deal with it instead. We'd pay a fee, naturally.'

'Love to. Just let me know exactly what you want.'

'It will be easier to explain with the book in front of us. I was just thinking. Mrs Martin lives somewhere quite close to here, doesn't she?' This is not in fact a change of subject, although it must sound like one.

'A different village. Greater Monckton. But only six miles away. You're really doing the rounds then, are you?'

Jarvis finds himself flushing. 'When I called here, there were two things I had in mind. One was to apologise, in a way, for what happened to your husband. The other was to see if there was anything I could do to make up. Some practical gesture. And what happens instead? I eat your food and I propose something that *you* can do to help *me* instead.'

'Oh, but it does help me!' Madge, thinking he was about to leave, has held out her hand to say goodbye a few minutes earlier, and has made no attempt to remove it from his grip as they continue to talk. 'It makes me feel useful. There's no greater gift you can offer to anyone than that.'

131

'I failed with Mrs Cunningham,' Jarvis says ruefully. 'Am I likely to do any better with Mrs Martin?'

'Penny was very upset, naturally. Well, we all were, but she hadn't been married all that long. She was very much in love with her husband. But she's young and good-looking. Sooner or later, I'm sure she'll find someone else – although of course that's not something anyone can say to her so soon. It's Candida I worry about more.'

'Mrs Cunningham said the same thing.'

'I think we'd all like to see Candida given the chance to make a new start in life. If you ever have a job she could do . . .'

'I'll bear that in mind. What I was getting at, though, was that if I arranged to see Mrs Martin next Sunday, perhaps I could bring a copy of the typescript round here myself instead of trusting it to the post.'

'Give me a ring.' Madge does now remove her hand. The evening is over – but Jarvis realises with amazement that he has been given a taste of the comfort which he himself hoped to bestow. Without any apparent effort, Madge Manderson has succeeded in lifting his spirits.

2

For four months now, ever since Helen put Monckton Hall on the market in January, time-wasters have been trooping round her home. She leaves the task of escorting possible buyers to the estate agent, but makes a point of greeting all of them personally. It is worth the effort just to see the flush of embarrassment on the faces of local acquaintances who are taking the opportunity to have a snoop.

It has not taken her long to recognise which of the visitors are genuinely looking for a property of this size; and the number is very small. It amazes her that so many people should apparently regard the inspection of other people's houses as a pleasant way of spending their weekends. The occasional arrival of a professional house-hunter, retained by an expatriate who is about to return to England or a firm which plans to relocate, comes as a pleasant change, but none of these has yet proved interested enough to make an offer. The Moncktons, it appears, are just that little bit too far from London.

Today's viewers, however, are different. They have arrived in an expensive Mercedes on a sunny day in May. The house is looking at its best. Although Helen may have let her own appearance go, she recognises the importance of keeping the property well groomed.

One contract agency regularly mows lawns, rakes gravel and trims the low box hedges of the formal garden: another polishes floors and windows. Inside and out, Monckton Hall is gleaming and tidy; and the chestnut avenue which leads up to the house is at its most magnificent.

Even during the first handshake Helen can see the excitement in the eyes of the wife and can sense the husband's wish to give her whatever she wants. It comes as little surprise when, after the tour ends, the couple first of all retreat for a few moments to talk privately and then tell the agent that they would like to go round the house again. 'We're interested,' they say before they leave; and Helen is prepared to believe that they are serious.

Patrick, the estate agent, phones up next day to report that an offer has been made, subject to survey and contract. Helen has no fears about the survey. Michael spent a small fortune on the house before they moved in, and they have maintained it conscientiously ever since. Nor is she in the mood to haggle about money, although for the sake of his own pride she gives Patrick permission to try for something nearer to the asking price.

'Just one thing, though,' he warns her. 'The offer is conditional on getting vacant possession before the end of July. I gather there's a baby on the way.'

'Oh. Will the Manor development be ready by then?' The same firm of estate agents is selling the sheltered housing units in Greater Monckton. Patrick does not handle new homes himself, but he knows that she has her name on the list of interested parties, and he has checked the position before ringing.

'I'm afraid not. November at the very earliest – and you can never trust a builder's dates.'

Helen considers this in silence. Although there is no particular reason why she should want to stay in the same area, she has lacked the energy to explore other possibilities. Patrick gives her just the right length of time to think before continuing to speak.

'But the conversions in the house itself are almost finished now, and I do really think, Mrs Cunningham, that one of those apartments would suit you better.'

'Everyone says that.'

'Well, perhaps everyone is right.' Patrick has visited Monckton Hall so often in the past few months that he must feel he has acquired the right to make personal statements of this kind. 'Will you let one of my colleagues at least show you round the two that are still unreserved?'

A little grumpily, Helen considers the question. But if other people can waste her time, why shouldn't she do a little snooping herself, even with no intention of buying? She agrees on an appointment.

The two flats prove to be very different. One is still unsold because it is the smallest; the other because it is the most expensive. The small one gives Helen cause to think. The bungalow which she has reserved in the sheltered housing development looks from the specifications and artist's drawing to be extremely well-designed and compactly fitted; but she has not yet seen more than lines on a plan and the trenches of foundations. As she moves around the modest rooms of this upper flat it does occur to her for the first time that perhaps she has been proposing to confine herself in too small a space. Everyone has been saying so: perhaps they, and Patrick, have indeed been right. And yet she is sincere in her wish not to move again after this. She wants to step straight into the third age: to establish herself in accommodation suitable for a pensioner, and to stay there.

It has been clever of the estate agent – Erica, on this occasion – to show her this cramped apartment first, because when they move downstairs the contrast is dazzling. The original drawing room of The Manor has been divided by a partition wall with a wide central arch to make a separate room for dining, but the effect is still one of spaciousness. Helen recognises that it would be possible to install some of her best furniture here, and even the large pictures. There would be room to give parties, and to entertain friends for dinner in something approaching her old style. She walks over to one of the four long windows and looks out across a formal terrace to a view of a small lake and an elegant row of willows in their fresh spring colours.

'The terrace garden goes with this flat,' Erica tells her. 'If you like gardening you could look after it yourself. But if not, there'll be gardeners to keep the whole of the parkland tidy and you could just pay a small annual charge for anything you'd like them to do.'

Helen makes no comment, and she remains silent while she inspects the rest of the accommodation. 'I'll have to think about it,' she says finally, and almost smiles at the memory of how often those same words have been spoken to her during the past three months.

The thinking needs time. There is a sense in which her earlier decision to move into sheltered housing has been a negative rather than a positive plan: she was saying to herself that she didn't want to be bothered with having to consider what she would do with the rest of her life. The Manor apartment has stirred her interest in the future – only slightly, as yet, but even that little is painful. She postpones a decision.

What cannot be postponed, however, is the need to organise her departure from Monckton Hall, in case the offer to buy it holds firm. Later on that same day she forces herself to go into Michael's study and sit at Michael's desk.

It has been one thing to plan for the disposal of furniture, but quite another thing to empty the house of her husband. By now Michael's clothes have gone from his dressing room, but all the rest of his most personal belongings are here. Also stacked on the desk are letters and statements from his accountant, solicitor and stockbroker. She has dealt with the first onslaught of the formalities necessary for probate, but there are still dozens of decisions to be made.

She is competent to make them. Helen has lived for many years as the leisured wife of a prosperous businessman, but as a young woman she was trained in office management and accountancy. When she first met Michael she was working as a freelance book-keeper, spending one day a month at each of twenty small farms to help keep their accounts in order. In the two years before Michael inherited the fruit farm which proved to be the basis of his future prosperity, his father had become confused, and Helen devoted extra hours to his affairs. It was because she often stayed to share the family evening meal that her friendship with Michael began to grow.

Although she ceased to travel round once they were married, she used her training to support Michael in the new venture which became Purefrew. Even after Lucy was born she continued to look after a good deal of the paperwork. All that is a long time ago, of course. Once the business became established and could afford to employ full-time office staff, she retired into the role of chairman's wife.

But there is a legacy from the working years of her youth. She is not one of those women who are frightened of figures. The complications of probate and the tax affairs of a dead man have made her grateful for the help of professionals, but she is perfectly capable of understanding their figures for herself.

Until today, however, she has not cared to interest herself in such matters at all. She has answered the unending streams of questions as best she can, but has made no attempt to study the uses made of her answers. Michael has left her well off: why bother with the details?

Except that unexpectedly now, as she attempts to put the papers into some sort of order, she finds herself becoming interested in those details. There is, for example, a list and valuation of Michael's share-holdings at the time of his death, together with several pages of detailed advice about which might be transferred directly to herself

135

and which would best be sold to cover the bequest to Lucy. Another valuation has arrived more recently, and she is interested to see that the value of the portfolio has increased over the six-month period. Interested enough, in fact, to fetch the daily newspaper and check how each individual holding is moving. Somewhere in the pile of papers are the stockbroker's newsletters which no doubt explain the movements of the market. She collects them together and then pulls towards her the corner of something transparent which she takes to be a document holder, so that she can file away everything relating to stocks and shares.

Her assumption is wrong. This is the transparent bag in which the police have sealed up those few of Michael's possessions which were salvaged from the crash. She has kept it pushed out of sight because she doesn't want to be reminded of the moment when his briefcase was flung out of the BMW: the moment when she was lying in Derek Forsyth's arms. But it can't be ignored for ever. Cautiously, as though it might contain an unexploded bomb, she breaks the seal.

There is nothing unexpected about the contents, most of which relate to the business negotiations in which he was engaged that day. There is a folder containing summaries of Purefrew's past accounts, and another which holds its projections for the future. Tucked away between them is Michael's diary.

The year, like Michael himself, is dead; there is no point in keeping this. But without thinking, before she tosses the diary away, she opens it at the third week in October. There, in the little section allowed for the day of his death, is the eleven o'clock appointment with Wright and King. And underneath it is written '10.30pm. D?'

That single letter causes Helen's heart to miss a beat. She has come across it once before, in the stubs of Michael's cheque book, which had to be checked off before his bank account could be closed. Who is D?

It doesn't come easily to her to search for clues. She has never been the kind of wife who inspects handkerchiefs for traces of lipstick. But if she doesn't resolve her suspicions about D, they will continue to nag at her mind. Methodically she begins to turn the pages of the diary back through the year.

D must live in London. The initial appears regularly on the days which Michael has set aside to watch test matches or one-day finals at Lord's. The London connection is confirmed when Helen reaches a page on which telephone numbers are scribbled; and the number for D is a familiar one. She remembers noticing it on the timed and itemised telephone bill which arrived at the end of October, and wondering at the time why the calls to it were always made so late at night. Now she knows.

It will be easy to check. She can call the telephone number herself and hear a woman answer. 'Hello. Daphne speaking.' Or Dorothy. Or Deirdre. But there's no need for that. She knows.

Softly at first Helen begins to laugh, but soon the laughter becomes hysterical, for she is crying at the same time. It is all quite clear. Had the Purefrew negotiations not been concluded early, Michael would, like Helen herself, have spent the night with a lover.

After a little while she brings herself under control with several deep breaths. Tossing the diary into a wastepaper basket she stands up and straightens her back: she needs a moment or two to think about this. She pulls on a cardigan, because by now the day has become cool, and steps outside, walking round and round the formal garden.

Can the guilt which has paralysed her mind since the moment she learned that she was a widow be erased by the conviction that Michael, too, was unfaithful? Logic says no. Since she had no knowledge of any extramarital fling on his part, her own behaviour can still not be excused. But little by little she is conscious of a softening of the anger she has felt ever since she heard the news of the accident: the anger with herself.

For the first time she is able to look back at her marriage and see it as it was. When the sexual relationship gradually faded away five or six years earlier, that must have suited both of them in the same way, for it made no difference to the strength of their friendship or the pleasure they still took in being with each other. If each of them separately was looking outside the marriage for company, that did not affect their relationship either. That's what she needs to hang on to: the fact that she has had a happy marriage. Happy through the years of lovemaking and happy through the more recent period just of companionship.

If Helen is confident in this memory of happiness, why is she crying again? It can only be that for the first time now she has broken through the barrier of her own guilt and is able at last to mourn for Michael. She allows the tears to flow without check as she continues to walk round and round the garden. She has forgiven Michael already; can she now begin to forgive herself?

137

3

The street in which Candida Brown lives is shabby and dirty, littered with empty cans and made noisy by the rattle of passing trains. Half a dozen black youths lean against a wall, staring at Jarvis's car in a manner which makes him uneasy. He is ostentatious about locking it up and setting the alarm, and turns round to keep an eye on it after he has rung the bell.

None of the young men moves. Probably it is a purely racist assumption that makes him nervous about what might happen if he lets the car out of his sight. Nevertheless, although he has called in the hope of finding Candida at home, it comes as a relief when the unsmiling woman who opens the door makes no suggestion of inviting him inside as she informs him that no, her daughter is not in. Somewhere out of sight a child begins to scream. Mrs Brown closes the door.

Well, it was an unplanned visit: an impulse triggered by the realisation, at the end of a lunch with a fellow publisher in Fulham, that a return via Shepherd's Bush would not prove too much of a diversion. It helps him, however, to understand why Helen Cunningham and Madge Manderson have both pressed Candida's claims rather than their own as the recipient of any practical help he may be able to offer. In her brief visit to his house he was impressed as well as touched by her attitude. This depressing area is no place for a young woman who is not just good-looking but also intelligent and sympathetic. Tom Harding would certainly have offered her a better life, had he lived. As he queues patiently in the heavy traffic around the Green, Jarvis is confirmed in his wish to help her in some way.

First of all, however, he has an arrangement to call on Mrs Martin. She has asked him to come no later than eleven on the Sunday he has proposed, because she is expecting visitors for lunch. This suits Jarvis well, since he has confidently and correctly hoped that Madge would offer lunch when he proposed a time for delivering the typescript of the cookery book to her on the same day.

The day of his visit is hot: one of those glorious May mornings when the doors of a furnace seem to open and allow summer to pour out for the first time. There is no cloud in the sky and no breeze on the ground; as he steps out of the car, he is enveloped by the balmy warmth of the air and the scents of many blossoming trees and shrubs.

For a moment before moving he gazes appreciatively at The Old Rectory, admiring its Georgian symmetry. He would have liked to move to just such a house himself when the decision was made, a few years earlier, to leave the London flat. But he always allowed Pamela to have the last word on domestic affairs, and she wanted a brand-new, labour-saving house. Ever since her death he has ceased to feel at home in it, but assumes that this is simply because he is lonely. Now for the first time he admits to himself that he has never really liked it – but he is still lacking in the emotional energy to start looking for somewhere else on his own.

Penny Martin proves to be very much younger than either of the two widows he has visited earlier. She is barelegged and barefooted and wearing a simple sun dress; her long blonde hair is strained off her face by an Alice band. But beneath this casual appearance Jarvis senses a sophisticated woman. She is not as immediately welcoming as Madge, nor as indifferent as Helen Cunningham. He is conscious that she is summing him up, trying to decide why he has come, and deliberately leaving the direction of the conversation to him. Fair enough.

His first comment is spontaneous. 'What a marvellous home you have here!'

Penny smiles. 'It's for sale. Can I interest you?'

'A little large for me, I think. Well, a great deal too large. Although the idea of living in such a restful setting is appealing.'

'Would you like me to give you the tour?' asks Penny. 'Not the sales pitch, but the picture of country living.'

'I'd be very interested. Thank you.' They are both equally postponing the moment when he will have to explain his presence.

'We'll start at the top, then. That way we finish up in the drawing room, which you're supposed to find irresistible.' She leads the way up one graciously proportioned staircase and then another, narrower one.

'Servants' attic originally, I imagine. My hobby room now.'

Jarvis goes across to the window and looks out. On the further side of a high stone wall stands a brand-new house surrounded by a brand-new lawn; it is still possible to see the lines which separate each strip of turf. A bearded man wearing only shorts and gloves is digging the bare earth which might one day be a flowerbed and flinging stones and lumps of concrete into a wheelbarrow as he excavates them. As though conscious that he is being watched, he looks up, staring directly into the window, and waves. Jarvis turns his head and sees that Penny is standing close behind him. Her cheeks flush slightly as she waves back.

On the nearer side of the wall – on a lawn which must once have been a tennis court – is someone he has seen before. Candida is

139

swinging gently on a chair suspended from a metal frame. Her sun dress is even more exiguous than Penny's, and her son wears nothing at all. As Jarvis watches, she sets the baby down on the grass and looks on, smiling, as he crawls away at top speed.

Jarvis feels a touch of envy. Candida has lost her man and with it her security, but she still has her child. He would have liked to have children himself, but no babies arrived to complete his family and both he and Pamela found it more satisfactory to press on with their busy working lives instead of investing time and emotion in treatment for infertility. Now, left alone, he is sorry. It is not that he would have liked to see a miniature version of himself, but rather that it would be easier to feel excited about the future if he had a personal stake of this kind in it. Lucky Candida!

'That's Candy.' Penny is following the direction of his gaze. 'Her boyfriend died in the accident as well. I suppose the accident is what you've come to talk about, is it?'

'Yes.' Jarvis wonders briefly whether to confess that he has already met Candida; but to do so may mean admitting that he has given no thought to the other victims of the crash until she put the idea into his head. 'I know there's nothing that words can do to make anything seem better, but I did want just to express my regret about what happened. And to see if there's any sort of support you might need.'

'I shall be all right, thank you. Are you going round all of us? You'll find that Helen, Helen Cunningham, needs help, but won't accept it. Madge Manderson – she'd probably be shocked if I said this to her face, but she seems to have blossomed in the past few months. I really don't believe she was allowed to have a single thought of her own while Harry was alive – except when she was playing bowls, because he didn't know anything about that. And now she's discovered that she's perfectly capable of running her own life, and she loves it. But Candy . . .' They look down together, watching as Daniel is scooped up and set down to start his escape again. 'Candy didn't have time to get started like the rest of us.'

'Perhaps I could have a chat with her while I'm here,' Jarvis suggested. 'See if there's anything . . . Mrs Martin, what are these?'

On a table set at right angles to the window about twenty paintings, cheerfully bright, are laid out. Some of them fill the whole of a sheet of paper; others are smaller and overlaid with a transparency on which a text has been handwritten in a neat italic. Jarvis finds that he has no need of the words to understand the story, which is set on a building site and obviously involves the kidnapping of a small yellow excavator by a group of boys and the adventures of the mother and father excavators as they set off to rescue it.

140

The machines are unmistakably machines, and yet with a few small touches they have been given individual characteristics. The mother is elegant and protective; the father is strong and easily enraged; the small kidnap victim, clearly the hero of the story, is resourceful and has a sense of humour as he rescues himself and takes revenge on the boys.

'I made some sketches while the site next door was being excavated.' Penny tells him. 'There was a JCB there for about three weeks and it moved so gracefully, I found it irresistible. Then someone suggested that I might do some more illustrations and turn them into a children's book. The pictures were easy, and I thought of a story. But I don't seem to manage the words so well.'

'These are delightful!' Jarvis exclaims, bending to examine the sheets more closely. 'Have you got a publisher?'

'Heavens, no. At the rate I'm going, it will be months before I finish writing it.'

'I'm a publisher myself,' Jarvis tells her. 'I specialise in illustrated books, for both children and adults. The Elliott Press. You can look me up in any of the yearbooks. I would very much like to introduce your characters to the world.'

Penny stares at him wide-eyed. 'Is it as easy as that to get published?'

'It's not usually easy at all,' Jarvis tells her. 'I turn down about ten books of this sort every week. But there's something different about these. The only question I'd want to ask is, if this book should prove popular, do you think you could do another?'

'Yes, of course. But the words . . . It's terribly difficult, getting the right bit of the story next to the right picture.'

Jarvis by now has had time to read a few paragraphs of the neat script and can see that she has been having problems. He thinks for a moment.

'Have you got any kind of personal computer?'

She shakes her head. 'Clive had a laptop, but that went back to the company.'

'Do you ever come to London, Mrs Martin?'

'Penny,' says Penny. 'Yes, quite often. I'm looking for a flat and a job.'

'If you were to bring these in to our offices, Penny, we could scan the pictures on to a screen and then it would be easy to arrange the text round them and go on fiddling with it until it was right. Even if you still wanted to write the words by hand in the end, you'd have a layout to work from.'

'I'm not sure . . .'

'I have a young assistant who would be delighted to help you.' He is thinking of Girl Friday, whose enthusiasm and natural flair would make up for any lack of experience on a project like this.

Penny looks at him with a directness which makes him realise that she is older than the summer simplicity of her appearance has first suggested.

'Are you making this offer – of publishing the book – as some sort of compensation, Mr Elliott?'

'My name's Jarvis. Since we're going to be colleagues. No, certainly not. I came here to say how sorry I was, and that was a personal thing. But I couldn't put my employees' jobs at risk by using the company to make uncommercial gestures. I think some publisher could have a big success with this. I'd like it to be me.'

She nods, believing him.

'That would be marvellous, then. I'd like it very much indeed.'

'Don't expect too much of it to start with,' he warns her, seeing from the brightness of her eyes how excited she is. 'This sort of book is expensive to produce and has to be sold fairly cheaply, so the royalty on a single copy doesn't amount to much. It's only very occasionally that something takes off like *Thomas the Tank Engine*. But if you enjoy doing it . . .'

'Yes, that's the thing!' exclaims Penny enthusiastically. 'I need something to keep me busy until I can find a job. Look, since you don't really want to buy this house, why don't we go into the garden? I'm longing to tell Candy what's happened.'

'Could you give me ten minutes with her first?' asks Jarvis. 'I hadn't expected her to be here, but since she is . . .'

'Sure. I'll be out soon with something to drink.' She leads the way downstairs and points out the door which opens to the garden. Candida shows no surprise when he joins her.

'Penny told me you were coming today. Was it because of what I said?'

'Yes,' says Jarvis. He sits down in an ordinary chair while Candida, keeping one eye on Daniel, continues to swing. 'I did feel very much ashamed that I hadn't been thinking at all about how the four of you must feel. And because you took me by surprise, I didn't really say the right things.'

'What are the right things?'

'I'd like to do something, anything, if I can, to make up. Not for losing Tom; I realise there's nothing to be done about that. But to improve your way of life, perhaps. I called at your house on Monday.'

'Oh, that was you, was it? I couldn't guess, from what Mum said. She told me you seemed impatient to be gone.'

'Only because you weren't there. Though I did feel a little anxious for my car. And I didn't like to think of you having to walk past that gang every time you leave home.'

'They're not a gang. Just haven't got jobs, that's all. They'd never hurt me, and they wouldn't have hurt your car, either, not while you were visiting our house. Most of them were potty-trained by my mum.'

'Well, all the same. I've been wondering since then whether you might like a bit more space for yourself and your baby. Fresher air. Not necessarily for ever, but while you work out what you might want for the future.'

'What are you suggesting?' Candida looks puzzled.

'You've seen the house I live in. Too big, really, for one person living alone. There'd be plenty of room for you and Daniel if you cared to move in and, well, look after it. You'd have a roof over your head, and a salary, and it would be nice for me not to be rattling around on my own. As you can imagine, I don't have much time for doing housework, or for shopping or cooking. Quite apart from the fact that I'm not very good at any of those things.'

His mention of the advantage to himself is intended to make the offer sound less like a favour to Candida and more like a business arrangement for mutual benefit, because he thinks this might be easier for her to accept. But it seems that he has judged wrongly. The puzzlement has disappeared from Candida's eyes, to be replaced by hostility. This too he manages to misunderstand.

'There's nothing, what shall I say, personal about this. I mean, obviously I'm not trying to seduce you or anything.'

It is not, as a matter of fact, as obvious as all that. Candida must know what an attractive young woman she is. But she can also tell that she is more than thirty years younger than himself and although she does not say in so many words, 'So I should hope!' her expression speaks for her. She does not even intend to put her refusal into words, although it takes him a moment to realise this.

'I thought, that day you came to seem me, that we were, well, in sympathy,' he says.

'Maybe that was so,' Candida agrees coolly. 'As two people who had each suffered equally. Not as master and servant.'

'To act as a housekeeper is quite different from being a servant.'

'In that case, I'm completely unqualified for the position you're kind enough to offer me. If you'll excuse me now, I'll go and give Daniel his lunch.' She picks up her son from the edge of the tennis

143

lawn, where he is nibbling at a blade of grass, and carries him into the house, leaving Jarvis in a state of some irritation.

Several minutes pass before Penny comes to join him, carrying a tray.

'I seem to have upset Candida,' he says, gratefully accepting a Pimm's. 'I was trying to suggest something which I thought might be helpful, but . . .'

'Yes, she told me.' Penny shows signs of amusement. 'The word "slave" came into it.'

'Oh, really!'

Penny sits down and lifts her own glass towards him. 'Cheers!' She takes a sip before beginning to swing gently, as Candida has done.

'I've only known Candy for a couple of years,' she says. 'But I suspect that as a schoolgirl she was very ambitious. She had to work hard to get to Oxford and she must have wanted to do something special with her degree. She put it all on hold because of the baby and Tom. That way of life has fallen through, so I expect she's beginning to feel ambitious again. But now, of course, it's more difficult. So that makes her unsettled, and perhaps being unsettled makes her a bit prickly. She saw your offer, I suppose, as giving you a clean house and a clean conscience at the same time.'

'She has a degree? Why didn't she tell me?'

'Why didn't you ask her?'

'I suppose because it never occurred to me that she might have any kind of qualification.'

'I'm not sure that a law degree *is* much of a qualification for anything in itself. That's part of the problem. Maybe if the compensation claim comes through she'll be able to complete a training. In the meantime, if you're really going to offer me a book contract, I shall employ Candy to check through it for me. She told me once that she'd like to specialise in contracts. I was going to ask if you'd like to stay for lunch. Jonathan, from next door, will be over soon. But –'

'But now you think that Candida may go on hunger strike if I'm still here?' Jarvis laughs. 'Kind thought, but I'm due somewhere else. In fact . . .' He stands up. 'I'll send you a contract this week. And then, if Candida approves it, perhaps you'll let me know when you'd like to bring the illustrations in to the office.' They shake hands and he makes his way back to the car.

He will be earlier than has been arranged, but somehow he doesn't think Madge will mind. The distance between the two villages is too short for even the slowest driving to make much difference, but he uses it to consider whether Candida's criticism is

144

justified. Is he genuinely using these visits to the four women merely to comfort them if possible? It is certainly true that the suggestions he has made both to Madge and to Penny are of advantage to himself. But that doesn't mean that the advantages aren't mutual. If he's got it wrong with Candida, it is because there was no clue – like Penny's drawings or Madge's cooking – to suggest what field he should explore. He has hurt her dignity, but he can already think of a way in which he can make up for that.

In the meantime, he has arrived at College Farm, where he confidently expects to be greeted by a friendly face and a delicious meal. As he reaches across the car for the folder of recipes from the bachelors' book, he is already smiling.

Chapter Eight

1

'I don't understand.'

The postman has just brought two letters addressed to Miss Candida Brown; the first one is making her frown in puzzlement. It contains the offer of a place on the Legal Practice Course due to start in October. This course will be part of her training if she wishes to become a solicitor – but how can she have been accepted for it when she hasn't applied? She would have needed to send off the necessary form before the end of December, and in December she was far too unhappy after Tom's death, far too exhausted by her work as a sales assistant and far too conscious of her lack of money to contemplate a further year of study.

'What's this, then?' asks Mrs Brown.

Candida passes the letter across the breakfast table. 'But I didn't apply,' she says.

'Yes, you did.' Her mother gives a nod of satisfaction. 'I posted the form.'

'I didn't even fill one in. How could you possibly –?'

'The year before, you filled it in. Left it in your bedroom when you went back to Oxford.'

'Ah!' It was in the middle of the Christmas vacation, seventeen months ago, that a pregnancy test revealed Daniel's presence and brought her career plans to an end.

'I changed the date,' Mrs Brown tells her proudly. 'It's only one year lost. And if this man Rufus gets you compensation, there's the money. Daniel can stay on here.' Mrs Brown has been quick to become a doting grandmother.

'I'm not sure . . .' Candida stares uncertainly down at the letter.

'You don't need to be sure, not yet. What you want, girl, is choices. That's what education's for: choosing. Maybe you make a wrong choice and kick yourself for a fool. But no choice at all, you get angry with the world. Like those boys who hang around in the street all day. This summer, you've got time to think. You collect your choices, one, two, three. Set them out and get it right. What's your other letter?'

The other letter is from Jarvis Elliott. Candida raises her eyebrows in surprise and slight amusement as she reads it.

'Well, what is it?'

'It's from the husband of the woman.' Her mother will know what she means by this vague statement. 'I told you, he turned up at Penny's house on Sunday. He's writing to say that he's sorry he offended me. And he wants me to call at his office.'

'What he do to offend you?' Mrs Brown is quick to take umbrage on her daughter's account.

'Not important.' Candida stares thoughtfully at the letter, wondering how to respond. Rufus has told her that she was an idiot to make personal contact with Jarvis, and no doubt he is right; perhaps she ought not to let it go any further. But the memory of their shared moment of sympathy is stronger than the indignation she felt at being invited to act as a skivvy in return for being kept off the streets. And if he has been insensitive, perhaps she has been too sharp. Collect your choices, her mother has said. If Jarvis Elliott has in mind to offer more than an apology, it will be foolish not to go.

On Friday of that same week, in his office, she hurries to get her own expression of regret in first.

'It was nice of you to write,' she says. 'I'm sorry if I was a bit prickly on Sunday. Ungracious. I'm sure you meant –'

'Entirely my fault,' Jarvis responds. 'I hadn't expected you to be there and I rushed in without stopping to think.' His hands make a gesture of helplessness. 'If I'm given a pen and paper and a bit of time, I can draft exactly what I want to say; but to be honest, I've never been very good at speaking the right words on the spur of the moment. As a matter of fact' – he smiles to take any sting out of his words – 'it was because I suspected you might be a prickly sort of person in that way that I phrased my suggestion as I did. I put too much emphasis on how useful the arrangement would be to me, because I didn't want you to feel that I was trying to do you a favour to make up for what you might think I owed you.'

'Although you were?' Candida is able to thread her way through the convolutions of his argument because she has already worked it out for herself.

147

'Yes.' His smile softens his face, just as his tears did a few weeks earlier, making him seem as vulnerable and huggable now as he was then. But now he is sitting in his own office, the head of his own business, and old enough to be her father. Candida naturally does not move to hug him.

'I don't propose to make the same mistake again. I would like to do you a good turn if I can. Not because I feel any need to clear my conscience. But because I did appreciate the gesture you made in coming to see me.'

He pauses, giving her a chance to comment if she wishes, and then continues.

'Another mistake I made, of course, was in not knowing anything about your background or training. Penny told me afterwards that you have a law degree. I have a temporary job here that I could offer you: something that might prove to be useful experience. May I go on?'

Candida grins her permission, feeling thoroughly at ease with him now that they have got Sunday's conversation out of the way. He is a kind man; they are not antagonists.

'One of my staff, Louise, who looks after rights and contracts, is expecting a baby and will be taking maternity leave. At the moment she plans to return. My experience in the past has been that very often when the baby actually arrives, the mother decides to give up work after all; but nobody will know that until the time comes. I need someone to hold the fort at least until the end of September. Would that sort of thing interest you? If you and the work got on well together, we might be able to consider some more permanent arrangement, but it would be as well to have this trial period first. And in case you think that I'm merely offering a superior kind of kitchen floor which needs scrubbing, I should say that I'm perfectly competent to take over Louise's work myself for a short time if I have to, although I've got enough on my plate already and I'd rather not.'

Candida's grin widens in pleasure at the suggestion; but there are questions to be asked.

'It sounds rather a responsible job. Would I be qualified?'

'You'd be inexperienced, certainly. However, if you were to start at once, Louise would still be here at first and you'd soon get the hang of all the routine matters and how to put everything on to computer. That's what we mainly need a replacement for, to make sure that everything slots smoothly into the system. We have a standard contract of our own and you wouldn't have any trouble with that because I negotiate any variations myself in any case. Where the

148

author has an agent with his own form of contract, you'd check it against earlier ones and with the correspondence. There's a book, *Publishing Agreements*.' He has a copy on his desk and now pushes it towards her. 'This would tell you what to look out for. But the main thing is that I'd always be here. And Louise would answer questions over the phone if there were any problems over something she'd started.'

Candida makes no attempt to disguise her pleasure. This time Jarvis has made a real effort to find something that would suit her, and he has got it right. The timing is good, as well. A job which finishes in September will allow her to take up the Legal Practice place – or instead to start as a management trainee if she is offered that as well. It is tempting to accept at once; but she remembers what her mother has said about setting out choices.

'May I think about it and tell you on Monday?' she asks.

'Of course you may. Is that your only question? Don't you want to ask what you'd be paid, for example?'

'I'm sure you wouldn't cheat me, Mr Elliott.'

'That attitude, if I may say so, is quite unsuitable for a rights and contracts manager. Here, take this with you for your weekend thinking.' It is a typed statement of terms of employment. She smiles her thanks as she stands up.

At half past six that evening, when Daniel is asleep and Mrs Brown has left for her weekly Bible-study class, Candida makes her way into the little-used front room. It seems the appropriate place in which formally to consider her future. Her mother has suggested that she should devote the summer to considering her choices, but there are some which can't wait. She cuts a sheet of paper into squares and begins to write on each.

First comes Jarvis Elliott's offer of a temporary job. That's easy. She has decided during the course of the afternoon that there is nothing to be lost and a great deal to be gained by accepting. She will enjoy working for Mr Elliott and it will be good experience in a field which appeals to her. She sets the square down on the left of the table, alone.

The next column is more complicated. There is the Legal Practice Course offer, which is firm but which will not be held open indefinitely.

There is the possibility that Louise may not return to work after her baby is born and that Candida may be offered the job permanently, if she has done well. That is something which will not be known until the last minute. Or there is a second possibility: that even if Louise comes back she may be glad to have an assistant.

There is the Wright and King management traineeship which is also only a possibility. She has made the short-list and was re-interviewed at the end of April: she should hear the verdict quite soon. Without being too cocky, she feels fairly confident that they will make an offer. It is one of the occasions on which the colour of her skin is a definite plus factor.

In addition to these, she has recently received a batch of job details from the university appointments board and has sent off several applications, although without any great enthusiasm for the work on offer. She writes all these down on a single square, but leaves them out of her calculations for the moment.

Does she still truly want to be a lawyer – and if so, what kind of lawyer? Does she want to become a businesswoman – and if so, in what kind of business? The whole of her future life hangs on what she is deciding now. That is an awesome thought. It comes almost as a relief when she is interrupted by a knock on the front door.

2

As Rufus waits on the doorstep for his knock to be answered, he is aware of being under scrutiny. He has come straight from the office and so is wearing a suit – which in this neighbourhood marks him as some kind of official. The young men lounging on the corner of the street, the children kicking a football about and their mothers peering from the windows across the way, all take note of any stranger. But they have seen him before, and they have seen Candida smile as she opens the door to him. There is no hostility in the staring, but only a lot of curiosity.

Candida is the most curious of all. She doesn't in so many words demand to know why he has called, but her expression expects an answer.

'I've come to take you out for a meal,' he tells her.

'I'm sorry, Rufus. I can't.'

The refusal is unexpected. It is not yet seven o'clock. 'Give me three good reasons why not,' he demands.

'The first is that I've eaten already this evening. The second is that the reason we ate early was because my mother was going out, and now she's gone, so I have to stay with Daniel.'

'I asked for three reasons.' He grins encouragingly and she smiles back, but without producing any further excuse. She doesn't need to. Rufus himself is well aware of the problem.

She must know that he is – to use a word which has been out-of-

150

date for years – courting her; but because he is refusing to express his feelings in words he is making it more difficult for her to push him away. He feels sure that by the look in his eyes and the way in which from time to time his fingers touch her hand he has made her aware that he loves her. But he is leaving it to her to alert him in whatever way she chooses to the moment when she has recovered from Tom's death and is ready to embark on a new relationship. Any other girl he would long ago have invited back to his flat; but for Candida he is prepared to wait.

'There's something I want to discuss with you,' he says. 'May I come in?'

She stands aside without speaking. He is surprised to see that the front room is for once in use.

'What's going on here?' He crosses to the table and looks down at the patchwork of paper squares.

'I'm plotting my future,' Candida tells him. 'By the autumn I shall have had a year off, sort of. A lot of people take a year's gap either before or after university. This won't seem such an unusual thing. But by September or October I need to be quite sure where I'm going and to have my foot firmly on the ladder which will get me there. These are some of the possibilities.'

Rufus reads the headings without comment. There is no mention of marriage or of any other possible relationship. Because his visit is unannounced he cannot reasonably view her plans as an intentionally hurtful message to himself, but the message is there. Candida, perhaps reading his thoughts, tries to soften the effect.

'You've been along this path yourself, Rufus. You know how important it is to get qualifications. And how difficult it is to go back to passing exams if you stop cramming for too long.'

'Yes.' But he has not really listened to the opinion before agreeing with it. His mind is on something else.

'As a matter of fact, it's about your future that I've come. Can we sit down?'

As she nods and pulls out a chair for herself, Rufus takes one of the empty squares of paper from the top of the pile. It is tempting to write on it 'Marry Rufus', but the temptation proves resistible. He needs some sign of readiness from Candida herself first, or else she is likely to push him away completely. Instead, in large capitals, he prints the words FORMULA FOUR, and pushes the paper towards her.

'What about Formula Four?'

'That's what I'm asking you. You've got this idea for a new drink. I've tasted it and I know how good it is. If you chose to develop it, you might well make a fortune – for other people as well as for your-self. Why should you spend your life at other people's beck and call?' He flicks his fingers toward the list of jobs for which she has applied. 'You could have your own business; be your own boss.'

Candida takes her time about answering. 'I did wonder about that at one time,' she admits. 'I was going to ask your advice. But when I thought about it more carefully, I realised that it isn't realistic, is it? Just making a few batches of something without having to get them tested or approved or preserved or bottled or sold is light years away from building up a business. If Tom had lived he would have made sure that the formula worked scientifically, and Purefrew would have started it on its way, and Wright and King would have had the capital to develop it and the sales organisation to market it. But on my own . . . no way!'

'You wouldn't be alone. That's what I want to talk about.'

As Candida waits patiently, he assembles his thoughts, pressing the fingers of each hand together. Now his mind, like his body, is dressed in a lawyer's suit.

'Helen Cunningham asked me to call on her a few weeks ago,' he says at last. 'She wants to sell Purefrew. Not surprising, really. She hasn't had anything to do with the running of it for years.'

'Is it an easy thing to do, selling a business?'

'Sometimes it can be; there are always people looking out for something ready-made that they can manage and improve them-selves. But in this case there may be problems. Obviously Michael Cunningham thought he'd got it all sewn up in the projected takeover; but when those negotiations fell through it left a tricky sit-uation. The normal second-best would be a management buy-out; but of course this particular firm has lost its two most senior managers, as well as Tom, who would have been the brains behind any expansion.'

'Couldn't Mrs Cunningham run the company herself as a sort of non-executive chairman?'

'She could, and in my opinion she should, at least for a while. Because what she has now is a stagnating company. The new man-aging director seems to be quite a bright chap who'd like to introduce new ideas and generally perk things up. But without more capital and some support from above, there's not much he can do. No one's going to pay much for the business in its present state. But – have you seen Helen recently?'

Candida shakes her head. 'Not since Christmas. She offered me some furniture and I called to thank her. She was very depressed.'

'When I saw her in April, she still was. She was having trouble selling her house, and probably she was feeling a bit ambivalent about whether she did or didn't want a buyer to come along soon. My personal opinion was that she needed a doctor more than a lawyer, but there wasn't much I could do about that. What she certainly needs is something to jolt her back into life again. Some kind of excitement. That's where you could come in. She doesn't really know much about Formula Four, except the name. Suppose you were to go and see her. Ask if Purefrew could be used to develop the new drink.'

'How?'

'The best arrangement would be for you to set up a little company of your own, which could go into partnership with Purefrew. I could help you with that aspect of it. Maybe it would only be possible on a small scale at first, but if you got it up and running you could go back to someone like Wright and King.'

'But you could do all that on your own, Rufus. Arranging mergers is your speciality, isn't it? I can give you the recipe if you like. As I said, the whole thing is too complicated for me to develop on my own anyway, so I never shall.'

'No.' Rufus responds with vehemence. 'If I take the idea to Helen she'll realise that I'm simply trying to cheer her up and she'll turn it down. But one thing that came out of our conversation is that she does feel concern for you and Penny and Madge. Especially you. Not that you're her responsibility in any way; but she's been left comfortably off and wants to be sure that you're keeping your head above water.'

There is a note of incredulity in Candida's laughter. 'Let me get this straight. You want to help Helen Cunningham and you think the only way to do it is to make her think she's helping me?'

'You have it in one. You're obviously going to make a good lawyer with that sharp mind of yours.'

'How shall I ever have time to become a lawyer if I'm busy becoming a millionairess? You must be joking, Rufus. Although Penny –'

She breaks off. Some thought has occurred to her, but she is apparently unwilling to express it. Instead she reminds him that she has no money to invest in such a project. 'And I've been brought up never to borrow.'

'You wouldn't necessarily need capital. The recipe could be your contribution. Although of course when the compensation comes through –'

'No.' Candida's rejection of that idea is definite. 'That will be for Daniel. So that we can have a home of our own.'

153

Rufus doesn't argue that point, but waits to hear if she has any other objections. If she has, it seems that she is not prepared to share them with him at this moment. Her hand makes a gesture towards the other choices which are spread out on the table. 'I'll have to think about it,' she tells him.

'Yes, of course.' But he grimaces with disappointment as they both stand up, and his longing for her cannot be completely controlled. For the first time in the six months of their acquaintance he kisses her goodbye. People kiss like this all the time nowadays: it is a chaste social kiss on the cheek, not a passionate kiss, but the tightness with which his hands grip her arms must surely tell her how much he is hoping that she will offer her lips.

For a second time he is disappointed.

3

The principle of flexitime is operated by the staff of the Elliott Press with more than the usual flexibility. By four o'clock on Friday afternoon almost everyone has hurried away to beat the rush-hour traffic. Jarvis, however, remains. Why should he hurry to return to his unwelcoming home? Instead, he takes pleasure in prowling round the empty building. It was built as a house, not as an office block, in a century when Bloomsbury was a pleasant place to live, and it still retains a little of its domestic quality; indeed, it is more homelike to him now than number 3 Kiln Close.

There is pride as well as comfort in his beating of the bounds. This is his achievement. He has provided not only employment but a congenial atmosphere in which to work. He has helped scores of authors and artists to achieve publication and has offered entertainment or instruction to thousands of readers. And there is no downside. No one can claim to be harmed by his products; no one can accuse him of being a harsh taskmaster. It has always been his belief that a happy ship sails smoothly.

He climbs the stairs to the offices which two hundred years earlier were bedrooms. Pat, who keeps the accounts, has the smallest, positively choosing to be confined with calculator and computer into a space too tight to allow of disturbance by other people. Azil and his assistants share the master bedroom, its wall now covered with workflow charts. The bedroom converted for Louise's use has a small dressing room attached to it. It is here that Jarvis discovers that he is not, as he thought, alone in the building.

Candida, at the end of her first week in the office, looks up as he appears in the doorway.

'How's it going?' he asks her. Louise has already assured him privately that the new member of staff has taken to the job like a duck to water.

'It's fascinating,' she tells him enthusiastically. 'But there's an awful lot to learn before Louise disappears.'

'No need to do overtime, though.'

'It's not five o'clock yet. And I don't find it easy to concentrate at home. My mother likes to know what I'm doing all the time. I thought, while everything was quiet, I'd just make a list of questions to ask Louise on Monday.'

Nodding approvingly, he looks over her shoulder. 'Video recordings? Where does that come up?'

'It doesn't. That will be the question. A lot of your books would make marvellous videos: the sort of thing that public libraries are renting out nowadays. The new flower-arranging book, for example, and a lot of the cookery books. But it doesn't seem at all clear in the contracts I've looked at so far who sells the rights or how any fees would be divided.'

'Don't let it spoil your weekend. You go down to the Moncktons quite often, do you?'

'Yes. Almost every Sunday. Penny's very hospitable. We hold each other's hand from time to time when we're feeling miserable. And of course it's marvellous for Daniel and me to have a breath of country air.'

'Do you feel miserable very often?'

'Well, I don't let myself. It breaks through from time to time, but mostly I can keep my eyes on the future. I wonder, Mr Elliott –'

She breaks off uncertainly. Jarvis is on the point of suggesting that she, like the rest of the staff, should call him by his Christian name, but he is sensitive enough to realise that something quite serious is troubling her and that he ought not to interrupt while she thinks it through.

'Well, I just wondered if I could talk to you. Ask your advice. A personal matter, nothing to do with work. But I expect you're in a hurry to get away.'

'Not in the least,' he tells her. 'No point in trying to leave until the traffic thins out a bit. Why don't we go down to my room? More comfortable.'

His room was once the first-floor drawing room of the house. It is handsome and spacious. The walls are lined with the file copies of every book he has published. His desk is near the window and at the

155

other end of the room half a dozen comfortable chairs are grouped round a table, ready to be used for editorial conferences or chats with authors. He points Candida to one of these and sits down to face her.

'What's worrying you?' he asks.

'Well, I have to make plans. For the rest of my life, really. It's a bit nerve-racking, wondering whether I'm going to make some terrible mistake. I mean, I'm here until the end of September, you said, and I shall enjoy that, I know. But after that . . .'

After that, Jarvis has every intention – unless some great disaster occurs – of asking her to stay on in some capacity. Girl Friday has had her chance to prove herself and has failed as far as the business side is concerned, although it may prove possible to use her as a free-lance reader and editor. But Candida's intelligence and application have impressed everyone who has met her and a single week has been long enough to assure him that she fits in well with the rest of his small staff. However, it is too soon to make any definite offer; and in any case it is clear that she has some specific problem in mind.

'I'm lucky, really,' she adds hastily. 'I have choices, and that's good, isn't it?'

'Yes and no. The *really* lucky people, I suspect, are the ones who feel a vocation – who know absolutely for sure that there's only one way ahead which will satisfy them, and who manage to achieve what they want. People like that never need to consider any alternatives. But choices and uncertainty go together, as presumably you're dis-covering. Choice can turn out to be a cause of stress. And some people, who start off by being glad that they have the power to choose, become upset when they realise that once they've chosen, they've lost that power.'

'Yes, that may be it. It's quite hard to reject something without wondering whether I'll be sorry later.'

'Well, suppose you start by telling me what your choices are.'

There is a long silence. Jarvis feels almost as though he can see inside Candida's brain and observe the neatness with which she is marshalling her thoughts, ready to present them as clearly as possible. Then, leaning slightly forwards, with her fingers pressing against each other as though she is praying, she gives him all the details.

He listens carefully, docketing each possibility as neatly in his own mind as it already lies in hers. When she comes to a halt, there is a second period of silence. Candida may presume that he is preparing to issue a single authoritative opinion, but this is not exactly the case.

Before he can continue with this conversation, he must resolve once and for all his attitude towards Candida herself. Everything about her – her slim, straight body, the smoothness of her skin, the

156

brightness of her eyes, the earnestness of her character – combines to make her an extremely attractive young woman, and it would be stupid to deny that he is indeed attracted to her. That is a fact to be first of all recognised and then dismissed. He is not prepared even to contemplate any casual sexual relationship with a member of his staff and he is sensible enough to recognise that a marriage between a woman of twenty-two and a man of fifty-five would be unwise for the man and disastrous for the woman.

Perhaps it would have been better if no such possibility had ever entered his thoughts. The second-best is to face the situation squarely and control it. Unexpectedly, into his mind flashes the memory of their first encounter, when they embraced each other in unhappy sympathy. There was no sexual strand in that conversation, and there must be none in this one – or ever. Candida is appealing to him for advice because she has no father to help her, and it is as a father speaking to a daughter that he now prepares to advise her.

4

Candida waits, grateful to realise that Jarvis is preparing to give her considered advice rather than a quick answer. When at last he speaks, it is in fact to ask a question.

'What's the most important consideration in your mind, Candida, when you're weighing the possibilities?'

'Daniel.' The answer comes without hesitation. If motherhood and professional ambition are in conflict, Daniel will win.

'Noted. But let me put it another way. In the context of working for a living, which of these things would you say most interests you? Money? Or people? Or objects, things?'

It is a good question, and she takes her time about answering it.

'Not precisely any of them,' she decides at last. 'I think the answer would be "words". Not in your sense, of publishing them. Not even in the sense of choosing exactly the right words to use. But working out the exact meaning of words that are already in place. That's what attracted me to law in the first place, I think. I never had any great visions of myself as a knight in shining armour saving people from prison. Or sending them there, come to that. But commercial law: where the important thing is what a document says and precisely what it means.'

'That's a good starting point.' Jarvis's voice is approving. 'Right. Let's go through your options. Starting with your friend Rufus's idea about setting up a soft-drink company and making your fortune.'

He pauses for a moment and his face creases into the soft, friendly smile which Candida finds particularly attractive.

'I'm going to speak very definitely on this one,' he tells her. 'That doesn't mean, of course, that I'll be hurt if you ignore my advice. Here goes, then. I've set up a business of my own, so I do know a little about it. Of the people who go in for this sort of thing, the most successful are the entrepreneurs whose primary aim is to make their fortunes. If you're that sort of person, then you know it right from the start, without having to ask anyone else. It's a kind of vocation. You've had to ask, so that's not you.'

Startled, Candida laughs. Only a few moments ago the future seemed to be a tangle of complications. It seems that Jarvis is going to hack his way straight through with a pair of shears. But he has not yet finished with Formula Four.

'There's also my sort of business-former, though,' he tells her. 'What I did was to create exactly the sort of life I wanted for myself, without having to rely on finding a congenial employer. Let's look at it from that point of view. You'd be going into a crowded market which already contains some very large players. You say that you'd be offering a healthy alternative to Coca-Cola, but you'd find Lucozade there before you and I understand that there's a range of fruit drinks currently sweeping the American market and bound to reach here soon. You mentioned all the scientific hurdles, but those would be nothing compared to the marketing costs. Speaking off the top of my head, I'd be amazed if you could get something like this off the ground for under two million. And you don't seem to me like someone who would be happy knowing that you owed a bank that kind of money, with bankruptcy looming at every setback.'

'You don't think I'd make a success of it.'

'No, I don't. In the publishing world it's possible to start small, without too many overheads, but with Formula Four you'd have to plunge straight into big business. You'd have to give it the whole of your life, almost twenty-four hours a day, and I think you'd fail. Say no to this one, Candida. If Helen Cunningham chooses to take a gamble, that's a different matter. She's got the facilities, presumably, to develop the idea to a certain extent and then use it to sell the company on. There's nothing to stop you letting her use your recipe, in return for a royalty if it's successful. You may not make your fortune that way, but you keep your peace of mind.'

'Thank you.' He has told Candida what she wants to hear. It was unfair of Rufus, she thinks, to make her feel that she alone has the power to draw Helen out of depression. Well, perhaps she does have that power, but there are easier ways of exercising it. She will ask Penny for advice on that point when next they meet.

Jarvis is still delivering his verdicts.

'I think you should say no to Wright and King as well. It doesn't sound as though you have any great interest in warehousing or distribution or retailing.'

'No. But it's a job. With a career structure.'

'No point in having a ladder to climb if you aren't going to enjoy the view from the top. Now then, let's think about the law. If you take this course, are you qualified at the end of it?'

Candida shakes her head. 'I'd have to be articled for another two years. And before you ask: no, it's not easy. There are only places for about half the people who apply. The latest report I saw said that only seven per cent of black applicants are accepted. Of course, I always reckoned that I was going to be one of the seven per cent. But although my law tutor must have given me a good reference to get me on to the course, my degree won't go down very well with any firm of solicitors who are looking for a First.'

Jarvis looks at her in an appraising way. 'Why have you chosen to consider the solicitor option?' he asks. 'The Bar would suit you better. It would be easier to specialise.'

'Yep. I thought quite hard about that. But pupillage is even harder to come by than articles. And you can't expect to earn a living wage for the first few years.'

'You can if you go for the Employed Bar and take a legal job in a general company. You might never be famous, but you'd get the sort of work that suits you.'

Candida gives a regretful shrug of the shoulders. 'Well, I haven't applied for the Inns of Court School, so that's not one of my choices.'

'I suppose your mother would like you to be a lawyer.'

'Oh, sure.'

'Parents are always keen to see their children in professions with recognised qualifications. I had trouble with mine, as well. But that's because a generation ago a professional job was a job for life and the middle classes – and those who aspired to join them – have always gone great guns on the principle of delayed gratification. Spend your youth slogging away in order to enjoy a prosperous middle age.'

'I don't believe it!' Candida exclaims, laughing. 'You're going to make me say no to the law as well!'

'I realise that what you've asked me is to advise on what might be best for *you*. But Daniel needs an advocate too. He deserves to have

159

as much of your undistracted time as you can afford to give him. I'm sure you agree with that.'

She nods, still waiting for his final opinion.

'What I'm going to suggest is that at least for four years, until Daniel starts school, what you need is an ordinary sort of job. Nine to five at the most: even shorter hours if you can find them. Something you can shut the door on, and enjoy your evenings and weekends. At the end of that time you could consider reading for the Bar as a mature student. But you might find by then that an ordinary job is what you really want, if it's a congenial one.'

Candida takes her time about considering this. What he is really telling her is that she must think of herself as an ordinary kind of person.

Because she was a high-flyer both at school and in her first two years at Oxford, she has always been encouraged to be ambitious. 'The sky's the limit!' she was told on the day she received the school prize for the best A-level grades of her year. Pregnancy clouded that sky, but because she loved Tom so much she was able to abandon her ambitions without regret. Perhaps, since his death, she has been trying too hard to pretend that nothing else has changed. All the same, this is a sobering moment. Jarvis is bringing her down to earth.

She knows him well enough by now to guess what he will say next. He is not the kind of man to demolish all her expectations and leave her with nothing. It is important that she should judge his motives correctly and she raises her eyes to stare intently into his.

What she sees reassures her. He is not like Rufus, who is behaving perfectly but making sure, all the same, that she knows what he wants. Jarvis has an even greater degree of self-control. Whatever he may be feeling, he is going to behave as a fatherly employer.

'I know you haven't had long,' he asks her now, 'but are you enjoying your work here?'

'Yes. Very much indeed.'

'I can offer you, if you'd like it, a little more security. An extra year from September, with the hope that we may both wish to continue the arrangement. Or it would give you time to consider alternative plans. You may find that there are ways of keeping up your legal studies part time: I wouldn't know about that. But I'd try to fit in if that was what you wanted. Go away and think about it. Discuss it with your friends. You asked me for impartial advice, and I don't want you to turn down my final suggestion just because it leads in the direction of my own advantage.'

'*Is* it to your advantage?' Candida asks. 'It seems to me that it's

160

entirely to mine. Are you suggesting this because of – because of your wife?'

Jarvis shakes his head. 'It has the advantage to me that I needn't have hysterics if Louise decides to take her full maternity leave and then disappear at the end of it. It has the advantage to me of replacing Girl Friday, whose apprenticeship will end in September just as we've all become accustomed to having someone young and willing to fill any gaps. And there's another thing.'

There is a very long pause. Candida can tell that he is wondering whether to say something that he will later regret.

'My parents are both dead,' he tells her at last. 'I have no brothers or sisters or children. Or wife, of course. One sister-in-law and her children, but they're a very self-sufficient family. I would very much like to be offered the privilege of becoming Daniel's adopted grandfather.'

Candida stares across the table at him, finding herself unexpectedly moved almost to tears. Once before, at their first meeting, their individual lonelinesses have reached out to touch each other. She can still recall the warmth of what was both a physical and an emotional contact. She had not expected it to create more than the most fleeting of relationships, and even now it is hard to believe that she can trust Jarvis to remain on the right side of such a razor-thin line.

Almost as though testing him, she stretches out her hand and puts it on the table. He rests his own hand on top of it and presses down gently. Like a psychic, she tries to interpret his feelings through that touch, and is reassured. Yes, he feels some kind of love for her, but it is a love that she is free to accept. He is not in competition with Tom. A grandfather for Daniel is a father for herself. Until this moment, with the offer on the table, she has perhaps never realised how much she wanted one. She bends her head to conceal the fact that she is about to cry.

'Thank you,' she says.

5

'I need some advice,' says Penny on Sunday, and Candida laughs aloud.

'Snap! That was what I was going to say to you.'

'I asked first.'

'Right. What is your problem, madam?'

'Holidays,' Penny tells her. 'There's a glimmer of hope on the job-hunting front. Nothing definite yet, but if it comes to anything I shall

161

be a slave to office hours again. So I'd like to get away just for a week or so first. But I don't know where I want to go or how I want to organise it.'

'What sort of thing did you enjoy before?'

'Before I met Clive –' Penny pauses for a moment. The years before she met Clive now seem unimaginably remote. She has an album full of photographs of a bright, flirtatious blonde in a sarong or bikini: is that young woman really her? 'Before I met Clive I used to enjoy the singles type of holiday. The West Indies. The Mediterranean. The kind of resort where everyone's young and hunting, but it doesn't matter because at the end of the fortnight you never need to see any of them again. I stopped that after we were married, naturally. Clive was nuts on sailing. We went to the Greek Islands, and along the Turkish coast: we had three marvellous trips. But I wouldn't want to do that sort of thing on my own.'

As her friend frowns with concentration, Penny continues to talk.

'It's difficult, you know. I don't want to be the young kind of single any more and I'm certainly not the elderly kind of single. People of my age are expected to be in couples.'

She is beginning to feel upset and is glad when the conversation is interrupted by the arrival of Jonathan Verne. Although the house next door is finished by now, he still takes it for granted that he will be welcome for Sunday lunch. Candida explains Penny's problem.

'Ah, well!' he says, and promptly disappears again. When he returns he is carrying a National Trust booklet.

'A working holiday, that's what you need. I do this every year, just for the pleasure of getting my hands dirty. There's a sort of community spirit. You're quite liable to find yourself sleeping in a dormitory. Nobody really knows or cares whether you're on your own: you're just part of a group. But if you came for the same weeks as me, I'd make sure that you never felt lonely.'

'When are you going?' Penny, turning the pages, is interested.

'Whenever it suits you.' He grins, and Penny flushes slightly as she turns over the pages. She is being invited to dig out ditches, repair dry-stone walls, coppice woodland, clear footpaths or make botanical surveys.

'I'll read it through tonight, if I may,' she tells Jonathan. He is opening his mouth to press her to agree; rather than let him speak she grabs at the first change of subject which comes to her mind. 'Have you heard about Helen Cunningham?' she asks Candida.

'What about her?'

'She's managed to sell her house. And has decided to take one of

162

the posh Manor flats after all, instead of slumming it in the retirement complex.'

'I *beg* your pardon!' Jonathan, as the architect responsible for both projects, puts on a show of indignation.

'You know what I mean,' Penny tells him. 'That sort of bungalow would have been far too small for someone like Helen.'

Candida is looking at her with an unusual degree of interest. 'So is she feeling more cheerful now that she's making plans for the future?'

'It seems to be the other way round.' Penny doesn't quite understand it herself. 'I get the impression that first of all something happened to lift her out of the gloom, and it was after that she became more positive about her plans.'

'Rufus said he saw her in April and she was terribly down in the dumps.'

'Quite right. But no longer. Now then, it's your turn, Candy. You said you wanted advice about something as well.'

But just as Helen's mood has apparently changed, so – it seems – has Candida's. She thinks for a moment and then shakes her head. 'I think you've answered my question before I needed to ask it.'

Puzzled, Penny waits for an explanation, but is not given one. She thinks over the conversation. Was Candida's problem in some way connected with Helen's state of mind? It doesn't seem likely. Perhaps she was going to suggest that she and Penny should go on holiday together, and has now stepped away from that idea in order to leave Jonathan a clear field. For a second time that morning Penny finds herself blushing.

Chapter Nine

1

Madge is devoting the summer to playing bowls. There is an outdoor green within walking distance of her home, but in spite of her enthusiasm for the game it has been difficult in the past for her to spend much time there. She was never, for example, able to sign up for club matches, because such games always extend to include tea, which would have made her late for Harry's supper. And although Julie, while she was alive, could be wheeled down to sit in front of the clubhouse, her presence was a distraction, making it impossible to concentrate on the game.

So for years Madge confined herself to friendly roll-ups which could be brought to an end at any time by a word of apology. This summer is different. As soon as the season opens at the beginning of May she pays daily visits to the club in order to practise: backhand and forehand, long and short jacks, drawing and firing. If anyone comes to join her, that's fine, but bowls is a game for which an opponent is not essential. A good many years ago some instinct told her that this was a game at which she might turn out to be quite good if she tried; now for the first time she can start trying.

She enters for competitions: not just the internal club competitions but the more important ones in which bowlers from all over the county compete for the chance to qualify for the national championships at Leamington. Getting to Leamington is the equivalent of getting to Wimbledon or Wembley in other fields. Madge is determined to achieve it one day, although it may be overambitious to hope for such success for a few years yet.

Successful or not, there is a buzz about reporting in at the venue appointed for the county competitions. The dates are fixed and two

164

rounds are played each day, so the clubhouse is crowded with women from a score of different clubs. She enjoys not only her freedom to drive herself there for the first time, but also the friendly but businesslike atmosphere when she arrives. Her life has for too long been confined in a narrow space, but now that space is expanding. She can feel herself metaphorically broadening her shoulders, pushing out her elbows, becoming solid and not to be ignored.

Because she has never signed up to play in county matches, her name is not known outside her own club; so her opponents in early rounds congratulate themselves on getting an easy draw against an inexperienced player and suffer the consequences of too casual an approach. By the end of June Madge has been knocked out of the County Fours and Triples, because all members of a team must come from the same club, and the Moncktons cannot provide her with sufficient support. But she and Gwen are still in the Pairs, and Madge on her own has reached the semifinal of the Two-Wood Singles. It is all very satisfactory.

She can't help laughing to herself sometimes as she drives home at the end of a county day. This is really a very frivolous and unproductive way of spending her life. But she decided quite early on after Harry's death that it would be a mistake to make any sudden decisions on large matters. Whether or not to move house, whether or not to look for a job or start a catering business of her own for a second time: these are not questions to be decided in a hurry. Quite apart from anything else, the fact that the decisions are hers and only hers to make comes as a relief rather than a cause of stress, so that every postponement is an increase in the time she can devote to pleasurable speculation. It is not indecision that prompts her to remain in her own house and refrain from looking for work, but a sense of horizons widening, of possibilities beckoning. After so many years cocooned within the demands of her husband and daughter it is a delight to spread her wings briefly: a butterfly fluttering and basking in the sunshine.

It doesn't matter if she's late home from any of these bowls days. Peter will forage for himself in the kitchen if he's hungry. He is still living at College Farm, but no longer as a paying lodger. With his health restored by three months of regular meals prepared to a careful dietary plan, he has imperceptibly become just a member of the household. For part of each day, after taking a long and lonely walk, he works on the book he is writing about his experiences in China; but when that is done he helps Madge to cultivate the vegetable plot, keep the car clean and cope with domestic emergencies. Best of all, he still reads poetry to her every evening; it is an hour which gives them both great pleasure.

By now Madge has discovered that Peter is only thirty-three years old. But she feels no wish to mother him, knowing that his years of solitary imprisonment have left him in as much need of space and privacy as she is herself. She is simply glad to be in a position to offer him a home. The mortgage on College Farm has been paid off by the insurance on Harry's death, and her living expenses are minimal: running the car is her only luxury. If Rufus Grant succeeds in winning compensation for the accident, that will be a bonus; but even without it she has no need to ask Peter for money.

Jarvis doesn't understand her relationship with Peter at all – but then, Madge herself is not at all clear about Jarvis, who, as the summer wears on, is becoming a regular visitor, at his own request. Why?

The first visit was easy enough to understand: a duty call – one of four – to make a kind of vicarious apology for his wife's aberration. His discovery that Madge would be capable of testing recipes for him was genuine enough, so the second call was sufficiently explained by the need to deliver the typescript safely. When he asked if he could return a week later, she assumed that he wanted to check that she was performing the test-cooking efficiently. Well, fair enough. But why does he keep on coming? Has he nowhere else to go?

The answer, she gradually realises as the weeks pass, is that no, he hasn't. As she comes to know him better, she's emboldened to put the question directly. He is still living in an area designed for family occupation, but surely, if he were to take a flat in London . . .

Jarvis shakes his head. 'There's a kind of deadness about London at the weekends. That's to say, there are plenty of people swarming around, looking for entertainment. There's a gay scene and a teen scene. But a man of my age is expected either to be in waiting on a female of some kind or else to be making for the golf club. Monday to Friday I'm as bright and bustling as the best of them, but Sundays are a bit flat, to be honest. That's no excuse for dumping myself on you, though. I'm sorry.'

Madge makes the expected noises about how glad she always is to see him, but she remains puzzled. Perhaps the fact that he is a publisher is misleading her. She is a great reader and, unlike some readers, looks at the name or colophon on the spine of each book to discover who has published it. Her mental picture of publishers is of intellectual men and women who congregate in clubs and attend international conferences and throw launch parties and are continually lunching with famous authors. Possibly such people do indeed exist, but she begins to realise that Jarvis is not one of them.

He spells out his position himself, in fact, when he becomes aware of her misapprehension on one Sunday in July.

'I'm just a small businessman, in a line of business which is riskier than most. I started my own company and I've built it up into a going concern and my end products are books, so that makes me a publisher. But it's not the people connected with books who excite me, but the books themselves. The look of them, the feel of them, even the smell of them. I'm not part of the literary world. I very rarely meet my authors at all – and if I do, they're not Iris Murdoch, they're people like Penny Martin. And when I talk to other publishers, it's usually about things like the Net Book Agreement or whether it's good or bad to have our books on sale next to the spaghetti in supermarkets. Culture doesn't come into it: just cash.'

The frankness of this admission makes Madge uneasy. He is insisting that she should get to know him; he is forcing himself on her in a more insidious manner than that of merely angling for Sunday lunches. She could always turn him away, claiming that she has other things to do on Sundays – but she is sorry for him. He knows that, of course; he is trading on it.

Next time he comes, she has prepared a tease. By now several weeks have passed since she finished testing the recipes in the cookery book and returned the manuscript to him with her comments. But she has kept copies of some of them.

'It occurs to me, rather late,' she says as she pours coffee for Peter and Jarvis, 'that getting those recipes tested by someone who knows how to cook isn't really a fair way of judging. Since they're intended for men on their own, it should be single men who have a stab at them. To make sure that they don't take even the most basic knowledge for granted. So today I'm forcing a kind of party game on the two of you. I want each of you to make a birthday cake for a child.'

'But neither of us has a child,' Jarvis points out.

'I had noticed. You have to pretend. You're divorced and it's your day for having the children. I've put out all the ingredients on the kitchen table.'

It amuses her to realise that she is becoming bossy. No doubt it is because she always acts as skip when she is on the bowling green, giving confident directions to the other members of her team. But she would never have dreamed of talking to Harry like that.

Peter – who is still not much of a talker – smiles his willingness to obey and goes out into the kitchen. Jarvis does not follow.

'I don't think I want to play that game,' he says. 'There are absolutely no circumstances in which I would want to make a birth-day cake.'

'You're going to publish the book.'

'And I've given it to an expert, you, to check through.'

Madge comes close to pointing out that he himself is the expert in being a single man, but manages to check the hurtful words in time.

Jarvis stirs his coffee noisily. He is working himself up to say something.

'Is Peter a permanent resident here?' he asks at last. 'Part of the family?'

In just such a way a small child who has originally welcomed a new baby into the family may suggest to his mother that it has out-stayed its welcome. Madge stares at Jarvis in astonishment. Is it possible that he's jealous?

'It's up to him,' she replies, shrugging her shoulders. 'He knows that he can stay or go as he pleases. Liberty Hall. I expect, when he's finished his book, he'll look for another job as a journalist. But he needed a rest. That's why he's here.'

'Will you miss him if he goes, when he goes?'

'I shall miss our poetry hours,' Madge admits. 'And it's nice hav-ing him around, even though I'm hardly aware that he's here. Yes, I shall miss him.'

'I suppose . . .' There is a cautious note in Jarvis's voice, as though he realises he is stepping on to thin ice. 'I suppose that when you've been married for so many years, it must be nice for you still to have somebody to look after.'

This conversation is making Madge uneasy. By making her answer sound casual she hopes to bring it quickly to an end.

'I didn't really look after Harry. He looked after me. I fed him and made our home comfortable, but that's different.'

'Your daughter, though.' By this time Jarvis knows about Julie and the cerebral palsy with which she was born. 'You had to look after her.'

'I don't want to talk about Julie.' But it's too late. Julie, darling dead Julie, is in the room with them, demanding attention although she has no words with which to speak. And something is happening to Madge. Something is swelling inside her head, as though air is pumping into a balloon to press against her brain. She is tempted to scream. She is tempted to faint. But in what is left of her common sense she knows that there is only one way to prick the balloon and reduce the pressure. She has been a widow now for more than nine months, and it is time to be honest with herself.

Harry was a tyrant in a small way. His motives were good. He bullied and imprisoned her because he loved her, and knowing that he loved her helped her to believe that she was happily married. Julie was an absolute tyrant. She was unable to ask for anything and so it was impossible ever to say no to her. It was somehow Madge's own fault that her daughter was so helpless, and therefore help could never be refused. It would have been unspeakably wicked to pray for release from this passive tyranny, and because of that she has allowed herself to be heartbroken by Julie's death. In this moment of honesty she recognises the truth.

Although she does not speak the words aloud, she articulates them inside her head. 'I'm glad that Julie is dead. Glad, glad, glad. And I'm not really sorry that Harry is dead. I'm free!' For six months already she has been revelling in her freedom, but has felt ashamed of the fact, attempting instead to think of herself as a widow in mourning. She has been honest enough not to play that part in public for long, but this is the first moment when her mind and heart are able to escape from the role. It is a brutal moment. It leaves her in a state of shock.

Neither at the time nor later does she know now long it takes for the balloon in her head to be pricked. Perhaps after all she has become faint, because she finds herself standing up with her head pressed against Jarvis's chest.

'I'm sorry, Madge, my dear; I'm sorry. I shouldn't have mentioned . . .'

Madge pulls herself away, shaking her head in a gesture which could mean either that it doesn't matter or that she doesn't wish to continue the conversation. Either way, she is probably giving a wrong impression, but this is not the time to correct it. She has something new to worry about now. Can it possibly be the case that Jarvis wishes to threaten her new freedom?

2

At four o'clock on a summer afternoon Penny fills the last gap in the stone wall which she has been repairing and takes a few steps backwards to survey her handiwork. Although she has never done anything of the kind before, she has been quick to develop a talent for dry-stone walling. Perhaps it is her training as a designer which helps her to hold in her memory the shape of a space and then quickly identify the piece of stone which will exactly fill it.

Most of the volunteers at the work camp have chosen to go out each day in pairs, so that they can divide the task and chatter companionably as they work, but Penny enjoys the silence of being alone. Somewhere below, out of sight beneath the swelling of the fell, Lake District holiday-makers in cars are sweating and fuming their way along the side of Lake Windermere in traffic jams, but in the high, fresh air Penny has seen only four hikers and half a dozen inquisitive sheep all day.

Jonathan's suggestion has provided her with exactly the kind of holiday she needed. He himself has been working on the repair of footpaths on a lower level, so that they have spent no time together during the working day, and there is no sense in which they are regarded as a couple. But she finds it comforting to know that there is someone looking out for her: someone who will save her a place at mealtimes or suggest – as he has done today – a late-afternoon walk together on the days when they are not rostered to help prepare supper.

He is due to collect her at five o'clock, so that they can start their walk from a high point. There is twenty minutes to go before she can expect him to arrive. The sun is shining, and she is just tired enough to welcome a period of relaxation, without feeling any great weariness. She makes herself comfortable on the grass and continues to stare proudly at the long stretch of wall which she has repaired in the past three days.

Staring is not the same as looking, but her attention is caught by the slightest of movements. A large spider has emerged from the section of undamaged wall with which her own construction has just linked up. It pauses for a moment in a patch of sunlight and then moves purposefully towards the new section and disappears into one of the cracks.

House-hunting! thinks Penny, smiling to herself. A new development of desirable residences. She hopes the spider will approve of her building standards.

That thought suggests others. Before long, no doubt, ants and woodlice will begin to make tentative explorations of possible new apartments. She begins to examine more closely the old section of wall, to see how many different inhabitants she can identify. In much the same way she once stared at the stones of Jonathan's walled garden; but then her interest was in texture and colour: the varied greens of mosses and lichens, the whites and greys and yellows of the rock.

Now, in contrast, her eyes are alert for movement. She registers the brief posing of a butterfly, the winged descent of a ladybird and its ploddingly determined journey of exploration. A worm which must have thought itself comfortably settled in the mud beneath a pile of fallen stones indignantly wriggles its way down towards the ground again. There must be mice around, she tells herself as she keeps very still; and although she has not been aware of many birds during the week, some will surely come in the nesting season to help themselves to the fragments of wool which the sheep have rubbed off against the edges of the stones.

Her eyes feed ideas into her mind, which rearranges them into new pictures of a life inside the wall which cannot be seen from outside. To turn these pictures into paintings would require an effort of imagination which she had not needed in her previous sketches of stones. The challenge excites her and absorbs all her concentration. She is still sitting cross-legged on the grass, staring at the wall, when she becomes conscious that Jonathan is standing behind her.

'I didn't hear you coming. Is it time for our walk, then?'

'It's time to get cleaned up for supper,' Jonathan tells her instead. 'Walking time was an hour ago. I came to collect you, but you were so deep in thought that I couldn't bear to disturb you, so I went off by myself.'

Penny looks down at her watch. Half past six! Gracious!

'Sorry,' she apologises. 'You're quite right. I was thinking. About life in the wall. There's so much going on. Come and look. I wondered whether it might make another book.'

Jonathan drops down to sit beside her. He glances at the wall, but is more interested in staring at Penny. She is aware of his gaze, but has not yet sufficiently emerged from her own train of thought to react to it.

'The thing is,' she says, thinking aloud, 'there are so many possibilities that it's difficult to choose. Because each different possibility would need to be worked up for a different sort of readership: a specific age. I mean, it could be mainly story, with pictures just as illustrations; or it could be mainly pictures, with only a few words on each page to make the pictures interesting. It could even be a book of puzzle pictures, with perhaps just a question underneath. You know: can you see what's caught in the spider's web? That sort of thing.'

Jonathan doesn't make any comment. This is not his subject. He is content to leave her to think it through without interruption. What he does do is to put his arm round her waist as they sit close together. Penny is aware of this as well, but again doesn't allow herself to be distracted. She gives a frustrated sigh.

'I do truly like this idea of producing books for children,' she tells him. 'Not necessarily always about the JCBs, though; that would be boring. I've enjoyed the summer. It's been marvellous, having something specific to do. To begin with, when Jarvis made that first offer,

171

I thought perhaps he was just being kind. Because of his wife and Clive. But he wouldn't have considered more than one if it were only for that reason. So now when he tells me they're good, I believe him, and I would like to do some more. To make it my job, in a way. But the stupid thing is, I don't actually have any contact with children at all. Except Daniel, and he's too young. I mean to say, it would be ridiculous, wouldn't it? A children's-book writer who doesn't know any children!'

She is trying to laugh, but really she is close to tears. Jonathan's arm tightens round her waist. He is trying to make her turn her head and cry on his shoulder. Although just managing to resist this, she has to delve in the pocket of her jeans for a handkerchief and blow her nose noisily.

'Do you wish you had children of your own?' he asks softly.

'Yes. Very much. We were going to. Just not straight away. It felt as though there was all the time in the world. I hadn't learned the *carpe diem* lesson: do it now; there may not be a tomorrow.'

'But there *is* a tomorrow. There's still time.'

Penny gives something between a sniff and a snort. She is still fighting this unexpected hurricane of regret.

'How old are you, Penny?'

'Thirty-two.'

'There you are, then. Not too late at all.'

'But –'

'It's not too late,' Jonathan repeats. 'The difficulty, from my point of view, is whether it's too early.'

'What do you mean?'

'I think I fell in love with you the first day I met you,' Jonathan tells her. 'You were so beautiful and so sad. I felt that I wouldn't mind being dead myself if someone like you would mourn me. Well, that didn't last long, of course. What I want now is to be alive with you for ever and ever. I want to marry you. I would have asked you months ago, but I was afraid that if I spoke too soon, while you were still in mourning for Clive, you'd push me away without even thinking about it. But now, well, if I don't say something soon, you'll sell the house, move away, forget all about me. I need you to know.'

Penny finds herself unable to speak. There is a sense in which she does know, has known for some time, what Jonathan has wanted to say; but she has not been ready to hear it. She is still not quite ready – and he is sufficiently sensitive to her feelings to recognise this.

'I'm not asking you now,' he tells her. 'To marry me, I mean. But I shall. Quite soon. I want you to think about it. Because we could have children, you and I. I'd want that. And I'd even let you have the

172

study painted dark green if you insisted.' Over the past six months he has frequently asked Penny's opinion about the decoration of his new house, but has not always accepted it. This concession on his part lightens the tension between them and he manages to grin as he scrambles to his feet and holds out both hands to lift her up.

There are limits, though, to his self-control. Penny feels herself being pulled towards him. He embraces her tightly, unable to conceal his longing; and when he kisses her, she accepts both the kiss and the embrace with gratitude and pleasure. As his lips move over her face and throat and his hands find their way beneath her work shirt to stroke her skin, she can tell how much he would like to tear away her clothing and make love to her then and there, on the springy turf: and almost with surprise Penny realises that she wants it too. But they both manage to control their feelings, pulling a little away from each other.

She finds it less easy to control her eyes, which express at the same time both doubt and delight. In the conflict between the two emotions, delight is the victor. Trembling from the intensity of Jonathan's kisses, Penny clutches his hand tightly as they walk slowly down the hill. She knows that she has answered the question which he has not yet asked. But the other question remains: is it too soon?

3

'Is it too soon?'

Candida is tempted to laugh aloud; not at her friend's question, but at the assumption that Candida herself is in any way qualified to act as a kind of agony aunt. Naturally, though, she resists the temptation. It is a hot and humid August day. Later there may be thunder, but for the moment the sun is shining and the atmosphere is heavy enough to make them both unusually lethargic. They are sitting in the garden of The Old Rectory and she can tell that Penny, who has just finished describing the events of her holiday, is serious – and anxious.

'You're the only one who can tell about your own feelings,' she answers. 'Are you really asking me what other people will think?'

Penny shakes her head. 'No. I'm not bothered about that. It's more that, yes, I know what I feel now, but shall I be ashamed of those feelings later on?'

Qualified or not, Candida realises that it is important to be decisive. For the past ten months Penny has been floating in limbo, with no job and no children to provide continuity after Clive's death, and not even any great attachment to her home. Candida has had the

173

responsibility for Daniel to concentrate her mind, but Penny has been on her own. Not everyone can cope with loneliness. Is she afraid that in marrying Jonathan she would be giving way to desperation rather than love?

Candida takes a moment to consider the couple. Because she has spent almost every Sunday for several months with Penny, she knows Jonathan well; he has frequently come to share their lunch. He has a good deal in common with Penny, for they are both interested in the shapes of things; and he also in some ways resembles Clive, especially in his love of the village in which he has chosen to live. It wouldn't be right to act as a matchmaker if the match were likely to prove unsuitable, but this one should work.

'Right,' says Candida. 'I'll tell you what I think. If you'd been unhappy with Clive, or even not particularly happy, you might think twice about marrying again. But it seems to me that it's the greatest compliment you could pay to Clive. Wanting to repeat, if you can, the happiness you had with him. You'd be sort of saying that marriage is marvellous, and it would be Clive who taught you that. He's never going to come back. One day, sooner or later, you'll want to start again, settle down with someone else. If you've met the right man already, it would be crazy to send him away. Marry Jonathan. Wait till after the first anniversary of the accident, because that's not going to be a happy day for any of us, but marry him straight away after that. And tell him now.'

'You think?'

'I'm sure.' Candida laughs. 'I'm saying what you want to hear, aren't I?'

'Yes.'

'Well, then.'

Penny shows by her smile how grateful she is for the reassurance. Then she looks quizzically at her friend.

'Doesn't the same argument apply to you?' she asks. 'You were happy with Tom? Why are you keeping Rufus at arm's length? And don't just say because of Daniel, because if Rufus doesn't mind, why should you?'

This is a trickier question. Yes, Candida loved Tom. Lying in her single bed at night, her body still aches with the memory of her love for him. Probably she could bring any further questioning to an end simply by saying that there will never be anyone else for her: but that may turn out not to be true. It is not easy to explain, without being disloyal, why she is in no hurry to rush into someone else's arms. She gives a deep sigh as she attempts to sort out her thoughts.

'When I was eighteen, the day I heard I'd got into Oxford, I felt as

174

though everything was going the way I planned. As though I could see my whole life straight ahead. And what I saw didn't include being a young wife and mother. No, sir!' Penny knows already that Daniel's arrival was unplanned, so no secrets are being revealed here. 'Having a baby pulled me into a kind of trap. A honey trap. Yes, of course I adored Tom. But it worried me when he gave up his doctorate work to support us. I thought he might regret it later.'

'And you wondered whether you might regret what happened yourself, as well?'

'I never let myself think that at the time. We would have married; we would have gone on being happy, I'm sure. But it wasn't a planned kind of happiness. So now, when I'm forced to make new plans, I don't necessarily want to take the same path. I mean maybe, one day; but not without having plenty of time to think about it. And I want always to have choices.' She is tempted to laugh as she realises how efficiently her mother's repeated admonitions have affected her: she is speaking with Mrs Brown's voice.

'One day,' says Penny, secure in her own new relationship, 'you'll fall head over heels in love again and all these plans and choices will fly out of the window.'

Candida shakes her head. 'I never really loved anyone before Tom. I'd been out on dates with boys at school, of course, but I didn't know how it felt to fall head over heels, as you say. I really couldn't see straight for a little while. Does that happen to everyone the first time?'

She pauses, because she has surprised herself by what she is revealing. She knows that the impression she makes on strangers is one of poise and self-confidence – it is something she has worked at – but she is not really at all sophisticated where relationships with men are concerned. Her strict upbringing, and the need to work hard at school if she was to earn a place at Oxford, combined to leave her still a virgin when she started at university. She has never been in love with anyone but Tom. 'Well, anyway,' she concludes, 'nothing like that can ever bowl me over again.'

'You'll want somebody –'

'Uh-uh. There's no rule that says you need to be in love with someone every day of your life, or to sleep with someone every night. Look at all the wives who have fallen out of love with their husbands but plod on because they can't get away.'

'There's a lot more to loving someone than sleeping with him,' Penny points out. 'It's the marvellous thing of having companionship, knowing that you come first with someone.'

'I'm in the opposite slot. Daniel comes first with me. We're looking at this from different sides, you and me. That doesn't mean that one choice is right and the other's wrong.'

'Your choice sounds very second-best to me.'

'It's a second choice, certainly. But then, my first choice wasn't really a choice at all. Just something that happened. In the end, looking after myself could turn out to be what's first-best. For a time. For me. But this discussion was supposed to be about you. When can I officially start to congratulate Jonathan?'

'Oh, heavens, don't say anything yet. I haven't told him . . . He hasn't asked.'

'He will. You will. I hope you'll be immensely happy. So! You'll stay on in Greater Monckton. Simply move next door. Become the Beatrix Potter of our times. And have dozens of children.'

'Two will be enough.' But the flush of pleasurable anticipation on Penny's face causes her friend to look at her sternly.

'That's not why, is it?' she asks. 'You're not grabbing at Jonathan just as a stud? Because if so . . .'

'Of course not.' Penny reacts with indignation. 'He wants a family as well. That's what's so marvellous: that we both want the same things.'

'In that case, you have my blessing, my child. Just let me know when your plans come off the secret list.'

They talk of other things. Daniel has taken his first uncertain steps, although only a mother could describe the movement as walking. Penny has been delighted by the proofs of her book, which is to be published in October, ready for Christmas – and Candida, in her new role as acting rights manager for the Elliott Press, is trying hard to interest foreign publishers in this particular book.

The future holds excitements for them both, and it is perhaps a natural progression in her train of thought that Candida should wonder aloud how Helen and Madge are getting on.

'Oh, Madge is on Cloud Nine,' Penny tells her. 'She got to Leamington this year.'

'What do you mean, got to Leamington?' The distance from the Moncktons to Leamington is not so great as to make a journey between the two any great achievement.

'It's apparently what every woman who plays bowls in England longs to do. I don't know exactly the details, but Madge won some competition for all the bowlers in the county, and that entitled her to go and play against the women who'd won in *their* counties to see who would become the national champion.'

'So is she the national champion?'

'Heavens, no. Knocked out in the first round once she got into the big league. But she didn't seem to mind that at all. It was the getting to Leamington that was the big thing. No one from the Lower Monckton club has ever done it before, apparently. They put up a poster, wishing her luck. It sounds as though she's come out of her shell in a big way. I didn't really know her terribly well before, in spite of living so near. She seemed a rather mousy sort of woman.'

'My impression too. Though I should point out that mice don't live in shells.' Candida pauses to consider Madge's situation. 'Jarvis talks about her a lot at the office, as a matter of fact. In an odd sort of way. I mean, if we're discussing that cookery book that he got her to test for, that's natural. But he sort of brings her name into other conversations, if you know what I mean. The excuse is that she's a friend of mine, but he must know that she isn't really. I think he's quite keen on her.'

'Well, maybe he's looking for a cook, just as you accused me of looking for a stud.'

'I didn't.' But her friend's grin shows that the accusation is not serious. 'So what about Mrs Cunningham?' To Candida, Helen Cunningham is still the boss's wife, to be spoken of with respect.

'She's practically a next-door neighbour now. Moved into one of The Manor flats just before I went on holiday. I told you, didn't I, that I saw her a few weeks ago, while she was measuring up in the flat, and she seemed like a different woman? As though she'd come to terms with things after looking terrible and behaving like a recluse for the first six months or so. Why don't we go and call on her? Welcome her to Greater Monckton.'

It's a good excuse for a stroll. Candida dries and dresses Daniel, who has been splashing happily in the little paddling pool which Penny gave him for his first birthday. Together they make their way through the park which was once part of The Manor's grounds. The retirement bungalows are up to roof-height by now, but the site is a mess of bricks and skips, concrete mixers and piles of sand. By contrast, the gardens which surround The Manor are immaculate.

Helen's flat is immaculate as well, although rather overcrowded with furniture and pictures. She herself is equally neat in her appearance, and her pleasure in greeting the unexpected visitors and showing them round the flat suggests that she was feeling bored before they arrived. But in spite of what Penny has earlier suggested, it seems to Candida that this is still an unhappy woman.

A casual remark of Penny's elicits an explanation for their hostess's depressed mood.

'How marvellously you've managed to get everything into its right

177

place in such a short time! Most people who move are still living in chaos three months later.'

'I haven't got everything in,' says Helen. 'Not Michael.'

There is an embarrassed silence. Candida and Penny agreed many months before that one of the worst aspects of bereavement was that other people hated talking about it. They vowed that they would each be prepared to talk and listen to each other, in sad moments as well as happy ones. But they are not on such terms with this older woman. They feel awkward at the thought that she is about to break down in front of them – and ashamed of their awkwardness.

Helen spares them that. She explains what she means in a normal tone of voice.

'I found it disconcerting sometimes, while I was still in Monckton Hall, coming face to face with Michael unexpectedly. Have you ever had that feeling? I mean, obviously not really, and I'm not talking about ghosts. But going into a room and suddenly being convinced that he was there with me. It was upsetting and comforting at the same time. Mostly comforting, though. We'd shared our home and our lives for so long, and he was still part of them. But here, in this flat, where he's never been – well, he's not here any more, and I hadn't expected that. Sometimes I wonder if I'll start to forget even what he looked like.' Her eyes flood with tears as she turns her head to stare at the row of photographs arranged along the top of a bureau. 'Perhaps I shall find myself remembering only a photographic image, and not a real person at all. Oh, well. You didn't come here to talk about that. Let me make you some tea. What would little Daniel like?'

'He'd love a biscuit. Thank you.' The visit becomes an ordinary social occasion, but the two younger women are sobered by the encounter. As they walk back later across the park, Penny speaks aloud the question which is in both their minds.

'Which is worse, do you think: to lose your future or to lose your past?'

'That's not the right question,' Candida tells her. 'We all four of us – no, I mean all five – lost our expected futures. Mrs Cunningham just as much as you or me. The difference lies in how long the future is in terms of years. You and I have got to make new plans and take action just because there are so many years to fill. But she hasn't got so long.' To Candida, as to Helen herself, sixty-one is old. 'It probably doesn't seem worth doing anything at all.'

'Is there anything we can do to help her, do you think?'

This is a question which Candida has had to consider once: when Rufus, in May, so unexpectedly appealed to her on Helen's behalf.

'That was something I wondered about a little while ago. But then you told me that something seemed to have happened to perk her up, so I put it out of my mind.'

'Yes, there was a change. There still is. She's not depressed in exactly the same way as before, when she seemed to have made herself ill with it. But she does seem terribly bored. Do you think there is some way in which we could help, then?'

Candida takes her time about answering. Jarvis will tell her she is being a fool. And she is under no obligation to help Helen, who is almost a stranger – and who is comfortably off, with no material needs. But today's visit has introduced her to a woman with a different need.

'Yes,' she says slowly. 'I think perhaps there is.'

4

Selling a house, buying a flat, disposing of furniture, moving in, getting things straight: all this activity has kept Helen busy. There was no time between May and August to sit around feeling depressed – and the discovery of Michael's diary and his appointments with the unknown D enabled her to put her feelings of guilt behind her. But by now all the business of moving is over, leaving her at a loss to know how to fill her days.

She has rejoined the bridge club, but limits herself to one session a week. In the days when she was married and busily occupied she used to feel sorry for what Derek privately describes as the Old Trouts Brigade, who turn up every day because they have nothing else to do: she is determined not to become one of their number.

What else? Once a week she writes to Lucy. There is a little gardening to be done on her terrace, and she takes care of her own housework – but once the flat has been furnished and tidied after the move, not much cleaning seems necessary. She makes the reading of a daily newspaper last longer than it deserves, and attempts some of the easier crosswords. She searches the television channels for something of interest, but has yet to discover any comedy which makes her smile. Almost in desperation, attempting to add some structure to her week, she allows herself to become a regular viewer of one of the soaps – but despises herself for it even as she switches on.

Only one activity has the power to penetrate her apathy. She has started to read the *Investors Chronicle* and, in addition, takes the *Financial Times* every Saturday now. She checks the prices of shares which she already owns and others in which she is interested; she reads comments and advice and makes notes, working out ways in which to improve her portfolio as earnestly as though it is a way of earning a living. It is only a third of the way through the tax year, but already she has reached the ridiculously low limit of tax-free gains; from now on every sale and reinvestment must promise a profit after taking into account the forty per cent levy on her gain. It is a challenge.

Planning her gambles adds spice to each Saturday, but Sundays are dull: boredom descends again. She goes to church on the one Sunday in three when the vicar holds a service in Greater Monckton, but out of a sense of duty rather than faith: she is, after all, one-sixth of the lady of the manor. So on the Sunday afternoon when Candida Brown and Penny Martin pay their unexpected visit, it gives her real pleasure to have their company for an hour.

After they have left, however, she finds herself more depressed than before. She ought not to have talked about missing Michael. They won't call on her again if they fear being exposed to her unhappiness. It's one of the lessons she has already learned: that a widow who wants company must learn to keep smiling.

There is something else as well. They are young. Although each of them has lost the man she loved, it is easy to tell that they are beginning to recover. They have their eyes on the future; they are making plans. It is all very natural, but it makes Helen particularly conscious that her own future holds nothing good. Just endless repetitions of what is not particularly interesting to start with. Even the artificial excitement of making profits from her switches of investment is tainted by the realisation that she doesn't really need any more money.

Prowling restlessly around the drawing room after she has cleared away the tea things, she stares for a second time that afternoon at the row of photographs. They are mostly of Michael and Lucy and the boys, but she is there herself as well, on her wedding day. Tall, slender and handsome, and radiant with happiness at the promise of a future in which nothing bad, surely, will ever happen. No bride ever thinks about the day when she will find herself a widow.

Candida and Penny are both good-looking and intelligent. As soon as they begin once more to send out the signals which indicate that they are ready to be loved again, lovers will come. There will never be another lover for Helen, because she doesn't want one. But what is there to look forward to, if not that?

If looking into the future reveals only emptiness, considering the past is not much better. What has she managed to achieve in her life? As a bookkeeper, forty years earlier, she had her uses, and in

Purefrew's early days she provided considerable practical help to Michael – but even that contribution ended more than thirty years ago. She has successfully brought up a child; but Lucy doesn't need her any longer. She has looked after Michael, but even before his death he had ceased to be a lover and now he is gone completely.

She opens a bottle of wine, without bothering to prepare any food to go with it. As she sips it throughout an empty evening she can feel herself sliding back into the wretchedness from which she thought she had escaped. Her earlier bout of depression was caused as much by guilt as by the sadness of bereavement, and she has believed this to be successfully banished by the discovery that Michael was guilty as well. This new depression is far worse, because it has no neat cause. Except one: that she is no longer young. From now on she will be doing nothing but kill time. What's the point?

At nine o'clock she abandons the battle to cheer herself up and goes to bed. Perhaps sleep will smother her melancholy. But sleep refuses to come at such an early hour. At ten o'clock she gets out of bed and searches the bathroom cabinet for the sleeping pills which her doctor prescribed several months earlier but which she ceased to need after she read Michael's diary. She takes two and settles back into bed.

They are slow to work. As she slides into a comfortable state of drowsiness, her unhappiness does indeed slide away – to be replaced by a new thought. A new day has nothing to offer her. How much simpler it will be if she never wakes up. No one will miss her. She is not an essential part of anyone's life. Why hang around for all the tedious and inevitable processes of illness and dying? Get it over with now.

In an odd way this presents itself to her not as an escape but as a positive course of action. She is taking her future into her own hands, and it is her own decision that it should be the shortest possible future. She swallows the last seven tablets which remain in the bottle.

Almost immediately a new thought occurs to her. Probably her doctor would have been careful to avoid prescribing to a depressed patient anything which might be lethal on its own. Hasn't she read somewhere that it's the addition of alcohol that is the real killer? With her eyes almost closed, she gropes her way to the drinks cupboard in the dining room and pours a large glass of whisky. Getting it all down is an effort, but at last she settles back into bed: not frightened, but at peace.

There is no one to awaken her next morning: no one to notice her absence from anything. It is two o'clock in the afternoon when Helen opens her eyes to find herself lying in a mess of vomit. So disgusting is the smell and the sliminess of it that she is promptly sick again. Staggering to the bathroom, she washes her hair and scrubs her body clean under the shower, but the bedroom mess remains.

Fighting nausea, she strips the bed, putting the duvet into the bath while she feeds sheets into the washing machine. Monckton Hall had its own separate laundry room, but here she is forced to use the kitchen and before long the whole flat is stinking. Luckily it is a hot day. Helen opens all the windows. This turns out to be a mistake, for at four o'clock one of the other Manor residents calls her name through the French windows which lead to the drawing room and steps inside before waiting for an answer.

Helen is still wearing the towelling robe that she put on after her shower. Her damp hair hangs limply round her shoulders. She knows that she looks pale and ill, and the smell still pervades every room in the flat.

'Oh, my dear!' exclaims her unwanted visitor. 'What happened?'

'Food poisoning. All right now.'

'But you must let Dr Hardie see you.' There is only one doctor in the Moncktons.

'Not necessary, thank you very much.'

'But really, yes. These things can be very serious. Why don't I ring him for you, while you go back to bed?'

'No, thank you. I really don't –'

But Mrs Mullens, damn her, has hurried off to do her mischief. Dr Hardie will come and ask questions, do tests, take specimens. Meanwhile Mrs Mullens will be gossiping, no doubt voicing suspicions which come near to the truth. In the hothouse of the Moncktons, everyone will soon guess what has happened. Shivering with cold in spite of the sunshine which is flooding into her drawing room, Helen sits down to think.

At his kindest, Dr Hardie may assume that she has been making a gesture: a cry for help. She can beat him on that one by acting the part of a cheerful woman who is not in need of help. Almost without noticing it Helen straightens her back and begins to breathe deeply to stiffen her resolve.

It will not be entirely an act. She has already decided that nothing like this is going to happen again, ever. The temptation to sleep and never wake was a great one, but her decision was not premeditated: it was made with a mind already confused by drowsiness. If there was any coherence at all in her thoughts as she drifted into unconsciousness, the picture she had of her own dead self was of a

182

peaceful, dignified figure lying between clean sheets in an immaculate flat. She knows now that it would not have been like that.

Helen is a fastidious woman. It may be the ultimate vanity to worry about one's deathbed appearance, but in that case she is vain. Under no circumstances will she ever succumb to such weakness again. It is a turning point in her life.

How long has she got? Two hours, probably, since Dr Hardie has a surgery from four until six. Defying her weakness she sets to work. By six o'clock the sheets and underblanket are tumble-dried and in the airing cupboard, the duvet has been soaked and scraped until there is nothing left which can be placed in a test tube, and the mattress has been shampooed. Helen has dried her hair and put it up, has applied slightly more make-up than usual and is wearing a linen jacket and skirt in which she looks neat and cool. The flat smells of air freshener, but that is the only giveaway.

When Dr Hardie arrives at half past six she expresses surprise that he has been called and admits to drinking perhaps slightly too much whisky on a stomach unsettled by some roast pork which she suspected even at the time and by now has thrown away. She is the same calm, dignified woman whom he has known for most of her years at Monckton Hall, and even his sympathy cannot break her story. That will not, of course, check the gossip which is probably already doing the rounds.

Before she goes to bed that night she has summoned all the strength of her character to bolster the earlier influences of vanity and disgust. Never again will she allow herself to slip into a death wish of depression. There are millions of people all over the world who are starving or who have seen their families massacred in front of their eyes. How different is her own condition. She is comfortably off and well fed: she has a daughter, grandchildren and friends. All she needs is a little courage, a little humour. To construct a new life for herself requires only an act of will; and she has the will.

It is remarkable how cheerful she suddenly feels; as though she needed to sink to the very bottom of a slough of despond before she could draw on the energy to fight her way out. It's over now: behind her for ever. Nodding her head in determination, she makes a second resolution. She needs to develop some kind of ambition. It doesn't matter what it is. An Open University degree, first prize in a flower-arranging competition, a resolve to master the art of portrait painting: anything will do. She allows herself three weeks to think of some activity in which success would actually give her pleasure – and discovers that the exploration of possibilities is in itself enough to raise her spirits.

5

Only a few days of the three weeks have passed when there is a phone call from Penny Martin to ask whether she and Candida may call again. Something in Penny's voice tells Helen that she has heard the gossip and has believed it. It may be because she has shared all the griefs of bereavement that she feels in a better position than most people to offer comfort.

Helen is no longer in need of comfort. By an act of will she has removed herself from the temptation of giving in. But in spite of that – or perhaps because of it – she looks forward to the small excitement of the Sunday visit.

After the preliminary chat is over, it is Candida who comes to the purpose of the visit.

'Rufus Grant came to see me a little while ago. He said you were thinking of selling Purefrew.'

'I'd like to, yes. But nobody seems to want it.'

'I had the impression from Rufus that one reason why Wright and King pulled out last year was that they'd been hoping to acquire the rights to what was called Formula Four, but they didn't want to develop the process themselves.'

Helen knows something about Formula Four, of course, but she has never tasted it. She has assumed that the formula was lost with Tom – or rather, she has hardly given the matter sufficient thought to assume anything at all. Now she looks at Candida with interest.

'Are you telling me that you know how to make it?'

'I'm the *only* one who knows how to make it. Mrs Cunningham, before we go any further, talking about trade secrets, I have to say formally that anything Penny and I tell you now will be in strict confidence.'

'Yes, of course.' Helen is still not clear what all this is about, but she is intrigued.

'Perhaps you'd like to taste it.' Candida takes a vacuum jug out of her large shoulder bag. 'This batch is freshly made this year and so it's the same as the samples Tom was offering around a year ago. Since then, actually, I've turned some of last year's batch into wine, but it tastes quite different, so I thought it would only complicate matters to bring that along as well.'

Helen fetches glasses so that they can all drink together. The first sip makes it easy to understand Michael's enthusiasm for the possibilities. The cool drink is instantly refreshing, with a tang which seems to clear her head. Draining the glass, she holds it out for a second helping.

'It's very more-ish, isn't it?' Penny agrees. As she speaks, she zips open a flat briefcase which she has been carrying and lays a set of designs on the table. 'This is how I thought it might look. In still and carbonated versions. Phitta and Phizz. I've taken out protection for a handful of trademark names, but those two seem the best.'

'That's very businesslike of you.' Helen studies the male and female shapes and listens as Penny explains how she hopes that it may be possible to pinch-seal them at the waist.

'Penny's real stroke of genius, in my opinion, is the different little heads,' Candida tells her enthusiastically. 'You could make a marvellous promotion out of them. You know, like a prize for anyone who gets a full set, but one variety would be terribly rare.'

'So what precisely have you in mind?' Helen asks. Again, it is Candida who acts as spokeswoman.

'Rufus's suggestion was that we should start up a company of our own. Penny and me and Madge and you – and, I suppose, Rufus himself as well. Well, Penny and I have discussed that, and it isn't what we want to do. But you own a business already. The right sort of business. You could take this over if you wanted to, just as your husband would have taken it over from Tom if . . . Well, you know.'

'But you would want to be part of it, surely? From the financial point of view, if nothing else.'

Penny has not yet contributed anything to the discussion except her drawings, but now she speaks to make it clear that she and Candida are in agreement.

'You, or your company, would have to invest a great deal of money before you got anything back,' she points out. 'It seems only fair that you should get most of the profit. The only reason for you to do it would be to make your fortune. What we'd ask each would be just a royalty: a tiny amount for every bottle sold. To Candida for the recipe and to me for the design. And we wouldn't expect anything at all until the first bottle was sold, so that would be one overhead you wouldn't have to worry about.'

'But if nothing came of it, you wouldn't get a penny.'

'It wouldn't have cost us anything, either,' Candida reminds her. 'We don't want to be bothered. It's as simple as that. You may not want to be bothered either. The idea's on offer if you want it, that's all. And I'm sure Rufus would be delighted to help if you asked him.'

'Rufus's original advice to Michael was that Purefrew was too small and undercapitalised to launch a new product on its own,' Helen remembers; and Candida nods in agreement.

'But you could work it up to the state it was at before,' she points out. 'In the hope that Wright and King would reopen negotiations. And if you took it just a bit further, you would probably get an even better deal for the company: not just a straight buy-out, but a proportion of the Formula Four profits as well.'

'You've taken my breath away!' Helen exclaims. That is so near to the truth that she feels unable to react immediately. 'Now that we've enjoyed your aperitif, how about some ordinary tea?' On this occasion, since she has had warning of their arrival, she has made one of the fresh raspberry and cream sponge cakes which Lucy always used to love. Only after she has handed round teacups does she ask the most important of the questions which Candida and Penny must be expecting.

'Since we're still talking confidentially, are you able to tell me what Phitta's main ingredient is? Is it something that is easily available?'

'It certainly is.' Candida laughs reassuringly. 'Local and cheap. Do you remember what the main crop was when you came to visit me in the Orchard Farm stable last year?'

Helen frowns as she tries to recall the scene. 'I can't remember anything except frost-blackened nettles,' she confesses.

'Well, that's it. Not left for the frost, but picked in the spring when the leaves are fresh and tender.'

'Nettles!'

'Nettles. There never seems to be any shortage, and if you went in for this in a big way you might find that farmers would be allowed to let them grow as part of the set-aside scheme. And something else that Tom was going to explore was the possibility of using the stems afterwards to make some kind of fibre, as a by-product. But I don't know anything about that. We don't expect you to make any comment now, Mrs Cunningham. You'll want to think about it. You may be happy just to let Purefrew jog along as it is. The financial rewards of developing something new would probably be more for your grandsons than yourself. This would be a sort of gamble, really, and you may not be that sort of person.'

They talk of other things: local village matters and Candida's job and the slow progress of the compensation claim. Only after her visitors have left does Helen sit down to consider their unexpected offer.

It is the word 'gamble' that has caught her interest. She is not a true gambler. She doesn't bet on horse races or football matches or Booker prizewinners. Although her recent interest in stocks and shares involves her in the possibility of losing money, she is careful never to stake more than she can afford to lose. In other words, she is not taking genuine risks – but nevertheless she likes to think of herself as someone who does not always play safe. That attitude is what in the past prompted her little adventures, her infidelities; nowadays she has realised that it is safer to play with money than with men.

What Candida has suggested would require a much higher stake and involve a real risk of loss – but it is all the more exciting for that. She thinks for a moment about her two grandsons and the pleasure it would give her to bequeath them a fortune. But Larry and Vince are the sons of a highly paid lawyer. She can't pretend to herself that she would be offering them a rags-to-riches transformation. No, if she decides to take up Formula Four, it will have to be because she is prepared to devote time and money to it for her own pleasure.

Why not? she asks herself. Time and money are what she has. She can stake them and still not be seriously at risk of either poverty or stress: it is a gamble only in the limited sense to which she has always confined herself.

And the rewards of success would not be only financial. Hasn't she just determined that she must set herself a goal and become single-minded in her ambition to achieve it? What could be better than the goal of making a fortune? Even to attempt it will be good for Purefrew, because she knows that her new, young managing director is a high-flyer. If she doesn't soon offer him a worthwhile target, he will leave to find one elsewhere.

Filled with new energy, she pulls from a drawer in her bureau the most up-to-date set of the Purefrew accounts as well as the valuation of her own assets. Although so many years have passed since she last made use of her bookkeeping skills, she is at home with numbers. From now on, she promises herself as she begins to scribble notes, she will take her responsibilities as chairwoman and owner of the company more seriously. It will be a pleasure.

It is hard to believe that only six days have passed since she allowed herself, almost without thinking, to give up on a life which had nothing further to offer her. She has not in fact needed the whole six days to change her attitude: a single moment of decision was enough. But now she must be grateful to Penny and Candida, who have undoubtedly heard enough local rumour to guess what happened and have found a perfect way to help her.

She has been offered exactly what she wanted: a genuine choice between achieving a goal or passing her remaining years in continuing lethargy. There is no contest. The choice was made before it was offered. And to put a new product on the market will be – well, fun.

Because after all, she thinks to herself as she makes up her mind, I'm only sixty-one.

6

In the darkness of a September evening Madge listens to Peter as he comes to the end of his evening's poetry reading – or rather, recital, for although the book lies open on his lap he cannot possibly see the words.

'Yet if you should forget me for a while
And afterwards remember, do not grieve:
For if the darkness and corruption leave
A vestige of the thoughts that once I had,
Better by far you should forget and smile
Than that you should remember and be sad.'

It was with one of Christina Rossetti's poems that Peter, nine months earlier, came into her life. Now, with another, he is leaving it. She knows that even before she asks the question.

'You're going?'

'Yes. But not, of course, into darkness and corruption.' She can hear his smile, although not see it. 'My book's finished. And I've been offered an appointment at an American college which special- ises in international affairs. I shall spend part of my time teaching and the rest of it bringing myself up to date in everything that happened while I was a prisoner. At the end of the year, I hope to have a choice between academic life and a return to journalism. Not necessarily in England.'

'I'm glad,' Madge tells him. 'About your job, I mean.'

'I've been trying all day to think of some way in which I can repay you. The debt I owe you is so immense that there's no sort of bread- and-butter letter or thank-you present that would come anywhere near being appropriate.'

'Debts cancel out,' Madge tells him cheerfully. 'If it hadn't been for you I should have been a stick insect by now. I'm glad we were able to help each other.'

That should be the end of the exchange, but it seems that Peter has after all thought of a thank-you present.

'The college I'm going to is near Boston,' he tells her. 'Give me a couple of weeks to get myself sorted out, and then I want you to come out and join me for a holiday. New England in the fall: all the marvellous autumn colours of the trees. We'll hire a car and drive all round. Will you do that?'

Madge is taken aback by the unexpectedness of the invitation –
and her first reaction is equally unexpected.

'I wonder whether I'm the only woman left in England who's
never yet been in an aeroplane!'

'You've never been abroad?'

'Oh, yes. But only by rail. As part of my training I spent six
months working in a restaurant in France. And had holidays there
later as well. But after I met Harry . . .'

Harry would never go abroad. Madge suspects that it was because
he spoke no foreign language. Her own fluent French would have
made it easy to organise a honeymoon in France, but that would have
deprived Harry of control, leaving him struggling to check timetables
or room rates or restaurant menus. At the time she sympathised with
the wish of a new husband to take charge of all the arrangements for
his bride – without realising that this was to set the pattern for the rest
of their marriage.

After Julie was born they were unable to take any holidays at all at
first, and when at last they were offered respite care for two weeks
every year, Harry claimed that they must never be too far from home
in case there was an emergency.

'I suppose I could have gone somewhere this summer,' Madge
says now. The thought has only just occurred to her. 'But I wanted to
play bowls.'

'Your season will be over in a fortnight's time. You can't use that
as an excuse. I shall write with a proper invitation as soon as I know
what's what. It depends on the time of the first frosts, but I'm told
that leaf-peeking time in Massachusetts starts round about 16
October.'

He stands up and moves towards the door. Since the first handshake with which he introduced himself in the dining room of
Cossets nine months earlier, they have never touched each other,
except accidentally. Certainly they have never kissed, and they do not
kiss now.

'I'll be gone before you get up in the morning,' he tells her.
'Leaving behind me my heartfelt thanks, dear Madge, for all you've
done. "Remember me when I am gone away."'

He is quoting, for a second time, the first line of the Rossetti poem.
But after the door closes behind him, leaving her alone in the darkness, it is the last two lines which Madge repeats aloud to herself.

'Better by far you should forget and smile
Than that you should remember and be sad.'

If what Peter calls the leaf-peeking starts on 16 October, she would
still be in New England on the anniversary of Harry's death. Would

189

it be right for her to be enjoying a holiday on a day which should be devoted to sadness and mourning?

Pushing that question to the back of her mind, she thinks instead about Peter. She has always known that he would leave as soon as he was fully recovered, so there can be no sadness there. She herself has helped him back to physical health and the remembrance and recording of his experiences have cleared his mind and given him the mental strength to take up his life again. She is glad for him, and not sorry for herself. One of the lessons his visit has taught her is that it is possible for two adults to live together without either needing to dominate the other, and in an odd way that will give her the confidence to live alone. There are no regrets of her own to spoil her pleasure in his new life, even though he has chosen to rebuild it in a distant country.

So she feels no loneliness next morning as she eats breakfast alone. Besides, Jarvis is coming for the day. No doubt Peter remembered that when he decided on the time of his departure.

It is amusing to notice the speed with which Jarvis recognises that something has changed, and to discover what it is. He has the sensitivity to other people's feelings that goes with an unselfish nature.

'Will you go?' he asks, when she tells him of Peter's invitation.

'No.' Lying in bed, she has had time to think about it. 'I didn't want to hurt his feelings by saying that on the spot. It was exactly the right thing for him to offer me; but turning it down is exactly the right thing as well. He'll be starting a new job. And he isn't really back into social living yet: he's bound to find it a strain, being part of a community. I'd only be a distraction. Besides, I'm going to take on the catering at the indoor bowls club for the winter season, to see how it goes, and that will start on 1 October. Peter knows I want to get back to work again. He'll understand.'

'I'm not sure that I do,' Jarvis says. 'Why do you want to tie yourself down to village life now that you're free to choose where you could live?'

'I have chosen. This is my choice.'

'But you're a city person.'

Madge shakes her head laughingly, realising that over the past few months she has given a wrong impression of herself. Because she is reluctant to talk too much about her life with Harry and Julie, she has probably moved too far in the opposite direction: asking Jarvis about his work and about life in London and matching his comments with happy memories of the years when she worked in the metropolis herself. But that was a long time ago, and probably much of the happiness was simply the result of being young. That's not some-

190

thing which can ever be recaptured. If she were to return now she would find the pace too fast and the atmosphere too noisy.

'I was once,' she agreed. 'But I've lived in the Moncktons for more than twenty years. If I'm going to build a new life for myself, this is where the foundations are set. I thought we might have a picnic today, since the sun's shining.'

The change of subject is to remind him that their plans for the day include a drive to a craft fair. One of Jarvis's authors has taken a stall for the pictures and greeting cards she makes out of dried flowers and he has supplied her with extra copies of her book to put on sale there. Since he has developed quite a strong list of illustrated craft books, it is worth investigating these fairs as possible regular sales points.

Later that day, however, after they have returned to College Farm, Madge finds herself once again being indirectly interrogated on the subject of her relationship with Peter. It is clear that Jarvis is hoping for reassurance on a subject which should never even have occurred to him.

'For heaven's sake!' she expostulates. 'You surely don't think that he was my toy boy?'

'I'm sorry.' Jarvis looks geninuely hangdog. 'It's impertinent of me even to wonder . . . But I *do* wonder. After being married for so long, Madge, don't you miss sex?'

Madge is taken aback by the frankness of the question. But presumably what he is really saying is that he himself is suffering in that regard since Pamela's death. So instead of suggesting that this is her private affair, she takes a moment to think.

Although it is so long ago, she still remembers vividly – perhaps because the period was so short and self-contained – the pleasures and excitements of her honeymoon and the few months which followed. Harry was a passionate lover, and her own passion matched his. Because they wanted to have a family, they were able to make love without anxiety. For a while.

After Julie's birth, everything changed. As soon as they realised the extent of their future commitment as parents, it was agreed between them that they would have no more children. They discussed respectively both vasectomy and sterilisation with their doctor. But Julie might die young, he told them. They might find that it was not too late . . . And so almost overnight their lovemaking ceased to be spontaneous. It was an expected time on an expected day of the week and Madge was driven almost to screaming point by the knowledge that Harry would use precisely the same phrase on every occasion to check that all contraceptive procedures had been followed. He was a belt-and-braces man who would neither leave

191

everything to her nor trust his own precautions entirely. What should have been an eagerly anticipated pleasure become a wifely duty. To be enjoyed while it lasted, certainly, but . . . No; it is not something she misses.

She has been silent for too long while she first of all works out what is a truthful answer and then decides not to give it. Jarvis can't wait any longer.

'I shouldn't have asked that question. I don't want to know. What I really want is something quite different. I want you. Will you, Madge? Now? Oh, Madge!'

Madge's eyes open wide in astonishment but she is given no time to reply. Jarvis is holding her, kissing her, pushing her back on the sofa, pressing his body against her, rolling off on to the floor with her, pulling at her clothes. What is going on? People in their fifties don't behave like this on the drawing-room carpet at five o'clock in the afternoon. But it seems that they do; and very nice it is too.

'Should I say I'm sorry?' asks Jarvis afterwards, his clothes in a jumble around him.

'Of course not. I should say thank you.' But that's not quite right either. As they continue to lie in each other's arms on the floor, with Jarvis's lips pressing lightly against her neck, Madge thinks the situation through. Excited and happy about what has just happened, she is nevertheless sufficiently clear in her mind to guess what will happen next and to decide on her reaction.

It turns out very much as she expects. Showered and tidy again, they have supper together in the kitchen. She is making coffee when Jarvis puts his first question.

'May I stay the night?'

'Yes. I'd like you to.' She smiles as she sets the cafetière down on the table between them and takes the hand which he stretches towards her.

'I want something more, as well. Will you marry me, Madge?'

'No, not that. I'm sorry, but I don't want to marry again. That's got nothing to do with you personally, Jarvis.'

Only the first of these two statements is accurate. It is true that over the past few months she has come to realise that marriage for her has been a form of imprisonment, and she is not prepared to surrender her new freedom so soon. But more particular in this case is the knowledge that she is not the right wife for Jarvis. He is a lonely man, looking for comfort, love and sex, and for the moment he can enjoy all these things in her company. But sooner or later he will encounter someone more suitable to be his second wife among his own circle.

When that time comes, he will find Madge ready to retreat from a love affair into a calmer friendship. She has already helped Peter, who was starved of food, back into normal life, and has said good-bye without a tear. Jarvis's starvation is of a different kind, but she can help him too.

For the moment he looks disappointed, but Madge smiles at him so cheerfully that he is forced to laugh. Probably he feels confident that he will be able to change her mind eventually. Still holding her hand as he stands up, he pulls her towards him again.

'I don't think I want coffee after all,' he tells her. 'May we leave the washing-up and go straight to bed?'

Chapter Ten

1

It is six o'clock on a January evening. Mr and Mrs Jonathan Verne are upstairs, changing out of their wedding clothes, while in Jonathan's drawing room the party buzz is beginning to quieten. The reception guests have ceased to circulate and have converged in small groups – village people, Penny's agency friends, family – to chat in desultory fashion as they wait.

Helen and Candida, Jarvis and Madge form one of these small groups. Rufus is not with them. Penny has met the young lawyer only two or three times, to discuss Clive's funeral arrangements or the progress of the compensation claim. That is business: she doesn't think of him as a personal friend, to be sent an invitation in his own right. All the same, she made it very clear that Candida's invitation was to be regarded as a double one, so that her friend could come with any companion she liked. Candida has chosen to ignore this hint. She doesn't want to be part of a couple. Instead, she chats with animation to the three people whom she has come to know so well over the past fifteen months.

Part of Madge's attention is elsewhere, listening for the quiet sounds of crockery and glasses being stacked and removed from the buffet table in the dining room. When Penny married Clive, four years earlier, all the contemporary social rituals were in place: the white dress, the marquee, the three-course meal, the dance floor, the professional photographer, the risqué speeches and embarrassing toasts, the cutting of the cake. Today's ceremony, by contrast, has been a small village affair, and Madge has been responsible for the modest catering.

Because she is a guest as well as the organiser, she has hired two

194

of her neighbours as assistants for the afternoon. Word has been quick to spread around the Moncktons that there is a little pin money to be earned by women who are not able to undertake full-time work, and Madge is becoming popular. This is just as well, since it takes the sting out of the gossip inevitably caused by the frequency of Jarvis's weekend visits.

Helen is as well aware as any of her neighbours of what is going on at College Farm. In view of her own past adventures she is in no position to criticise, but she is certainly surprised. Even in her best wedding clothes, Madge is hardly a glamorous figure. Although she has thrown off the starved look of a year earlier, she has always been far too thin: no breasts, no hips, no curves at all. Her grey hair is neatly cut, but she makes no attempt to improve her appearance with make-up. Yet her eyes are bright and her expression is vivacious and Jarvis is presumably lonely and finding it difficult to stand alone as far as his private life is concerned.

That is something Helen herself has managed. Certainly she is lonely. She misses her evening chats with Michael and she has become extremely conscious over the past year how much of ordinary social life is geared to couples. Invitations to dinner arrive only rarely nowadays, even from people she has regularly entertained over a long period. But she is learning to accept that particular kind of loneliness. There are other ways to fill her days and evenings, and she makes it a rule that there must be at least one entry under every date in her diary, even if it is for nothing more than a favourite television programme. The important thing is that there should be something to look forward to every day.

Much of her success in achieving this is thanks to Candida. Helen has thrown herself wholeheartedly behind the decision to investigate the possibilities of Formula Four. After applying her rusty book-keeping skills to an examination of Purefrew's accounts, she has drawn up a budget for future research and development. Enough nettle-bearing land has been discovered and reserved to allow for the making of a generous trial batch. The leaves will not be ready for harvest until May, but in the meantime she has secured the enthusiastic support of the new managing director and has found a graduate scientist – even younger than Tom Harding – who is prepared to offer occasional hours of work in order to finance his studies. Already he has analysed samples of Candida's previous brew and expressed approval; small flasks of the liquid are even now being exposed to heat and cold and different kinds of contamination to see how it may be affected. There is a feeling of excitement at Purefrew these days, and Helen, as she takes the chair at the monthly board meetings, shares in it.

And so she has successfully thrown off the guilt and depression which for so long caused her to neglect her appearance and take no interest in the future. Her long white hair is neatly dressed into a French pleat beneath a large and expensive hat. For the ceremony in the church she was not ashamed to wear the mink coat which Michael gave her on their twenty-fifth wedding anniversary, but by now this has been discarded to reveal a black and white silk suit. Her figure is good and in the way she holds herself she expresses a self-confidence which reflects something more important than merely the knowledge that she is correctly dressed for the occasion. Like Madge, she has learned to make the best of a situation which she would never have chosen.

Candida, standing beside her, is just as tall as Helen. Her posture is even straighter and her figure much slimmer; she has no need of expensive clothes. Her natural elegance attracts the eye of everyone in the room, but she is unconscious of this as she talks to Jarvis. Although the two of them now meet on every working day, they both enjoy the different kind of conversation which becomes possible on a social occasion. Jarvis recognises that if it had not been for Candida's visit he would never have met Madge, and his gratitude is especially warm at moments like this, when he is holding Madge's hand.

And now Penny comes running down the stairs, ready to leave for what is to be a skiing honeymoon. She moves quickly round the room, kissing her friends as she thanks them for coming and says goodbye. She leaves Candida until the last, and the two young women draw a little apart from the others as they embrace and then move together towards the front door.

'You look beautiful,' says Candida simply, and the compliment is true. Penny has always been good-looking, but the shock of bereavement and her slow struggle back to happiness have added a new maturity to her earlier prettiness. Jonathan is a lucky man; and Jonathan's children will be lucky children as well.

'If I had a bouquet, you're the one I'd throw it to,' Penny replies, smiling. 'Don't spend too long on your own, Candy. Remember how marvellous it is to be loved; to be the most important person in someone's life.' And then she is off, clutching Jonathan's hand as they run from the brightly lit house to the car which is waiting in the darkness outside.

After they have left, Candida is depressed by a feeling of anti-climax and the knowledge that a change has occurred in her own life as well as in Penny's. For more than a year she has spent almost every Sunday in Greater Monckton. No doubt she will still be invited occasionally, but it will not be the same. Jonathan will no longer be the neighbour whose visits have been almost as regular as her own, but the host; someone who may want to entertain different friends, or enjoy quiet Sundays alone with his wife. There is no reason why the friendship of the two women should not continue, but from now on Jonathan will always come first for Penny.

The other guests retreat from the cold January air to the warmth of the house. Standing alone in the doorway, Candida considers what Penny has just said and sets it against her own determination to survive on her own. If she thinks of herself as standing alone, is she kidding herself? She has a son whom she adores and a job which she enjoys. She has recently moved into a small but comfortable flat and she has enough money to pay the rent and to think of herself as financially secure. Should she choose, in a little while, to resurrect her old ambitions and acquire a professional qualification, she will be able to do so. But none of this could she have achieved without help.

It is Rufus who has pursued the claim for compensation for Tom's death so successfully that she could have bought a flat outright had she chosen to do so. He has also introduced her to a financial adviser who has persuaded her to invest the sum to produce income instead, so that she will not be tied down if later she chooses a different life.

It is Jarvis who has given her a job for which she was completely unqualified but perfectly suited. By now she has mastered it and can think of herself as genuinely useful; but not many people would have offered her such a chance.

Most of all, it is her mother, the only person she can trust to love Daniel enough, who has made it possible for her to work.

In other words, she has learned that it is not in fact possible for her to stand alone, as she so firmly determined to do after Tom's death. People have been kind to her, and she is grateful to them: she has needed support and has been given it.

All the same, she has achieved independence of a sort. She is in control of her own life. If at some point in the future she finds that she is taking a wrong path, the power to change it will be in her own hands. One of the lessons she has learned in the past two years is that nothing is for ever.

Like the others – Helen and Madge, Penny and Jarvis – Candida has resolved to make the best of the tragic situation into which she was pitchforked, and has made her choices, but what she has chosen is not to make any lasting decisions just yet, so that all the choices remain. Penny, for one – and perhaps the others as well – may find that hard to understand; but Candida is content with her decision. She has survived.

You have been reading a novel published by Piatkus Books. We hope you have enjoyed it and that you would like to read more of our titles. Please ask for them in your local library or bookshop.

If you would like to be put on our mailing list to receive details of new publications, please send a large stamped addressed envelope (UK only) to:

Piatkus Books: 5 Windmill Street
London W1P 1HF

PIATKUS

The sign of a good book